MR. MONK
GOES TO THE FIREHOUSE

A Novel by
Lee Goldberg

Based on the television series created by
Andy Breckman

A SIGNET BOOK

SIGNET
Published by New American Library, a division of
Penguin Group (USA) Inc., 375 Hudson Street,
New York, New York 10014, USA
Penguin Group (Canada), 90 Eglinton Avenue East, Suite 700, Toronto,
Ontario M4P 2Y3, Canada (a division of Pearson Penguin Canada Inc.)
Penguin Books Ltd., 80 Strand, London WC2R 0RL, England
Penguin Ireland, 25 St. Stephen's Green, Dublin 2,
Ireland (a division of Penguin Books Ltd.)
Penguin Group (Australia), 250 Camberwell Road, Camberwell, Victoria 3124,
Australia (a division of Pearson Australia Group Pty. Ltd.)
Penguin Books India Pvt. Ltd., 11 Community Centre, Panchsheel Park,
New Delhi - 110 017, India
Penguin Group (NZ), 67 Apollo Drive, Rosedale, North Shore 0632,
New Zealand (a division of Pearson New Zealand Ltd.)
Penguin Books (South Africa) (Pty.) Ltd., 24 Sturdee Avenue,
Rosebank, Johannesburg 2196, South Africa

Penguin Books Ltd., Registered Offices:
80 Strand, London WC2R 0RL, England

First published by Signet, an imprint of New American Library,
a division of Penguin Group (USA) Inc.

First Printing, January 2006
10   9

PUBLISHER'S NOTE
This is a work of fiction. Names, characters, places, and incidents either are the
product of the author's imagination or are used fictitiously, and any resemblance
to actual persons, living or dead, business establishments, events, or locales is
entirely coincidental.
    The publisher does not have any control over and does not assume any respon-
sibility for author or third-party Web sites or their content.

To Tony Shalhoub,
the one and only Monk.

Mr. Monk Goes to the Firehouse was adapted into the *Monk* episode "Mr. Monk Can't See a Thing," written by Lee Goldberg & William Rabkin. There are some significant differences between the two (Monk isn't blind in the book), but if you have seen the episode, you may experience some déjà vu, so please don't operate heavy machinery while reading this novel.

ACKNOWLEDGMENTS

First and foremost, I want to thank Andy Breckman for creating in Adrian Monk one of the funniest and most original detectives in television history, and for letting me tell some stories about the character, first on the TV series and now in print. It has been great fun and a real pleasure for me.

I'd also like to thank William Rabkin and the writing staff of *Monk*—Tom Scharpling, David Breckman, Daniel Dratch, Hy Conrad, and Joe Toplyn—for all the inspiration and laughter.

I am indebted to Richard Yokley, Kelsey Lancaster, and Dr. D. P. Lyle for their technical advice; to Gina Maccoby for her wheeling and dealing; to Martha Bushko and Kerry Donovan for their enthusiasm and editorial support; to Tod Goldberg for reading all the drafts, and, finally, to my wife, Valerie, and daughter, Madison, for putting up with me while I compulsively obsessed over this book.

I was born and raised in the Bay Area, but the native San Franciscans among you might notice I've taken a few geographical liberties with my depiction of the city. I hope I'll still be welcome next time I visit.

1

Mr. Monk and the Termites

My name is Natalie Teeger. You've never heard of me, and that's okay, because the fact is I'm nobody special. By that I mean I'm not famous. I haven't done anything or accomplished something that you'd recognize me for. I'm just another anonymous shopper pushing her cart down the aisle at Wal-Mart.

Of course, I had bigger things planned for myself. When I was nine I dreamed of being one of Charlie's Angels. It wasn't because I wanted to fight crime or run around braless—I was looking forward to the day I'd fill out enough to wear one. Sadly, I'm still waiting. I admired the Angels because they were strong, independent, and had a sassy attitude. Most of all, I liked how those women took care of themselves.

In that way, I guess my dream came true, though not quite the way I expected. I've made a profession out of taking care of myself, my twelve-year-old daughter, Julie, and one other person: Adrian Monk.

You haven't heard of me, but if you live in San Francisco and you watch the news or read the paper, you've probably heard of Monk, because he *is* famous. He's a brilliant detective who solves murders that have baffled the police, which amazes me, since he is utterly incapable of handling the simplest aspects of day-to-day life. If that's the price of genius, then I'm glad I'm not one.

Usually taking care of Monk is just a day job, but that changed the week termites were found in his apartment building. By Monk, of course. He spotted a pinprick-sized hole in a piece of siding and knew it was fresh. He knew because he keeps track of all the irregularities in the siding.

When I asked him why he does that, he looked at me quizzically and said, "Doesn't everybody?"

That's Monk for you.

Since Monk's building was going to be tented and fumigated, his landlord told him he'd have to stay with friends or go to a hotel for a couple of days. That was a problem, because the only friends Monk has are Capt. Leland Stottlemeyer and Lt. Randy Disher of the San Francisco Police Department and me. But I'm not really his friend so much as I am his employee, and, considering how little he pays me to drive him around and run his errands, I'm barely that.

I went to Stottlemeyer first, since he used to be Monk's partner on the force, and asked if he'd take him in. But Stottlemeyer said his wife would leave him if he brought Monk home. Stottlemeyer said he'd leave, too, if Monk showed up. I went to Disher next, but he lives in a one-bedroom apartment, so there wasn't room for another person, though I have a feeling he would have found some room if it were me who needed a place to stay. Or any other woman under the age of thirty with a pulse.

So Monk and I started to look for a hotel. That wouldn't be a big deal for most people, but Adrian Monk isn't like most people. Look at how he dresses.

He wears his shirts buttoned up to the neck. They have to be 100 percent cotton, off-white, with exactly eight buttons, a size-sixteen neck and a thirty-two sleeve. All even numbers. Make a note of that; it's important.

His pants are pleated and cuffed, with eight belt loops (most pants have seven, so his have to be specially tailored), a thirty-four waist, and thirty-four length, but after the pant legs are cuffed, the inseam is thirty-two. His shoes, all twelve identical pairs, are brown and a size ten. More even numbers. It's no accident or coincidence. This stuff really matters to him.

He's obviously got an obsessive-compulsive disorder of some kind. I don't know exactly what kind because I'm not a nurse, like his previous assistant, Sharona, who left him abruptly to remarry her ex-husband (who, I hear, wasn't such a great guy, but after working with Monk for a short time, I understand why that wouldn't really matter. If I had an ex-husband I could return to, I would).

I have no professional qualifications whatsoever. My last job before this one was bartending, but I've also worked as a waitress, yoga instructor, house sitter, and blackjack dealer, among other things. But I know from talking to Stottlemeyer that Monk wasn't always so bad. Monk's condition became a lot worse after his wife was murdered a few years ago.

I can truly sympathize with that. My husband, Mitch, a fighter pilot, was killed in Kosovo, and I went kind of nuts for a long time myself. Not Monk nuts, of course—*normal* nuts.

Maybe that's why Monk and I get along better than anybody (particularly me) ever thought we would. Sure, he irritates me, but I know a lot of his peculiarities come from a deep and unrelenting heartbreak that nobody, and I mean *nobody*, should ever have to go through.

So I cut him a lot of slack, but even I have my limits.

Which brings me back to finding a hotel room for Monk. To begin with, we could look only at four-star hotels, because four is an even number, and a place with only two stars couldn't possibly meet Monk's standard of cleanliness. He wouldn't put his dog in a two-star hotel—if he had a dog, which he doesn't, and never would, because dogs are animals who lick themselves and drink out of toilets.

The first place we went to on that rainy Friday

was the Belmont in Union Square, one of the finest hotels in San Francisco.

Monk insisted on visiting every vacant room the grand old Belmont had before deciding which one to occupy. He looked only at even-numbered rooms on even-numbered floors, of course. Although the rooms were identically furnished and laid out the same way on every floor, he found something wrong with each one. For instance, one room didn't feel symmetrical enough. Another room was too symmetrical. One had no symmetry at all.

All the bathrooms were decorated with some expensive floral wallpaper from Italy. But if the strips of wallpaper didn't line up just right, if the flowers and their stems didn't match up exactly on either side of the cut, Monk declared the room uninhabitable.

By the tenth room, the hotel manager was guzzling little bottles of vodka from the minibar, and I was tempted to join him. Monk was on his knees, examining the wallpaper under the bathroom counter, wallpaper that nobody would ever see unless they were on their knees under the bathroom counter, and pointing out "a critical mismatch," and that's when I cracked. I couldn't take it anymore, and I did something I never would have done if I hadn't been under extreme emotional and mental duress.

I told Monk he could stay with us.

I said it just to end my immediate suffering, not realizing in that instant of profound weakness the full, horrific ramifications of my actions. But before I could take it back, Monk immediately accepted my invitation, and the hotel manager nearly kissed me in gratitude.

"But I don't want to hear any complaints about how my house is arranged or how dirty you think it is or how many 'critical mismatches' there are," I said to Monk as we started down the stairs to the lobby.

"I'm sure it's perfect," Monk said.

"That's exactly what I'm talking about, Mr. Monk. You're starting already."

He looked at me blankly. "All I said was that I'm sure it's perfect. Most people would take that as the sincere compliment it was meant to be."

"But most people don't mean 'perfect' when they say 'perfect.' "

"Of course they do," Monk said.

"No, they mean pleasant, or nice, or comfortable. They don't actually mean perfect in the sense that everything will be, well, *perfect*. You do."

"Give me some credit." Monk shook his head.

I gaped at him in disbelief.

"You wouldn't stay in that hotel room we just saw because the floral pattern of the wallpaper didn't match under the sink."

"That's different," he said. "That was a safety issue."

"How could that possibly be a safety issue?" I said.

"It reveals shoddy craftsmanship. If they were that haphazard with wallpaper, imagine what the rest of the construction work was like," Monk said. "I bet a mild earthquake is all it would take to bring this entire building down."

"The building is going to fall because the wall-paper doesn't match up?"

"This place should be condemned."

We reached the lobby and Monk stopped in his tracks.

"What?" I said.

"We should warn the others," Monk said.

"What others?" I asked.

"The hotel guests," Monk said. "They should be informed of the situation."

"That the wallpaper doesn't match," I said.

"It's a safety issue," he said. "I'll call them later."

I didn't bother arguing with him. Frankly I was just relieved to get out of the hotel without stumbling over a dead body. I know that sounds ridiculous, but when you're with Adrian Monk, corpses have a way of turning up all over the place. But, as I would soon find out, it was only a temporary reprieve.

Monk lived in a Deco-style apartment building on Pine, a twilight zone of affordability that straddled the northernmost edge of the Western District, with its upper-middle-class families, and the southwest corner of Pacific Heights, with its old money, elaborately ornate Victorians, and lush gardens high above the city.

On this sunny Saturday morning, Monk was waiting for me on the rain-slicked sidewalk, watching the uniformed nannies from Pacific Heights and Juicy Coutured housewives from the Western District pushing babies in Peg Perego strollers up and down the hill to Alta Plaza Park and its views of the marina, the bay, and the Golden Gate.

Monk stood with two large, identical suitcases, one on either side of him, a forlorn expression on his face. He wore his brown, four-button overcoat, his hands stuffed deep into the pockets, which made him seem smaller somehow.

There was something touching about the way he looked, like a sad, lonely kid going off to camp for the first time. I wanted to hug him, but fortunately for both of us, the feeling passed quickly.

Parking is impossible on a weekend in that neighborhood, so I double-parked in front of his building, which was so streamlined that it looked more aerodynamic than my car.

I got out and gestured toward his two suitcases. "You're only staying for a few days, Mr. Monk."

"I know," he said. "That's why I packed light."

I opened the back of my Cherokee and then reached for one of his suitcases. I nearly dislocated my shoulder. "What do you have in here, gold bricks?"

"Eight pairs of shoes," he said.

"You brought enough shoes to wear one pair a day for over a week."

"I'm roughing it," Monk said.

"That can't be all you have in here." I wrestled his suitcase into the back of my car. "It's too heavy."

"I've also packed fourteen pairs of socks, fourteen shirts, fourteen pairs of pants, fourteen—"

"Fourteen?" I asked. "Why fourteen?"

"I know it's playing close to the edge, but that's who I am. A man who lives on the edge. It's exciting," Monk said. "Do you think I packed enough clothes?"

"You have plenty," I said.

"Maybe I should get more."

"You're fine," I said.

"Maybe just two more pairs."

"Of what?"

"Everything," he said.

"I thought you were a man who lives on the edge," I said.

"What if the edge moves?"

"It won't," I said.

"If you say so," Monk said. "But if it does, we'll rue this day."

I was ruing it already. And I wasn't even sure what "ruing" meant.

Monk stood there, his other suitcase beside him. I motioned to it.

"Aren't you going to stick that in the car, Mr. Monk, or were you planning to leave it here?"

"You're saying you want me to put the suitcase in your car?"

"You thought I was going to do it for you?"

"It's your car," he said.

"So?"

He shrugged. "I thought you had a system."

"My system is that you put your own stuff in my car."

"But you took one of my suitcases and loaded it in the car," he said.

"I was being polite," I said. "I wasn't indicating a preference for loading the car myself."

"That's good to know." Monk picked up his

suitcase and slid it in beside the other one. "I was respecting your space."

I think he was just being lazy, but you never know for sure with Monk. Even if he were, I wouldn't call him on it, because he's my boss and I want to keep my job. Besides, it gave me the opening I was waiting for to address a touchy subject.

"Of course you were, Mr. Monk, and that's really great. I appreciate that, because Julie and I have our own way of doing things that's not exactly the same as yours."

"Like what?"

Oh, my God, I thought. *Where to begin?* "Well, for one thing, we don't boil our toothbrushes each day after we use them."

His eyes went wide. "That's *so* wrong."

"After we wash our hands, we don't always use a fresh, sterile towel to dry them."

"Didn't your parents teach you *anything* about personal hygiene?"

"The point is, Mr. Monk, I hope that while you stay with us you'll be able to respect our differences and accept us for who we are."

"Hippies," he said.

There was a word I hadn't heard in decades and that certainly never applied to me. I let it pass.

"All I want is for the three of us to get along," I said.

"You don't smoke pot, do you?"

"No, of course not. What kind of person do you think I am? Wait—don't answer that. What I'm trying to say, Mr. Monk, is that in my house, I'm the boss."

"As long as I don't have to smoke any weed."

"You don't," I said.

"Groovy."

And with that, he got into my car and buckled his seat belt.

2

Mr. Monk Moves In

I live in Noe Valley. It's south of the much more colorful and well-known Castro District, with its energetic gay community, and to the west of the multiethnic Mission District, which is surely next in line to be conquered by the unstoppable forces of gentrification, Williams-Sonoma catalogs gripped in their fists.

Noe Valley feels like a small town, far away from the urban hustle and chaos of San Francisco, when, in reality, the bustling Civic Center, overrun with politicians and vagrants, is only about twenty blocks away, on the north side of a very steep hill.

When Mitch and I bought our place, Noe Valley was still a working-class neighborhood. Everybody seemed to drive a Volkswagen Rabbit, and all the houses were slightly neglected, in need of a fresh coat of paint and a little loving attention.

Now everybody is driving a minivan or SUV, there's scaffolding up in front of every other house, and Twenty-fourth Street—a shopping district that was once lined with bakeries, diners, and barbershops—is overrun with patisseries, bistros, and stylists. But the neighborhood hasn't gone completely upscale. There remain lots of homes in need of care (like mine), and enough little gift shops, secondhand bookstores, and mom-and-pop pizza places that Noe has managed to hold on to its quirky, Bohemian character (equal parts of which are now authentic and manufactured). It's still very much a bedroom community, filled with young, struggling families and comfortable retirees with nary a tourist in sight.

On the drive down Divisadero to my house, Monk asked me to adjust my seat so it was even with his. I explained to him that if I did that, I wouldn't be able to reach important things like the gas pedal, the brakes, and the steering wheel. When I suggested instead that he move his seat, he ignored me and began fiddling with the passenger's-side mirror so it was tilted at the same angle as the mirror on the driver's side, which I'm sure he figured would compensate for the natural imbalance created by the uneven seats.

I don't get the logic either. That's why I keep a bottle of Advil in my glove compartment at all times. Not for him, of course. For me.

When we got to my little Victorian row house, I let Monk get his own suitcases out of the car while I rushed inside for one last look around for things that might set him off. It's not like he hadn't visited my place before, but this was the first time he was staying there for more than an hour or two. Little things that he might have been able to summon the willpower to overlook before might become intolerable now.

Standing there in my open doorway, looking at my small living room, I realized my house was a Monk minefield. The decor is what I like to call thrift-shop chic, the furniture and lamps an eclectic mix of styles and eras. There is some Art Deco here and a little seventies chintz there, because I bought whatever happened to catch my eye and meet my meager budget. My approach to interior design was to have no approach at all.

In other words, my entire house, and my entire life, was the antithesis of Adrian Monk. There was nothing I could do to change that now. All I could do was open the door wide, welcome him in, and brace myself for the worst.

So that's exactly what I did. He stepped in, surveyed the house as if for the first time, and smiled contentedly.

"We made the right decision," he said. "This is much better than a hotel."

It was the last thing I ever expected him to say. "Really? Why?"

"It feels lived-in," he said.

"I thought you didn't like things that were lived-in," I said.

"There's a difference between a hotel room that's been continuously occupied by thousands of different people and a home that's . . . " His voice trailed off for a moment. And then he looked at me a little wistfully and said, "A home."

I smiled. In his own way, that may have been the nicest thing he'd ever said to me. "Let me show you where you'll be staying, Mr. Monk."

I led him down the hall, past Julie's closed door, which had a big, hand-drawn, yellow warning sign taped to it that said: PRIVATE PROPERTY. NO TRESPASSING. STAY OUT. KNOCK BEFORE ENTERING. Since it's usually just the two of us in the house, the sign struck me as adolescent overkill. I had a sign like that taped to my door, too, when I was her age, but I had brothers to worry about. She had only me. Below that sign, Julie had also taped up a diamond-shaped DANGER! HAZARDOUS WASTE placard that she'd found somewhere.

Monk glanced at the placard, then at me. "That's a joke, right?"

I nodded.

"It's very humorous." He tried to chuckle, but it came out sounding more like he was choking. "Do you confirm it periodically?"

"Confirm what?"

"That it's a joke," he said. "Children can be very mischievous, you know. When I was eight, I once went a whole day without washing my hands."

"You're lucky you survived."

Monk sighed and nodded his head. "When you're young, you think you're immortal."

I gestured to the room beside my daughter's. "This is our guest room."

Actually, until the night before it had been our junk room, where we stored all the clutter we couldn't fit into the rest of the house. Now it was all temporarily jammed into my garage.

Monk took a few steps into the room and regarded the furnishings. There was a full-size bed, the first one Mitch and I ever bought, and the walls were decorated with some cheaply framed sketches of London, Paris, and Berlin landmarks that we bought from street-corner artists when we eloped to Europe. The dresser was a garage-sale find with one missing drawer knob, a flaw I hoped Monk wouldn't notice but knew that he would. It was his astonishing powers of observation that made him such a great detective. He could probably tell by glancing at the sketch of Notre Dame if the artist was left- or right-handed, what he ate for lunch, and whether or not he smothered his elderly grandmother with a pillow.

Monk set his suitcases down at the foot of the bed. "It's charming."

"Really?"

This was working out much better than I'd hoped, though I noticed he was shielding his eyes from the dresser as if it were emitting a blinding glare.

"Oh, yes," he said. "It oozes charm."

Before I could ask him what he meant, exactly, by "oozes," someone rang the doorbell. I excused myself and went to see who was at the door.

There was a burly guy with a clipboard standing on my porch. Behind him I could see two men unloading a refrigerator from a moving truck in front of my house.

"Does Adrian Monk reside here?" the man asked. He smelled of Old Spice and Cutty Sark. I wasn't sure which was more unsettling to me: the mingling of odors or the fact that I could identify them.

"No, I reside here," I said. "Mr. Monk is just a guest."

"Whatever," he said, then turned and whistled to the guys on the street. "Start unloading the truck."

"Whoa," I said, stepping out onto the porch. "What are you unloading?"

"Your stuff," he said, thrusting the clipboard and pen at me. "Sign here."

I looked at the papers on the clipboard. It was a moving-company invoice listing all the furniture, dishware, bedding, and appliances they were transporting from Monk's house to mine. *This* was Monk's idea of roughing it?

"It's about time you got here," I heard Monk say behind me. I turned to see him holding the door open for the two guys hauling in his refrigerator. "Be careful with that."

"Hold it," I shouted at the movers, and then I turned to Monk. "What is all this?"

"Just a few necessities."

"There's a big difference between staying with someone and moving in."

"I know that," he said.

"Then how do you explain this?" I pointed at his refrigerator.

"I have special dietary needs."

"So you brought your own refrigerator and all the food that's in it?"

"I didn't want to be a bother," he said.

I waved the clipboard at him.

"This is everything you own, Mr. Monk," I said. "To accommodate all of your belongings, I'd have to move everything of mine out of the house."

Monk gestured to the movers. "I'm sure they'd be glad to help. They're professionals."

I took a deep breath, shoved the clipboard into the burly man's hands, and said to him, "You're taking all of this back where you got it."

"They can't," Monk said.

"Why not?"

"The building is tented by now," Monk said. "And filled with poison."

"Then you'll just have to put it in storage, Mr. Monk, or leave it on the front lawn. Because it's not going in this house."

I stomped back inside, slammed the door, and left Monk to work things out with the movers.

It was only when I was standing in the middle of my living room, trying hard to control my anger, that I finally realized that I'd been home for fifteen minutes and hadn't seen or heard my daughter. I went to her door and knocked.

"Julie?" I pressed my ear to her door. "Are you in there?"

"Yes," she said softly. "Stop putting your ear to my door."

I stepped back guiltily, even though I knew she couldn't have seen me. "Are you all right?"

"I'm fine."

"Mr. Monk is here," I said.

"I know," she replied.

"Is that why you're hiding in your room?"

"I'm not hiding."

"I thought you liked Mr. Monk."

"I do," she said.

I'm human and a single mother, and I was already pretty keyed up by Monk and the movers, so I wasn't in the mood for petulant behavior.

"Then get your butt out here and be polite," I said.

"I can't," she said.

"Why not?"

"Because he'll think I'm a baby," she said, and then I heard what sounded like a muffled sob.

I immediately felt a pang of guilt for snapping at her instead of being the intuitive, caring, all-knowing mom I should be. I decided to ignore the warning signs on her door and heed the one I heard in her voice. I opened her door.

Julie was sitting on her bed, tears streaming down her cheeks. She'd taken out all the stuffed animals that she'd stowed deep in her closet six months ago, after declaring she was "too grown-up" for them. Now she'd gathered them all around her and was hugging them close.

I got onto the bed beside Julie and put my arm around her. "What's wrong, sweetie?"

"You'll think it's stupid." She sniffled.

I kissed her cheek. "I promise I won't."

"Maddie called," she said, referring to one of

her friends from school. "Sparky is dead. He was killed."

And with that she started sobbing. Completely lost, I drew her close and stroked her hair. I hated to ask, but I had to . . .

"Who is Sparky?"

Julie lifted her head, sniffled hard, and wiped the tears from her eyes. "The firehouse dalmatian. The one that Firefighter Joe brings to school every year during his talk about fire safety."

"Oh, that Sparky." I still had no idea what she was talking about. "What happened?"

"Someone hit him on the head last night with a pickax," Julie said with a shiver. "Who would want to murder an adorable, trusting, innocent dog?"

"I don't know," I said.

She started to cry again and hugged me tight.

"I'll find out," Monk said softly.

Julie and I both looked up to see Monk standing in the doorway. How long had he been there?

"You will?" Julie asked.

"It's what I do." Monk shifted his weight. "Solving murders is kind of my thing."

Julie reached for a Kleenex on her nightstand, blew her nose, and tossed the wadded-up tissue toward her garbage can. She missed.

"Do you really think you can catch the person who killed Sparky?" she asked.

Monk stared at the tissue on the floor as if he were expecting it to crawl away. "Yes."

Julie turned to me. "Can we afford him?"

It was a good question. I looked back at Monk,

who was watching the tissue and twisting his neck like he had a kink in it.

"Can we?" I asked him.

"I'll bring the killer to justice if you will do me one huge favor."

"What?" Julie asked.

I hoped it didn't involve letting him move everything he owned into my house, because that wasn't going to happen, no matter how many puppies, baby seals, or bunny rabbits were murdered.

"Pick up that tissue, place it in a sealed plastic bag, and remove it from this house immediately."

"I can do that," she said.

"Thank you." Monk looked at me and tipped his head toward the placard on her door. "It's no joke."

3

Mr. Monk and the Fire Truck

Saturday is Julie's "activity day." Tae kwon do. Soccer practice. Hip-hop class. And, of course, the inevitable birthday party. Let's be honest here: No parent wants to spend their weekends chauffeuring their kids around. So I organized a carpool schedule with the other neighborhood mothers (it's always the mothers who get stuck with this drudgery). That particular Saturday happened to be one of my carpool days off, so another overworked, dead-tired mother was driving a bunch of unruly kids to their classes, practices, and birthday parties.

I always intend to spend that special "alone" time pampering myself with a good book, or a long walk, or a luxurious soak in a hot bath. But I inevitably end up running errands and catching up on all the things I've fallen behind on, like doing laundry, shopping for groceries, cleaning up the house, and paying bills.

So on that Saturday afternoon I was free to assist Monk, who been hired by my daughter to investigate the murder of a firehouse dalmatian.

Our first stop was the fire station, which was over in North Beach, the neighborhood between Chinatown and Fisherman's Wharf. There's no beach there, of course—that was buried under a landfill, and the waterfront extended farther north decades ago, so the name is kind of a cheat. It's perhaps better known locally as Little Italy, even though now there're as many Chinese living there as Italians, so maybe that name is a cheat, too.

North Beach is also known for beat writer Jack Kerouac, and stripper Carol Doda, whose enormous hooters used to be up in lights in front of the Condor Club. There are a few remaining vestiges of the neighborhood's beatnik past, mostly for the sake of the tourists. A couple strip joints still cling to life on Broadway, but their seedy allure is almost comically dated, and they're losing ground fast to coffeehouses and art galleries.

Gentrification, beautification, and renovation are everywhere, my friends. It's not just happening with buildings and neighborhoods. Go down to L.A. and you can see they're gentrifying, beautifying, and renovating people there now, too.

The streets were still damp from Friday's intermittent rains, but the skies were clear and bright, with a crisp, cold wind blowing off the white-capped bay. I could smell the sea, mingled with a hint of fried food wafting up from Chinatown.

The firehouse was on top of a hill with dramatic views of the Transamerica Pyramid and Coit Tower.

It was a redbrick building from the mid-1900s with a stone carving of the SFFD emblem, an eagle with its talons gripping crisscrossed axes over licking flames, mounted above the arched garage doors.

"When I was a kid," Monk said, "I wanted to be a firefighter."

"You did?" I said.

"I loved everything about it," he said. "Except the firefighting part."

"Then what was it about being a firefighter that you loved?"

"This."

Monk turned to the firehouse and opened his arms as if to embrace the sight in front of him. Both of the garage doors were open, letting the breeze stream into the station, where half a dozen firemen scrubbed and shined the two gleaming fire trucks, the sunshine glinting off the sparkling chrome and polished red metal.

"Isn't it great?" He sighed.

I followed his gaze as he took in the fire hoses, neatly folded atop one another on the fire trucks; the spotless cement floors of the garage scrubbed and mopped to a marblelike sheen; the neat rows of fire hats, coats, and helmets aligned in open racks of dazzling steel; the pickaxes, shovels, and other tools mounted on the wall in order of size, shape, and function. The beauty of cleanliness, efficiency, and order.

His eyes were wide in childlike awe and appreciation. He was ten years old again, though I must confess that in a lot of ways I'm not convinced he's ever really grown up.

Monk approached the captain, who stood beside a rolling cart of neatly folded white towels and a laundry basket, watching his men at work. His short-sleeved blue uniform was perfectly pressed and starched, his badge gleaming so bright that it was nearly pure light. He was in his fifties, with the kind of hard, chiseled features that only soldiers, comic-book characters, and statues usually possess.

"May I help you?" the captain asked.

"Actually, we'd like to help you," Monk said. "I'm Adrian Monk and this is my assistant, Natalie Teeger."

"I'm Captain Mantooth." He offered his hand to Monk. "You're the detective, right?"

Monk shook his hand, then held his open palm out to me for a disinfectant wipe. I gave him one. If Mantooth was offended, he didn't show it.

"I've been hired to investigate Sparky's murder," Monk said as he wiped his hands.

"Are you working for Joe?" Mantooth asked.

"Who is Joe?" Monk replied, and handed the wipe back to me.

"Firefighter Joe," I supplied, stuffing the wipe into a Baggie in my purse. By the end of a day my purse was usually overflowing with little Baggies of wipes. "He and Sparky were a team."

"They were much more than that, Miss Teeger," Mantooth said. "Joe Cochran rescued that dog from the pound ten years ago, and they have been inseparable ever since. Sparky wasn't my dog, but I still feel like we lost one of our men last night. We all do."

Monk picked up one of the folded towels from the cart and gestured to the fire truck. "May I?"

Mantooth shrugged. "Sure."

Monk went over to the truck and buffed one of the sparkling chrome headlights. When he turned back to us he had a big, boyish grin on his face.

"Wow," he said.

The captain and I watched Monk polish a valve. The other firemen on the truck watched him, too. I could see we might be there for a while, so I decided to press on.

"Can you tell us what happened last night?"

"We responded to a residential fire four blocks from here. Must have been around ten o'clock, but I can check the logs for the exact time. A woman fell asleep on her sofa while she was smoking a cigarette. It's the most common cause of fire death worldwide and easily the most preventable," Mantooth said. "We knocked the fire down and got back here about two A.M. We knew something was wrong the minute we pulled into the garage. Usually Sparky runs out to greet us, tail wagging. But he didn't this time. . . ."

Monk approached us, but it wasn't to ask a question or actually participate in some meaningful way in his own investigation. It was to drop his used towel into a basket and get a fresh one.

"This is so cool," he said, then grinned giddily at us both and got to work scrubbing a spotless door handle. Mantooth couldn't stop staring at him.

"Were there any signs of a break-in?" I asked.

"No," he replied, tearing his gaze away from Monk and back to me. "The firehouse wasn't locked."

"Was it unusual to leave the firehouse open and the dog by himself?"

"Not at all," Mantooth said. "That's one of the reasons, historically, that we have dalmatians. They guard the firehouse. Joe is full of facts like that. He can tell you all about dalmatians."

"Has anyone ever tried to steal anything from the firehouse before?"

"Not before and not last night," Mantooth said. "As far as I can tell, nothing is missing. It's a safe neighborhood, or at least it used to be."

I didn't know what to ask next, so I turned to Monk, who was, after all, the legendary detective around here.

"Mr. Monk?" I said.

He kept polishing.

"*Mr. Monk,*" I repeated, more firmly this time. He turned around. "Isn't there something you'd like to ask Captain Mantooth?"

Monk snapped his fingers. "Of course. Thank you for reminding me."

He tossed the dirty towel in the basket and looked at the captain. "Do you have any of those honorary-fireman badges?"

"You mean the ones we give the kids?"

"No, the ones you give the honorary firemen," Monk said.

"I think so," Mantooth said. "Would you like one?"

Monk nodded. Mantooth went back to the office. Monk looked at me.

"Wow."

"Is that all you're going to say?"

"Yippee."

"Don't you have any questions you'd like to ask about the murder? Like what happened here that night?"

"I already know."

"You *do*?"

"I've known since we walked in," he said.

"How?"

He drew a triangle in the air with his hands. "Simple geometry."

There's nothing simple about geometry. I flunked it in high school, and I'm occasionally awakened by this nightmare that Mr. Ross, my tenth-grade math teacher, hunts me down and makes me take the final exam again.

"Is there a way we could keep geometry out of this?" I said.

"The dog was over there." Monk pointed to the far right-hand side of the station house. "Point one of the triangle. That was his favorite spot to lie down when the trucks were away."

"How do you know?"

"You can see where he's scratched the wall with his paws," Monk said.

I followed his gaze and squinted. Sure enough, there were some light scratches the dog must have made when he was stretching or rolling over or lying against the wall.

"When the fire trucks are gone, that spot gave Sparky a clear view of the garage doors," Monk said. "When the fire trucks were here, they blocked the view from there, so he slept in his basket in the kitchen, where he could get table scraps and also enjoy more foot traffic."

He tipped his head toward the kitchen, and I saw the edge of the dog's basket inside the open doorway. I could see a rubber hot-dog chew toy in the basket.

I couldn't figure out how, or when, Monk noticed the scratches and the dog bed. It seemed to me that from the moment we got there all his attention had been on the fire trucks. But I was wrong.

Monk cocked his head, looked around the station, then took a few steps forward, as if he were placing his feet in a set of footprints in the sand.

"The murderer crept in through the open garage and reached this point, the second point in our triangle, when the dog saw him and charged," Monk said. "He looked around for something to defend himself with and spotted those."

Monk whirled around to face the axes, shovels, and rakes neatly arranged along the wall to the left of us, every tool in its proper place. At least I knew why that had attracted Monk's attention.

"He ran over there, the dog closing in on him. He grabbed the pickax off the wall and swung it at the dog at the last possible second." Monk took a few steps forward and stopped near the open racks of coats, helmets, and boots. He tapped the floor with his foot. "Sparky died right here. The third point in our triangle."

"How can you be sure?"

"Simple geometry," Monk said again.

"He's right, Miss Teeger," the captain said, coming up behind me. "That's exactly where we found the poor dog when we got back, right here in front of the turnouts."

"The what?" I said.

"It's what we call our firefighting gear," he said. "All the stuff we wear into a fire."

Monk looked past me. "Uh-oh."

"Uh-oh, what?" I asked.

He went over to the rack of heavy fire coats, which were all aligned front-to-back in a neat row. One of the coats was hanging from a hanger that was facing a different direction from the others.

Naturally, Monk took the coat off the hanger, turned the hanger around, and hung the coat up again, careful to make sure the shoulders lined up with the ones behind and the ones in front.

Mantooth shook his head in amazement. "He's more of a stickler for order than I am."

"Than anybody," I said.

"I wish all my guys were like him."

"Be careful what you wish for," I said.

Monk came back and wagged his hands in front of me for some wipes. I reached into my purse and gave him two.

"Are you absolutely sure nothing has been stolen from the firehouse?" Monk said while cleaning his hands.

"All of the equipment is accounted for, and none of the guys have reported anything missing from their lockers," Mantooth said.

I was getting confused all over again.

"How can you kill a dog that isn't there?"

"You could poison his food."

I thought about it. The killer staked out the station on a day he knew that Joe wouldn't be working, waited for everyone to leave to fight a fire, then sneaked inside to poison the food. But instead the killer was attacked by the dog he'd come to kill, a dog that wasn't supposed to be there, and had to protect himself with the pickax.

It could have happened that way.

Or the other way.

Either way, it wasn't too complicated. I could deal with it.

"Or the dog was killed by accident," Monk said, confusing things for me all over again. "And the guy was in the firehouse for an entirely different reason."

"Like what?" I said. With that question, I gave up trying to make sense of the case. That was Monk's job, not mine.

"I don't know," Monk said. "But I once solved a murder that was all about a penny. . . ."

The house that had caught fire was still standing, but the first floor was charred and gutted, the windows broken and rimmed by black where flames had licked out. The property was cordoned off with yellow caution tape, and several firefighters picked through the rubble while others hosed things down.

The smell of smoke was heavy in the air, the streets and gutters inundated with soot-blackened water, the storm drains clogged with burned debris. There was a fire truck, a black-and-white, an SFFD sedan, and an unmarked police car parked in front of the house.

The people in the neighborhood were out on their porches and milling on the sidewalks, looking at the house and talking animatedly among themselves. There's nothing like a fire to bring a community together.

The burned house was one of a half dozen identically bland, blockish town houses built side by side in the 1950s. They must have been designed by somebody who was really into the "international modern style" popularized by Le Corbusier, Richard Neutra, and Mies Van Der Rohe, only done artlessly and on the cheap (as you can probably tell, I took a few architecture courses and have been waiting for an opportunity to show off what little I remember). The town houses were unadorned by moldings, eschewing style for function, and the doors and windows were flush with the flat walls around them, making the places stand out in sharp (and, if you ask me, offensive) contrast to the gables, cornices, and bay windows of the utterly charming Victorian homes across the street.

I wondered how many of the neighbors were thinking the same thing I was: Architecturally speaking, it was a shame the fire didn't burn down all six of the ugly town houses on that side of the street. The neighbors' homes, by contrast, were wood-frame Eastlake Victorians standing shoulder-to-shoulder, narrow and tall. Each house had the requisite bay windows to increase the available light, decorative gables to add some individual flair, and tiny garages that were barely able to fit a single car.

The uniformed officer guarding the fire scene recognized Monk, lifted up the yellow caution tape, and nodded us past.

The interior of the living room was a gutted, scorched skeleton of what it once was, with the charred furniture and melted TV still eerily in place. An African-American woman in a bright blue SFFD windbreaker with the words ARSON INVESTI-GATOR written in big yellow letters on the back examined the rubble in the far corner of what was left of the room. Her hair was braided with color-ful white and pink beads. Julie had been nagging me to let her do that to her hair, which would have been okay with me if it didn't cost $120.

Monk stepped in gingerly, trying not to get a speck of soot on himself, which was impossible. We'd barely come through the door when we were greeted by a familiar face.

Captain Leland Stottlemeyer stood off to one side, smoking a fat cigar, his wide tie loosened at his open collar. He was a perpetually weary man, with a mustache that seemed to grow bushier as his hairline receded. He didn't look pleased to see us.

"What are you doing here, Monk?" he said.

"We came to talk to one of the firefighters," Monk said. "The firehouse dog was killed last night."

"You're investigating pet deaths now?" Stot-tlemeyer said.

"It's for a very special client," Monk said.

I couldn't help smiling, and Stottlemeyer noticed. In that instant he knew the client was me, or someone close to me. Stottlemeyer is a detective too, after all.

"We were told that this fire was an accident," I said.

"It probably was," Stottlemeyer said. "But since a lady died, we have to treat this like a crime scene until the arson investigator makes her determination. So we send someone down to stand around until then. It's routine."

"So why didn't you send Lieutenant Disher?"

Stottlemeyer shrugged. "It's been raining all week and it's a sunny day. I wanted to get out. Gives me a chance to smoke my cigar."

Monk sneezed. And then sneezed again.

"Whoever lived here had cats," Monk said.

"How do you know?" Stottlemeyer said.

"I'm allergic to cats."

"You're allergic to plastic fruit, dandelions, and brown rice, and that's just for starters," Stottlemeyer said. "How can you tell it's cat dander that's making you sneeze?"

Monk sneezed. "That was definitely a cat sneeze."

"You can tell the difference between your sneezes?" I asked.

"Sure," Monk said. "Can't everybody?"

Stottlemeyer took a deep drag on his cigar, then flicked his ashes on the floor.

Monk stared at him.

"What?" Stottlemeyer said.

"Aren't you going to pick those up?"

"They're ashes, Monk. Take a look around. The entire place is in ashes."

"Those are cigar ashes," Monk said.

"Oh." Stottlemeyer nodded his head knowingly. "They don't belong with the other ashes."

Monk smiled. "I knew you'd see reason."

"Not really." Stottlemeyer flicked his cigar again. Monk lunged forward, catching the ashes in his cupped hands before they could hit the ground.

Monk looked up, relieved. And then he sneezed, but managed not to blow the ashes out of his hands. "Anyone have a Baggie?"

Stottlemeyer glared at him, mashed out his cigar against the blackened wall, and dropped the stub in Monk's open hands.

"You can take the pleasure out of anything, Monk. You know that? Talk to Gayle, the arson investigator." Stottlemeyer tipped his head toward the African-American woman in the SFFD windbreaker. "I'm sure she can help you."

Monk made his way to the woman, walking like a man carrying a vial of nitroglycerine through a minefield. He moved cautiously and deliberately, careful not to get soot on his clothes or spill a single fleck of cigar ash from his hands.

Stottlemeyer and I observed his slow progress. It was strangely fascinating.

"How are you holding up with Monk as a houseguest?" Stottlemeyer asked me.

"It's only been a few hours."

"A few hours with Monk can seem like decades," he said. He took a pen from his pocket, scrawled something on the back of a business card, and handed it to me. "This is my home number. If you need a break, give me a call. I can take him out to the car wash."

"Thank you, Captain," I said. "That's very nice of you."

"You and I are the only ones who take care of him. We have to back each other up."

"We're sort of like partners."

"Sort of," Stottlemeyer said.

"He likes the car wash?"

"Loves it," Stottlemeyer said.

Monk finally reached the arson investigator, who was bent over with her back to him, examining something on the floor. I heard him clear his throat to get her attention. Gayle straightened up and turned around.

"Hello, Gayle. I'm Adrian Monk. I'm a consultant to the police." Monk shrugged a shoulder to draw her attention to the Junior Firefighter badge on his lapel. "And I'm one of your brothers."

She raised an eyebrow. "Is that so?"

"Could I have a Baggie?"

She took a clear plastic evidence bag out of the pocket of her windbreaker.

"Could you hold it open for me?"

She did. He emptied his ashes and the cigar stub into the bag and clapped his hands together, brushing off whatever microscopic traces might have been left. And then he brushed them a couple dozen more times for good measure.

"Thank you," Monk said, and left her holding the bag, his attention drawn to the coffee table. Its thick glass top and metal legs had survived the

"How about something that you wouldn't think of as important?" Monk said. "Something so insignificant, obscure, and unremarkable that nobody would necessarily miss it?"

"Then how would we know if it was gone?"

"I once solved a murder where it turned out all the killer was after was a piece of paper jammed in a copying machine."

"We don't have a copying machine."

"I once solved a murder where it turned out all the killer was after was a rock in a goldfish aquarium."

"We don't have any goldfish."

Monk glanced at me. "This is going to be a tough one."

"Come to think of it," Mantooth said, "we're missing two towels."

"What kind of towels?" Monk asked.

"The ones we use to clean and polish the fire truck," Mantooth replied. "We had thirty-four the day before the fire and thirty-two afterward. I know this sounds silly, but I'm kind of compulsive about keeping track of the towels."

"It sounds perfectly natural to me," Monk said. He'd found a kindred spirit.

"Do you really think someone would come in here to steal two towels?" the captain said.

Monk shrugged. "Where do you keep them?"

"In the basement, by the washer and dryer."

This was getting ridiculous. There was no way someone killed a dog over a couple of towels. So to stop the insanity, I piped up with a question of my own.

"Captain Mantooth," I said, "can you think of any reason someone would want to harm Sparky?"

"You'd have to ask Joe," Mantooth said. "He was closer to that dog than he was to any of us. When he went off duty, he'd take Sparky home with him."

"Where can we find Joe now?"

"He's still on duty, but he didn't want to be here, not today, not without Sparky," Mantooth said. "So I sent him back to the scene of the house fire to oversee the cleanup and assist the arson investigators. He should still be there."

"Thank you, Captain," Monk said. "This has been wonderful."

"You're welcome back anytime, Mr. Monk."

Monk started to go when Mantooth called out to him: "Wait, you don't want to leave without this."

The captain pinned a badge on Monk's lapel. The badge was a red helmet atop an emblem of a fire truck encircled by a golden fire hose and the words JUNIOR FIREFIGHTER in block letters. Across the bottom it read: SAN FRANCISCO FIRE DEPARTMENT.

Monk looked down at it and smiled. "Wow."

4

Mr. Monk and the Ruined Weekend

Since the scene of the previous night's fire was only four blocks away, and it was such a beautiful day, I thought it would be nice if we walked, even though it meant a steep climb uphill back to the car. I didn't even mind that Monk counted and tapped each parking meter we passed along the way. I was too preoccupied trying to make sense of what we'd just learned at the firehouse.

If the guy's plan was to kill Sparky, why didn't he bring a weapon with him? If he came to steal something, and killed Sparky in self-defense, how come nothing was missing?

I asked Monk the same questions. Between his parking meter count, which I will spare you, he answered them. Sort of.

"He could have been staking out the station house for days, waiting for them to leave to fight a fire so he could murder the dog," Monk said.

"Why would he want to do that?"

"Maybe the dog urinated on his roses."

I could see how that could strike Monk as a compelling motive for murder.

"So assuming this insane gardener was that intent on killing Sparky," I said, "why did he wait for the dog to go after him? Why didn't he just walk up to the dog and clobber him with a baseball bat or something?"

"He would have had to bring the baseball bat with him," Monk said. "And then he'd have to dispose of it later. Then there's the risk that it might be found and could somehow be traced back to him."

"And if he keeps it, it might link him to the crime later," I said.

Monk nodded.

It made sense. The case wasn't so confusing after all.

"On the other hand," Monk said, "maybe he didn't expect Sparky to be there."

"But Sparky was always there," I said.

"Only when Joe was on duty," Monk said. "Otherwise Joe took the dog home with him."

It had been only a few minutes since Captain Mantooth had told us that, and already I'd forgotten it. I obviously wasn't cut out for detective work.

"So you think Sparky's murder was an accident," I said. "You think the killer was after something else and got caught by the dog."

"Not necessarily," Monk said. "He could still have been going there to murder Sparky."

I was getting confused all over again.

"How can you kill a dog that isn't there?"

"You could poison his food."

I thought about it. The killer staked out the station on a day he knew that Joe wouldn't be working, waited for everyone to leave to fight a fire, then sneaked inside to poison the food. But instead the killer was attacked by the dog he'd come to kill, a dog that wasn't supposed to be there, and had to protect himself with the pickax.

It could have happened that way.

Or the other way.

Either way, it wasn't too complicated. I could deal with it.

"Or the dog was killed by accident," Monk said, confusing things for me all over again. "And the guy was in the firehouse for an entirely different reason."

"Like what?" I said. With that question, I gave up trying to make sense of the case. That was Monk's job, not mine.

"I don't know," Monk said. "But I once solved a murder that was all about a penny. . . ."

The house that had caught fire was still standing, but the first floor was charred and gutted, the windows broken and rimmed by black where flames had licked out. The property was cordoned off with yellow caution tape, and several firefighters picked through the rubble while others hosed things down.

The smell of smoke was heavy in the air, the streets and gutters inundated with soot-blackened water, the storm drains clogged with burned debris. There was a fire truck, a black-and-white, an SFFD sedan, and an unmarked police car parked in front of the house.

The people in the neighborhood were out on their porches and milling on the sidewalks, looking at the house and talking animatedly among themselves. There's nothing like a fire to bring a community together.

The burned house was one of a half dozen identically bland, blockish town houses built side by side in the 1950s. They must have been designed by somebody who was really into the "international modern style" popularized by Le Corbusier, Richard Neutra, and Mies Van Der Rohe, only done artlessly and on the cheap (as you can probably tell, I took a few architecture courses and have been waiting for an opportunity to show off what little I remember). The town houses were unadorned by moldings, eschewing style for function, and the doors and windows were flush with the flat walls around them, making the places stand out in sharp (and, if you ask me, offensive) contrast to the gables, cornices, and bay windows of the utterly charming Victorian homes across the street.

I wondered how many of the neighbors were thinking the same thing I was: Architecturally speaking, it was a shame the fire didn't burn down all six of the ugly town houses on that side of the street. The neighbors' homes, by contrast, were wood-frame Eastlake Victorians standing shoulder-to-shoulder, narrow and tall. Each house had the requisite bay windows to increase the available light, decorative gables to add some individual flair, and tiny garages that were barely able to fit a single car.

The uniformed officer guarding the fire scene recognized Monk, lifted up the yellow caution tape, and nodded us past.

The interior of the living room was a gutted, scorched skeleton of what it once was, with the charred furniture and melted TV still eerily in place. An African-American woman in a bright blue SFFD windbreaker with the words ARSON INVESTI-GATOR written in big yellow letters on the back examined the rubble in the far corner of what was left of the room. Her hair was braided with colorful white and pink beads. Julie had been nagging me to let her do that to her hair, which would have been okay with me if it didn't cost $120.

Monk stepped in gingerly, trying not to get a speck of soot on himself, which was impossible. We'd barely come through the door when we were greeted by a familiar face.

Captain Leland Stottlemeyer stood off to one side, smoking a fat cigar, his wide tie loosened at his open collar. He was a perpetually weary man, with a mustache that seemed to grow bushier as his hairline receded. He didn't look pleased to see us.

"What are you doing here, Monk?" he said.

"We came to talk to one of the firefighters," Monk said. "The firehouse dog was killed last night."

"You're investigating pet deaths now?" Stottlemeyer said.

"It's for a very special client," Monk said.

I couldn't help smiling, and Stottlemeyer noticed. In that instant he knew the client was me, or someone close to me. Stottlemeyer is a detective too, after all.

"We were told that this fire was an accident," I said.

"It probably was," Stottlemeyer said. "But since a lady died, we have to treat this like a crime scene until the arson investigator makes her determination. So we send someone down to stand around until then. It's routine."

"So why didn't you send Lieutenant Disher?"

Stottlemeyer shrugged. "It's been raining all week and it's a sunny day. I wanted to get out. Gives me a chance to smoke my cigar."

Monk sneezed. And then sneezed again.

"Whoever lived here had cats," Monk said.

"How do you know?" Stottlemeyer said.

"I'm allergic to cats."

"You're allergic to plastic fruit, dandelions, and brown rice, and that's just for starters," Stottlemeyer said. "How can you tell it's cat dander that's making you sneeze?"

Monk sneezed. "That was definitely a cat sneeze."

"You can tell the difference between your sneezes?" I asked.

"Sure," Monk said. "Can't everybody?"

Stottlemeyer took a deep drag on his cigar, then flicked his ashes on the floor.

Monk stared at him.

"What?" Stottlemeyer said.

"Aren't you going to pick those up?"

"They're ashes, Monk. Take a look around. The entire place is in ashes."

"Those are cigar ashes," Monk said.

"Oh." Stottlemeyer nodded his head knowingly. "They don't belong with the other ashes."

Monk smiled. "I knew you'd see reason."

"Not really." Stottlemeyer flicked his cigar again. Monk lunged forward, catching the ashes in his cupped hands before they could hit the ground.

Monk looked up, relieved. And then he sneezed, but managed not to blow the ashes out of his hands. "Anyone have a Baggie?"

Stottlemeyer glared at him, mashed out his cigar against the blackened wall, and dropped the stub in Monk's open hands.

"You can take the pleasure out of anything, Monk. You know that? Talk to Gayle, the arson investigator." Stottlemeyer tipped his head toward the African-American woman in the SFFD windbreaker. "I'm sure she can help you."

Monk made his way to the woman, walking like a man carrying a vial of nitroglycerine through a minefield. He moved cautiously and deliberately, careful not to get soot on his clothes or spill a single fleck of cigar ash from his hands.

Stottlemeyer and I observed his slow progress. It was strangely fascinating.

"How are you holding up with Monk as a houseguest?" Stottlemeyer asked me.

"It's only been a few hours."

"A few hours with Monk can seem like decades," he said. He took a pen from his pocket, scrawled something on the back of a business card, and handed it to me. "This is my home number. If you need a break, give me a call. I can take him out to the car wash."

"Thank you, Captain," I said. "That's very nice of you."

"You and I are the only ones who take care of him. We have to back each other up."

"We're sort of like partners."

"Sort of," Stottlemeyer said.

"He likes the car wash?"

"Loves it," Stottlemeyer said.

Monk finally reached the arson investigator, who was bent over with her back to him, examining something on the floor. I heard him clear his throat to get her attention. Gayle straightened up and turned around.

"Hello, Gayle. I'm Adrian Monk. I'm a consultant to the police." Monk shrugged a shoulder to draw her attention to the Junior Firefighter badge on his lapel. "And I'm one of your brothers."

She raised an eyebrow. "Is that so?"

"Could I have a Baggie?"

She took a clear plastic evidence bag out of the pocket of her windbreaker.

"Could you hold it open for me?"

She did. He emptied his ashes and the cigar stub into the bag and clapped his hands together, brushing off whatever microscopic traces might have been left. And then he brushed them a couple dozen more times for good measure.

"Thank you," Monk said, and left her holding the bag, his attention drawn to the coffee table. Its thick glass top and metal legs had survived the fire virtually unscathed. The table was in front of a pile of springs and ashes that I guessed was once the couch. More springs and ashes, the remains of two armchairs, were on the other side of the table.

Gayle sealed the bag and, with nowhere else to put it, reluctantly shoved it into her pocket to throw out later. I knew exactly how she felt.

"Where was the body found?" Monk asked, squatting beside the coffee table and squinting at an ashtray, a mug, and a glob of plastic that resembled a TV remote.

Gayle glanced at Stottlemeyer for approval, and he nodded.

"On the couch," she said.

"Where on the couch?"

The investigator pointed to the end of the couch farthest from Monk. "She was sitting in that corner, her hand on the armrest. The cigarette fell from her fingers and landed on a stack of newspapers on the floor, setting them aflame. The fire spread from there, engulfing the couch, the drapes, and eventually the entire room. She had piles of old newspapers. Matches and cigarettes everywhere. It was like kindling, a fire waiting to happen."

Monk made his way over to the TV, looking from it to the couch, then to the remains of the chairs.

"Have you found any traces of an accelerant?" Stottlemeyer asked the arson investigator.

"Nope," Gayle said. "The cigarette definitely caused this fire. It looks like an accident."

Monk nodded in agreement. "That's what it looks like."

"Great," Stottlemeyer said. "I can make it home early tonight and enjoy my Sunday off."

"But it's not," Monk said.

"Excuse me?" Gayle said with attitude, hands on her hips.

"It's not an accident," Monk said. "It's murder."

"Oh, hell," Stottlemeyer said.

"He's wrong," Gayle said.

"No, he's not," Stottlemeyer said miserably. "When it comes to murder, he's never wrong."

"I've been doing this job for ten years." Gayle opened her coat to show Monk the badge pinned on her uniform. "This is a *real* fire department badge, Mr. Monk. And I can tell you there is absolutely no evidence of arson."

Monk made his way to what had been the edge of the couch. "You said she died right here."

"Yes," Gayle said. "Her name was Esther Stoval, sixty-four years old, and a widow. The neighbors say she was a chain-smoker. Always had a cigarette in her mouth or in her hand."

"Did she live here alone?" Monk asked.

"With about a dozen cats," Gayle said. "They fled in the fire and have been coming back all day. We've got them out back waiting for Animal Control."

"Damn," Stottlemeyer muttered, then looked at me. "Can you tell the difference between one of your sneezes and another?"

"No," I said.

"Me neither," he said with relief. "So it's not just me."

"It's not just you," I said.

"If she was by herself, why was she sitting here?" Monk asked. "At this edge of the couch?"

"Because it was comfortable?" Gayle said. "What difference does it make?"

"Her coffee mug, her TV remote, and her ashtray are on the coffee table at the other end of the couch," Monk said.

I followed his gaze. The remote was a melted lump of plastic on the glass, but the mug and the ashtray were intact.

"If she sat there, she could see the TV," Monk said, gesturing to the other side of the couch. "But sitting here, where her body was found, the TV is blocked by that chair. Why would she want to look at an empty chair?"

Stottlemeyer looked back and forth between the couch and the TV and the remains of the chair.

"She wouldn't, not unless someone was sitting in it," Stottlemeyer said. "Someone else was here."

Gayle looked at Monk. "Damn."

She was impressed.

I was pretty impressed, too. That was twice in one day I'd seen Monk extrapolate a whole chain of events based on where a person—or a dog— happened to be sitting.

Who knew sitting could be so important?

Stottlemeyer took out his cell phone, flipped it open, and made a call. "Randy? It's me. Go down to the morgue. Tell the ME to move Esther Stoval's autopsy to the front of the line. It's a homicide. If you have any Sunday plans, cancel them."

He snapped his cell phone shut and glanced at

Monk. "I'm glad you stopped by, Monk. This one might have slipped past us."

And that's when I remembered why we'd stopped by in the first place.

5

Mr. Monk Learns to Share

We found Firefighter Joe Cochran sitting on an overturned bucket in the backyard, pouring milk into bowls and letting the cats crawl languorously all over him. He was a big man in his early thirties, who radiated strength and stoicism, qualities that seemed at odds with the tenderness he was showing to the cats. He stroked them gently, nuzzled them against his stubble-covered cheeks, and purred to them. For a moment I found myself wishing I could trade places with one of those cats.

The thought startled me. I've been involved with a few men since Mitch died, but none of them seriously, and none lately. I'd managed not to think about men for a long time, and was a little unnerved by how close to the surface those feelings really were. All it took was one glance at a rugged and tough, but sweet and tender, fireman to bring them all back.

My God, who was I kidding? Any woman would have felt the same way. He was the cover of a romance novel come to life. I just hoped when he spoke he didn't have a high, squeaky voice or a horrible lisp.

Repulsed, Monk stopped in his tracks. "How can he do that?"

"He's obviously a man who loves animals," I said.

"I'm not," Monk said.

"Really?" I said in mock surprise.

"You go talk to him," Monk said. "I'll stay here."

"Don't you want to ask him some questions?"

"I can read lips."

"You can?" I asked.

"This is as good a time as any to learn," Monk said.

I was hardly a natural at this detecting business, as I'd proved already. On the other hand, wouldn't it be nice to talk to Joe without Monk there?

"I can ask him to come over," I offered weakly.

"No," Monk said. "The cats might follow him. I could sneeze to death. It's a horrible way to die."

"Fine," I said, glancing back at Joe. My heart fluttered. It felt like high school all over again. "Any advice for me?"

"Remember to enunciate."

I took a deep breath and headed over to the hunky fireman. Hunky. Those were the terms in which I was thinking. How was I going to ask probing, sleuthful questions of Firefighter Joe when I'd mentally devolved into an adolescent girl?

"Joe Cochran?"

He looked up at me. "Yes, ma'am?"

Ma'am. He was brawny and polite. And God, what a smile.

"I'm Natalie Teeger," I said. "I work for Adrian Monk, the detective."

I motioned to Monk, who waved.

Joe rose to his feet and waved at Monk. The cats leaped off of him. "Why won't he come over here?"

"It's a long story," I said. "The reason we're here is because my daughter, Julie, is a student in one of the middle-school classes you visit each year. She heard about what happened to Sparky."

At the mention of his dog's name, Joe's eyes grew moist. It endeared him to me even more.

"The kids care that much?" he said.

"So much that she hired Mr. Monk to find whoever killed him."

"Excuse me." He turned his back to me and took a few steps away before wiping the tears from his eyes. I can't tell you how much I wanted to hold him, and comfort him, and wipe those tears away myself.

I swallowed hard and waited. After a moment he faced me again. "Forgive me, Miss Teeger."

"It's okay. Call me Natalie, please."

"As long as you call me Joe." He overturned another bucket, set it down beside his own, and offered me a seat. I took it.

Monk whistled and stirred the air with his finger. I got the message.

"Do you mind if we turn around?" I said, turning so I faced Monk.

"Why?" Joe asked.

"Mr. Monk needs to see our faces," I said. "He reads lips."

"Is he deaf?"

"No," I said.

"Okay," he said. "Is he a good detective?"

"The best," I said. "But eccentric."

"If he can find the son of a bitch who killed Sparky, I don't care if he likes to run naked through Golden Gate Park singing show tunes." He immediately caught himself, his cheeks reddening in embarrassment. "Oh, my God. I forgot. Can he really read lips?"

"I doubt it," I said, and waved at Monk. He gave me a thumbs-up.

Joe exhaled, relieved, and picked up one of the cats. "What do you need to know, Natalie?"

I liked hearing him say my name. Did I mention his voice wasn't the least bit squeaky?

"Do you know of anyone who'd want to hurt Sparky?"

His face tightened, but he continued to gently stroke the cat. "Only one person. Gregorio Dumas. He lives a few doors down from the station house."

That would certainly make it easy for him to know when the company responded to a fire and if the station was empty.

"What does he have against Sparky?"

"Love," Joe said. "Sparky was smitten with Letitia, Gregorio's French poodle."

"And Mr. Dumas didn't approve of the relationship?"

"Letitia is a show dog," Joe said. "Gregorio was afraid Sparky would ruin her career. He warned me that if he caught Sparky in his yard again, he'd kill him."

"Anybody else have a problem with your dog?"

Joe shook his head no. "Sparky was a smart, sweet, trusting animal. I'd take him to the cancer ward at the children's hospital, and he was so good with those kids, even the tiniest, frailest child. Everybody loved him."

"Somebody didn't," I said, and immediately regretted it.

His eyes started to tear up again, but this time he didn't try to hide it from me. "He wasn't just a dog to me, Natalie. He was my best friend. I know how corny that sounds, 'a boy and his dog.' But this job, and the hours I keep, aren't conducive to relationships, if you know what I mean."

Unfortunately, I did. Being a single mother who works for an obsessive-compulsive detective doesn't make for a great social life, either.

"I spend a lot of time alone. But I wasn't really alone, not with Sparky," he said. "Now I am. He was all I had. I feel gutted and totally adrift. Do you know what that's like?"

I took his hand, gave it a squeeze, and nodded. "Yeah, I do."

I suddenly felt self-conscious. I withdrew my hand and stood up.

"Mr. Monk will find whoever did this, Joe."

"How can you be sure?"

"Because he's Monk."

"I'm told he's got a long story," Joe said. "I'd like to hear it sometime."

"Here are my numbers," I said, writing them down on a piece of paper. "Please give me a call if you think of anything later that might help Mr. Monk's investigation." I took a deep breath. "Or if you want to hear that story."

"I will," he said with a smile.

I didn't know what else to say, so I just smiled back at him and headed back to Monk, who hadn't so much as taken a step from where he had been standing.

"How much of that did you get?" I asked.

"Just the part about enemas, Astroturf, and Wayne Newton's hair."

"None of those things came up."

"I see," Monk said. "I must have been reading the subtext."

There was subtext all right, but that sure as hell wasn't it.

For dinner I made Julie, Monk, and myself Dijon chicken breasts, petite peas, and mashed potatoes. Monk helped by counting out the peas onto our plates (we each had exactly twenty-four peas per serving) and laying them out in rows. He also served our mashed potatoes with an ice-cream scoop so they formed neat balls, which he carefully smoothed out with a butter knife.

Julie watched all this with rapt attention. It took her mind off her sadness, that's for sure.

While we ate, I filled her in on what we'd learned so far, which didn't sound very substantive to me but seemed to impress her. She gave Monk a hug and went back to her room to IM her friends.

I told her once that when I was her age we didn't have instant messaging to communicate with our friends. We used something called a telephone. You know what she said to me?

"I'm glad I live in the modern age."

I felt like a dinosaur.

Monk insisted on doing the dishes after dinner, and I didn't argue with him. While he worked I sat at the table and relaxed with a glass of wine. I decided there were some definite benefits to having a clean freak as a houseguest. I wondered what it would take to get him to do the laundry, but then I imagined him trying to sort our bras and panties without touching them, or even looking at them, and knew it would never work. On the other hand, it might be amusing to watch.

The phone rang. What would some anonymous cold caller in Bangladesh try to sell me tonight? I was tempted to let Monk answer the phone and put Rajid through the living hell he deserved, but I was merciful and snatched up the receiver myself.

"Hello," I said.

"Natalie Teeger? This is Joe Cochran. I hope I'm not bothering you."

He was, but in a good way. I reached for my

glass of wine and took a preemptive gulp to slow down my heart. It didn't work.

"Not at all," I lied.

"I was wondering if you might be interested in having dinner with me sometime," he said.

"That would be nice," I said, trying to sound casual about it when, in fact, I wanted to scream with glee.

"Is tomorrow too soon? My next night off duty isn't for a couple of days."

"Tomorrow works for me." Ten minutes from now would have worked for me, too, but I didn't want to seem too eager. We set a time and I gave him my address.

When I hung up the phone, Monk was drying the dishes and giving me a look.

"What?" I said.

"You're going on a date with Firefighter Joe?"

"It appears that way," I said, smiling giddily.

"Who is going to take care of Julie?"

I wasn't as concerned about that as I was about who would take care of *him*. I'd have to sit Julie down for a detailed briefing.

"I was hoping you'd keep an eye on her for me," I said. Then I lied, "A sitter is going to be hard to get on such short notice. Do you mind?"

"Will there be any shenanigans?"

"I don't think so," I said.

"Will I have to organize any activities?"

"She'll probably just stay in her room," I said. "She's at that age."

"Me too," Monk said.

*　　*　　*

On Sunday mornings, Julie and I like to get into our grungiest old sweats, grab the Sunday *Chronicle* off the porch, and go to the Valley Bakery, where we order blueberry muffins, coffee for me, hot chocolate for her, and forage through the paper.

Julie likes to read the comics, of course, and the capsule movie reviews in the Datebook, also known as the pink section for its colored pages. Each review is accompanied by a drawing of a little man in a bowler hat sitting in a movie theater chair. For a great movie he leaps out of his chair, hands clapping, eyes bugging out, hat flying off his head. If the movie stinks, he slumps in his seat, sound asleep.

Sometimes, as I go through the week, I picture that guy sitting in his chair, reviewing my life as it plays out in front of him. Most of the time he's sitting ramrod straight in his seat, mildly interested, which is a mediocre review. Rarely do I imagine him leaping out of his chair in ecstatic glee on my account.

After breakfast we take a long walk up a very steep hill to Delores Park, where the view of the Castro, the Civic Center, and the Financial District is spectacular. But that's not the view we go to see. We like to sit under a palm tree on the grassy knoll and people-watch. We see all kinds of people of every race in every possible combination.

Take the couples, for instance. We see men and women, men and men, women and women, and people who fall somewhere in between. We see mimes performing, kids playing, families picnicking, bands playing, groups protesting—all of it against the panoramic downtown backdrop. It's the best show in town.

We usually stay in the park for an hour or so, talking about the week that was and the week that's coming, and then, once we've caught our breath and had our fill of the show, we make the easy walk downhill. Once we get home, around noonish, we take our showers, change into fresh clothes, and do whatever chores and errands need doing.

But our routine was shaken up on that Sunday by a couple of things. First there was the weather. The city was socked in by thick fog and soaked by drizzle. And then there was Monk.

He woke me up at six A.M. with his incessant scrubbing. I dragged myself out of bed in my T-shirt and sweats to find him in the hall bathroom.

Monk, his hands in dish gloves, was on his knees in the bathtub polishing the drain. He was wearing a matched set of pajamas, and sheepskin slippers, which would have been adorable if he weren't an adult.

Obviously I'd cleaned the bathroom before he arrived, but not to the point that you needed sunglasses to tolerate the glare off the linoleum, which was what he'd done to it. On the sink there was a bar of soap still in its wrapper, a brand-new toothbrush enclosed in plastic, and a fresh tube of toothpaste. His electric razor was plugged into the outlet.

"It's six o'clock in the morning, Mr. Monk," I whispered so as not to wake Julie.

"I didn't know you're such an early riser."

"I'm not," I said. "What are you doing?"

"Getting ready to take a shower," he said.

"You do this before every shower?"

"And after," he said.

I shook my head and trudged to the kitchen. He was still in there two hours later. Julie was up by then and she was sitting at the table in her bathrobe, eating a bowl of cereal and shaking her leg.

"I really have to go to the bathroom, Mom."

"I'm sure Mr. Monk will be out in a minute," I said.

"You said that an hour ago," she said. "I've had two glasses of orange juice since then."

"That wasn't very smart, was it?"

"I didn't think he'd be in there forever," she said. "Couldn't you knock?"

"Is it that bad?"

"It's that bad," she said.

So we both got up and went to the bathroom door. I knocked.

"Mr. Monk?" I said. "We really need to use the bathroom."

"Does it have to be this one?" he asked from behind the door.

"It's the only one in the house," I said.

He opened the door, still holding his toothbrush. The bathroom gleamed the way it had at six. There was no sign at all that he'd used it. Julie bounced and shifted her weight from foot to foot.

"How well do you know the neighbors?" he asked.

"Not that well," I said. "We're going to have to share this bathroom."

"I don't see how that is going to work," he said.

Julie groaned in frustration, pushed past Monk, and went straight for the toilet. He scrambled out of the bathroom in terror and slammed the door closed behind him before she could even lift up the lid of the toilet seat.

Monk stood there looking at me. I looked at him.

"There's only one bathroom and three of us," I said.

"It's barbaric," he said. "Does the health department know about this?"

"You'll just have to get used to it."

"How can you live this way?" he said.

"If you paid me more," I said, "I wouldn't have to."

That shut him up. I knew it would.

The only thing stronger than Monk's compulsion for cleanliness and order is his stinginess with money.

6

Mr. Monk Meets the Queen

I spent an hour acting as Julie's social secretary, arranging a playdate for her at the home of one of her friends so she would be under a parent's supervision for the day while I assisted Monk on his investigation.

Since, technically, Monk was working for Julie, she didn't mind that I was dumping her at her friend's house. It didn't hurt that her friend had an Xbox, a PlayStation, a Game Boy, and every other computer game gizmo ever devised by man. The downside for me was that Julie would come home demanding, for the hundredth time, that I buy her all that stuff, too.

Monk and I were out the door at 10 A.M. The first stop Monk wanted to make was at the home of Gregorio Dumas, the man who lived across the street from the firehouse and was, according to

Firefighter Joe, Sparky's only enemy and therefore our number one suspect.

We knocked on Gregorio Dumas's front door a half hour later. He look as if he patronized the same groomer as his dog. His fluffy mane of golden hair was styled into an enormous, flowing pompadour. His silhouette reminded me of a French poodle, which, by the way, was the animal he happened to own.

Coincidence? I don't think so.

The guy was short and fat, with gold rings on every finger and necklaces and medallions draped around his neck. All his bling had a tacky canine theme, like the enormous, diamond-encrusted dog bone on the gold chain around his neck. He stood at his front door in a silk kimono, smirking with haughty superiority and evident distaste at his guests on the stoop, who happened to be Mr. Monk and me. Behind the two of us was the fire station where Sparky was killed.

"You obviously like dogs," Monk said after introducing us and explaining why were there.

"You *are* a detective," Gregorio said in a voice that was equal parts Ricardo Montalban and Fran Drescher. "Are all your deductions as brilliant as that?"

He stepped aside to let us in. It looked like he'd inherited his home furnishings from an elderly relative who did a lot of shopping at Levitz in 1978. The upholstery reminded me of the Impala station wagon my parents used to have.

An entire wall of shelves overflowed with dog show trophies, award ribbons, and framed photos of Letitia and her proud owner. Seeing the pictures, I was convinced I was right about their sharing the same groomer.

"If you like dogs so much," Monk said, "you must be heartbroken about what happened to Sparky."

"He was a rapist," Gregorio said. "A canine sex offender."

"C'mon," I said. "We're talking about dogs here."

"Letitia is not a dog; she's a symbol of perfection and beauty, the reigning queen of the canine world," Gregorio said. "Or she was until Sparky ruined her life."

He swept his arm in front of the wall of honors. "She's won hundreds of American Kennel Club competitions, including Best in Show at the Tournament of Champions. Letitia earned over sixty thousand dollars in prize money and endorsements last year alone."

"So you're living off your dog," Monk said.

"She enjoys the fruits of her success," Gregorio said. "She lives better than I do."

"She couldn't live worse," Monk muttered.

Gregorio led us through the kitchen. The laundry room was a modified pantry, and Monk paused to look in at a fresh load of clothes, underwear, and towels folded on the dryer.

"Mr. Monk," I said, drawing his attention away before he started to refold everything or, worse, began giving his lecture on the importance of separating clothes by type of garment into their own stacks.

Gregorio opened the door to the backyard, which was dominated by a miniature Victorian cottage with a cedar-shingled roof, gables, cupola, bay windows, and a wraparound porch with flower boxes. There were a bunch of rubber chew toys on the porch, including a bone, a squeaky ball, a hot dog, and a cat. There was a high fence ringed with razor wire surrounding the yard.

"You've got to treat royalty like royalty," Gregorio said.

"All that," I said, "for a dog? I could live in there."

"How many bathrooms does it have?" Monk asked.

"Show dogs are judged by teeth, muscle tone, bone structure, coat texture, and, most important, how they carry themselves. Their gait, their balance, how all the elements fit together. A dog who lives in a castle walks like a queen. That's what she was, a queen."

"You keep talking about Letitia in the past tense," Monk said. "What happened to her?"

"Sparky's lust," Gregorio said. He whistled for the dog.

Letitia bounded out of her mansion. The French poodle still had her astonishingly white, fluffy hair and her regal bearing, but she was almost as rotund as her owner.

"Sparky knocked her up," Gregorio said.

She went straight for Monk and shoved her nose toward his crotch. Monk blocked her with his hands and squealed when her wet nose made contact with his skin.

"I've been hit," he said, backing into the living room while the dog pushed him along, trying to get her nose past his hands.

"Now she's just a pregnant bitch," Gregorio said as he returned to the living room. I followed him. "Soon she'll be fat and swollen with big, bloated udders. But that's nothing compared to what she's going to look like after she squeezes out a litter of puppies."

Monk grabbed a pillow from the couch and placed it protectively in front of his groin. So the enthusiastic dog angled around for a sniff at his butt instead. He dropped into a chair, covered his lap with the pillow, and pinched his knees together.

I could have helped Monk, of course. But after the morning ordeal with the bathroom, I was enjoying some payback.

"Surely she can get back into shape," I said. After all, I thought, I bounced back to my old form after my pregnancy, didn't I?

"Sagging teats, wrinkly skin, bloodshot eyes; that's her future," he said. "A shriveled-up shell of her old self. I warned those firemen something bad would happen if they let their spotted monster run wild through the neighborhood whenever they left the station."

There was a mirror on the wall. I looked at my reflection, wondering if that was what Joe was going to see at dinner tonight: sagging teats, wrinkly skin, bloodshot eyes.

"It's not like she bred with a show dog. Sparky was common street trash," Gregorio said. "Can you imagine what those mixed-breed mongrel monsters are gonna look like? I won't shed any tears over Sparky."

Letitia jumped up on the couch beside Monk and started licking his cheek.

"Help," Monk squeaked.

"Sounds like you hated Sparky enough to kill him," I said.

"Except I didn't," Gregorio said.

"Is that the best you can do?" I said.

"Help," Monk squeaked again.

I grabbed Letitia by the collar and pulled her away from Monk, who bolted out the front door and closed it behind him.

"If I was gonna kill him, I would have done it before he knocked up Letitia," Gregorio said, taking Letitia from me. "What good would it do me now?"

"How about revenge?" Monk said from outside, his voice muffled by the door.

"I won't say it didn't cross my mind," Gregorio said.

"What?" Monk said.

"*It crossed my mind*," Gregorio yelled. "But I'm suing the San Francisco Fire Department for Letitia's lost earning potential instead."

"Where were you last night between ten P.M. and two A.M.?" I asked Gregorio.

"Here," Gregorio said. "Alone."

"That's not much of an alibi," I said.

"I don't need one," Gregorio said. "Because I didn't do it."

"Could you speak up?" Monk called out.

"*I didn't do it,*" Gregorio yelled back. "*Ask the fireman.*"

Monk opened the door a crack, just enough to stick his face in. "What fireman?"

"The one I saw coming out of the station about ten thirty," Gregorio said.

"But they all left at ten to fight a fire," I said.

"I know that. Don't you think I've got ears? It's a real joy to live across the street from a fire station, let me tell you. Anyway, the blaring sirens at ten; then a half hour later that damn hell-dog of theirs starts barking. I looked out my window to see if he was trotting over here to defile Letitia some more, but the barking stopped and I didn't see anything. Five minutes later, Letitia starts barking, so I look out the window again, thinking Sparky's on his way over for some action, and I see a fireman walking out."

"How do you know it was a fireman?" Monk asked.

"I could see his helmet and heavy coat," Gregorio said.

"But not his face," I said.

"He had his back to me," Gregorio said. "And it was nighttime, and he was across the street. Now if you will excuse me, I've got things to do."

He ushered me to the door. The instant I stepped outside, Monk waved his hands frantically in front of me, as if ants were swarming all over them.

"Wipe, wipe, wipe," he said.

I gave him about thirty of them as we walked to the car, which was parked in front of the fire station.

"I need to shower," Monk said. "For a year."

"Who does he think he's kidding?" I said. "He expects us to believe that a fireman killed Sparky? How lame is that? He's just trying to deflect attention from himself."

"He's not the guy," Monk said.

"How can you say that? Sparky knocked up his cash cow—or cash poodle—whatever. The point is, Gregorio lost sixty thousand dollars per year. That's plenty of motive for murder, and he lives right across from the fire station, so he knows exactly when the firemen come and go."

"He's not the guy," Monk said.

"He admitted he loathed Sparky and that he knew the firemen left at ten," I said. "It probably happened just like you said. He went over there to poison the dog food or something and Sparky surprised him."

"He's not the guy," Monk said.

"Will you please stop saying that?" I asked. "Did you see his hair? He's got to be the guy. How do you know he's not the guy?"

"He's too fat," Monk said. "He never could have made it to the pickax before Sparky took him down. But he's lying."

"About what?"

"He was in the fire station the night Sparky was killed."

"How do you know?"

"His laundry," Monk said. "I saw the two missing firehouse towels folded with his socks. Can you believe that? With his socks."

"Why didn't you say anything?"

"I was busy defending myself from that vicious dog and its slavering jaws of death."

I suspected the slavering part was what concerned him the most. Then again, if I lick my lips, he accuses me of slavering.

"Gregorio Dumas is still in possession of stolen property," I said. "Though you've got to wonder why he took the towels in the first place."

"I do," Monk said. "I also wonder how Sparky got Letitia pregnant."

"I could explain that to you," I said. "But do I really have to?"

"I don't mean how he did it, but how he was *able* to do it."

"He's a dog, she's a dog, I think that's all that really matters to dogs," I said. "That's why they call them dogs."

"What I mean is, the backyard is protected by a fence topped with flesh-cutting razor wire. How did Sparky get into the yard?"

"Maybe the fence was installed after the deed was done?"

We didn't get a chance to ponder the question because my cell phone rang. It was Stottlemeyer. He wanted to see Monk in his office right away.

Stottlemeyer's office was more than just an office. It was his refuge. Here he could do all the things his wife wouldn't let him do at home. He could smoke cigars. Eat junk food. Pick his nose.

He could take off his shoes, put his stockinged feet up on the desk, and browse *Sports Illustrated*'s swimsuit issue. The office was also filled with all the stuff she wouldn't let him display around their house, like his baseball memorabilia, his *Serpico* movie poster, his collection of cigar labels, and the bullet that was dug out of his shoulder a few years back.

So as much, and as often, as Stottlemeyer complained about having to work late and on weekends, I knew he took more comfort and solace in being in his office than he was willing to admit.

"I hate coming in here on my day off," Stottlemeyer said as we gathered in his office. The bullpen outside was sparsely occupied by three or four detectives.

Stottlemeyer was wearing a sweatshirt, jeans, and tennis shoes to remind himself, and anyone who saw him, that he was supposed to be home relaxing.

Lieutenant Randall Disher, by comparison, was in his usual ill-fitting, off-the-rack suit and tie, as if it were any other day of the week. He idolized Stottlemeyer, so he was never entirely comfortable around him. A tremor of eager-to-please anxiety underscored his every word and action.

"We could use your help on this one, Monk," Stottlemeyer said. "And since you're the one who brought this unsolvable homicide to our attention, I think you've got a duty to solve it for us."

"Unsolvable?" Monk asked. "There's no such thing."

"That's the spirit," Stottlemeyer said. "Tell him what we have, Randy."

Disher referred to his notebook. "Ordinarily in these kinds of accidents, where someone falls asleep while smoking, it's not the fire that kills them but the smoke."

"Did the medical examiner find smoke or soot particles in the victim's lungs or nasal passages?" Monk asked.

"No," Stottlemeyer said. "Meaning Esther Stoval was dead before the fire started."

"There you go," Monk said. "It's murder. You solved it. What's the unsolvable part?"

"We're getting to that," Stottlemeyer said. "Go on, Randy. Tell him the rest."

"The ME found bits of fabric in her windpipe and petechial hemorrhages in the conjuntivae of her eyes that come from increased pressure in the veins when—"

"Yadda, yadda, yadda," Stottlemeyer interrupted him. "In other words, she was smothered with a pillow."

"But we'll never get anything off the murder weapon because it was incinerated in the fire," Disher said. "Along with any fingerprints or other trace evidence that the killer might have left in the room."

"We've got no witnesses, either," Stottlemeyer said. "We canvassed the neighborhood. Nobody saw or heard anything."

"So you're saying you can prove it was murder but not who did it," Monk said. "And you'll never be able to prove who did it because all the evidence went up in flames."

"You got it," Stottlemeyer said. "We're looking at the perfect murder."

Monk tilted his head from one side to the other. I've seen him do that before. It's like he's trying to loosen up a stiff neck, but I think what really goes on is that his mind refuses to accept some fact he's seen or heard.

"I don't think so," Monk said.

"You already see the mistake the killer made?" Stottlemeyer said.

Monk nodded. "He shouldn't have killed Esther Stoval."

"You got anything more substantial than that for us to run with?" Stottlemeyer asked.

"Not yet," Monk said. "But I'm working on it."

"That's good to hear," Stottlemeyer said. "It's a start."

"What do you know about the victim?" I asked.

"From talking to the neighbors, we know that Esther was a miserable, chain-smoking harridan whom nobody liked," Stottlemeyer said. "Worse than that, she stood in the way of everybody on her block getting stinking rich."

He explained that Lucas Breen, a developer known for rejuvenating tired neighborhoods with innovative mixed-use developments, wanted to demolish those six ugly town houses and build a Victorian-style condominium and retail project. Esther Stoval was the only homeowner on the block who wouldn't sell, enraging her neighbors, who'd already sold their places to Breen and whose deals were contingent on her selling as well.

"Looks like there's no shortage of suspects," I said.

"They all could have done it," Stottlemeyer said. "They could have stood in a line and taken turns holding the pillow to her face. But we have no way of proving any of them were in that house the night it burned down."

"Maybe because none of them did it," Disher said.

"Where are you going with this, Randy?" Stottlemeyer asked.

"I have a theory," Disher said. "It's a little out-of-the-box."

"That's okay," Stottlemeyer said.

"What if it's the cats?" Disher said.

"The cats," Stottlemeyer said. "How could it be the cats?"

"There was this great Robert Culp movie. There are these scientists doing research in a remote lab in the Arctic on the effects of isolation on monkeys. The scientists are getting killed one by one, and no one knows who the killer is. The surviving scientists are afraid to turn their backs on one another," Disher said. "Pretty soon, it's down to just Robert Culp and one other guy and—"

"It's the monkeys," Monk said. "They turned the tables on the scientists and manipulated them into killing one another."

"How did you know?" Disher said.

Stottlemeyer sighed. "Because you started telling us that endless story to support your inane theory that the cats killed Esther Stoval."

"What if the cats purposely tipped the pillow onto her face and, while one of them sat on it, another one knocked the cigarette onto the newspapers?" Disher said. "What if it was an act of feline rebellion against their cruel master?"

"That isn't out-of-the-box thinking, Randy," Stottlemeyer said. "It's out-of-your-mind thinking."

"Cats are very clever, Captain," Disher said.

"Stop," Stottlemeyer said.

Disher started to speak again, but Stottlemeyer held up his hand to halt him.

"One more word and I'll shoot you," Stottlemeyer said, then looked imploringly at Monk. "Now do you see how badly we need you on this?"

7

Mr. Monk and the Buttons

The fog lifted Sunday afternoon, but dark clouds gathered over the city, pushed by a cold wind that made the torn, yellow caution tape outside Esther Stoval's scorched house dance in the air like party streamers.

Although there wasn't actually a party going on, the young couple living next door, Neal and Kate Finney, definitely had a skip to their step as they loaded up a U-Haul truck with moving boxes. They lived in one of the five town houses slated for demolition to make way for Lucas Breen's proposed condominium and retail complex.

"We only had minor smoke and water damage, but now that Mrs. Stoval is dead, there's really no reason to stick around another day." Kate wheeled a hand truck stacked high with boxes down to the U-Haul. "The house belongs to Lucas Breen's company now, which means we'll finally get our check."

"Honolulu, here we come," Neal said from inside the truck. He wore a loud Hawaiian shirt and cargo shorts despite the chilly weather. That's how enthusiastic he was.

"You aren't even trying to hide how happy you are that she's dead," Monk said.

"Nope," Neal said.

"You were her next-door neighbors. She stood between the building of the new condo complex and your big payday. Now she's dead and you're on the next plane to Hawaii," Monk said. "Aren't you concerned about how this makes you look?"

"We'll be sure to leave the police our forwarding address." Kate wheeled the boxes up to her husband, slid the hand truck out from under the stack, and headed back to the house for another load.

"You have the best possible motive for killing her, and you aren't even bothering to hide it," Monk said.

"It's our best defense," Neal said as he organized the boxes in the truck. "With all we had to gain, we'd have to be complete morons to torch her place."

"That could be your cunning plan," Monk said. "It's so obvious that you did it that nobody would think you did it, even though you did do it."

"We were out to dinner at Ruggerios with two other couples when the fire happened," Neal said. "Had I known what was going on, I would have ordered two more bottles of wine and picked up the check for everybody."

"A lonely old woman was killed in that fire," I said. "Doesn't that mean anything to you?"

"You don't know anything about Esther Stoval or what it was like living next door to her. So don't judge me, lady."

I didn't like these people or their selfishness and unadulterated greed. Did they sell their souls to Lucas Breen along with their home?

I thought about my own house and what it meant to me. Mitch and I found it, fell in love with it, and bought it together. Our daughter was born under its roof. I can still feel his presence in the walls, in the air, in the light streaming through the windows. Next to Julie, it's the last true attachment to him I have left. I couldn't sell it, no matter how much my neighbors pressured me.

"Did it occur to you for even one second that she might have refused to sell not just to be obstinate or for the evil pleasure of denying you wealth?" I said. "Maybe her house had deep, sentimental value to her. Maybe she loved living here and didn't want to move."

"She could have stayed," Kate said, wheeling some more boxes out of the house. "The developer offered to give her one of the condos in the new complex rent-free for the rest of her life, in addition to the good money he was paying her for her house. You can't get much more generous than that. And she still said no."

"It's not the same thing." Disgusted, I walked

away until I was out of earshot but still within sight of Monk if he needed me. I couldn't stand to be near these people for another minute.

Monk stuck around and asked a few more questions. I don't know what they were. Maybe he asked them what it was like living without a soul. Maybe he asked them what it was like to value money more than another person's right to happiness. But knowing Monk, he probably asked them to rearrange the boxes in the truck into even stacks of eight with the same sides facing out.

Aubrey Brudnick was a professional intellectual in his forties who worked at a San Francisco think tank and lived next door to the late Esther Stoval.

"I'm paid for my thoughts," he said, talking through his nose and chewing on his pipe. "If I can't think, I starve, and that is why I loathed Esther Stoval."

Judging by his double chins and potbelly, it wouldn't have hurt him to starve a little. He wore a blue cable-knit sweater over a white T-shirt, brown corduroy slacks, and black leather Ecco running shoes. His feet were up on his book-cluttered desk, which faced a window that looked out on the charred rubble of Esther's house.

"You couldn't think with her around?" Monk asked.

"It wasn't so much her," Brudnick said. "It was her cats."

"We heard she took in a lot of strays," I said.

"There were dozens of them. And they weren't

simply strays," Brudnick said. "They were exotics. She trolled the shelters looking for rare breeds. Just a few days ago she brought home a Turkish Van, a fluffy breed also known as the White Ringtail and the Russian Longhair."

He reached for a large book on his desk, found the page he was looking for, and passed it to me. It was a book on cat breeds, and he'd turned to the listing for the Turkish Van, a white cat with a cashmere-like coat.

"You kept track of her cats?" Monk said.

"It's a failing of mine. If a bird flies by, I need to know what it is. If a car is parked out front, I need to know its history. If I hear someone whistling a tune, I need to know the name and the complete biography of its composer," Brudnick said. "My intellectual curiosity is my great failing as well as my gift."

"I know the feeling," Monk said.

"That's one of the reasons I found her cats so distracting. Every time I saw one, I had to research the damn animal," Brudnick said. "The other thing, of course, was the smell. Her house was like an enormous litter box, and on breezy days the smell carried, along with all that dander."

"Did you do anything about it?" Monk said.

"I spoke to her," Brudnick said. "But she told me to mind my own business, which, coming from her, I found rather ironic."

"Why is that?"

"Because the old crone was always peeking in my windows, sorting through the mail in my box, and reading my magazines," Brudnick said. "I started walking through my house naked just so I could get a little privacy."

Monk shuddered at the thought, and so did I.

"You never thought about taking more direct action?" Monk said.

"You mean like burning her house down?"

Monk nodded. Brudnick smiled.

"I thought about it every day," Brudnick said. "Instead I sold out to Lucas Breen and looked forward to a new home in the near future, far away from Esther and her feline menagerie."

"So Esther wasn't just making your life a living hell," I said. "She was also standing between you and a fortune."

"She wasn't my favorite neighbor on the block; that's true. But I didn't wish any violence upon her."

"Where were you between nine and ten P.M. on Friday night?" Monk asked.

"Enjoying a hot bath and the latest issue of *American Spectator*," Brudnick said.

That was an image that would haunt me.

"Were you alone?" Monk asked.

"Sadly, yes," Brudnick said. "It's been some time since I've found a lady who'll share a bath and *American Spectator* with me."

He looked at me and smiled. I think it's a credit to me and my astonishing powers of self-control that I didn't vomit or run screaming out of his house at that moment.

"Did you see or hear anything unusual that night?" Monk said.

"Not until her house went up in flames," Brudnick said. "That was certainly unusual."

It was depressing. Esther's other neighbors on her side of the street had the same attitude about her as the Finneys and Brudnick did. Nobody saw anything, nobody heard anything, and nobody cared. They were all eagerly awaiting their checks and the wrecking ball.

We went across the street to see what the other neighbors had to say, the ones without the sales of their homes on the line, who didn't profit quite so directly from Esther's death.

We found Burton Joyner, a scrawny, unemployed software engineer, in his garage, working under the hood of an old AMC Pacer, a car that looked like a pregnant Ford Pinto—which was, by the way, the first car I ever owned, until my dad heard they could explode if a bug hit the windshield and bought me a Plymouth Duster instead. Joyner also had an AMC Gremlin and an AMC Ambassador parked at the curb.

"I'll be honest with you, Mr. Monk. I'm glad she's gone," Joyner said, tightening something with his wrench.

"She's not gone," I said. "You make it sound like she moved to Palm Springs. She was murdered."

"Esther was a victim of the bad karma she created," Joyner said. "She was a mean, vindictive person who made life unpleasant for everybody in the neighborhood. You can feel the difference on the street already. The stress level has gone way down."

"And the property values will go way up," Monk said. "Once the new development is built."

"The development isn't really important to me. It won't change my circumstances much, so I've stayed out of it. I'm the kind of guy who likes to get along with people." Joyner leaned back and wiped his hands on his jeans, smearing them with grease. "Live and let live is what I say."

"Me too," Monk said. "You wiped your hands on your pants."

"Esther wasn't like you and me. She'd sit at her window with binoculars, taking notes and pictures, intruding on things that were none of her business. She saw me watching a ball game on ESPN, so she called the cable company and ratted me out for hijacking their signal with an illegal converter box."

"Were you?" I asked.

"That's not the point," Joyner said. "How was sitting in my recliner in my living room, watching a ball game on TV, hurting her?"

"You stained your pants," Monk said.

"It's okay; they're my work pants," Joyner said. "I'll give you another example. My hobby is collecting and restoring old AMC cars. I've had to sell a couple of them to create some cash flow until I can find another job. Esther took pictures of people buying cars from me and filed a complaint with the city clerk, who fined me two thousand dollars for operating a business out of my home without a license."

"What did she have against you?" Monk said.

"Absolutely nothing. I never did a thing to her.

She treated everybody that way. She had a certain view of life and expected everyone to conform to it. How crazy is that?"

"Super crazy," Monk said. "You can go change your pants. We'll wait here."

"I don't want to change my pants."

"You really should," Monk said.

"I'm fine in these."

"You'll thank me later."

"No, I won't," Joyner said. "Do you have any more questions? I'd like to get back to my work."

"Where were you Friday night between nine and ten P.M.?" Monk asked.

"I was here at home, doing my laundry."

"I see," Monk said. "So you don't deny you have a pair of clean pants you could change into?"

"What's the matter with you?" Joyner said.

"Think about the karma your pants are creating," Monk said. "Did you see anybody visit Esther Friday night?"

Joyner shook his head. "I don't spy on my neighbors; I don't keep track of who comes and goes or what they're watching on TV."

He wiped his hands on his shirt—deliberately, I think—picked up his wrench, and got back to work.

"Why did you do that?" Monk said to him. "Now you have to change your shirt, too."

"Let's go, Mr. Monk," I said. "We have other neighbors to talk to."

"But we can't just leave him like that," Monk said:

"Let's go." I tugged on his overcoat and led him away.

Monk came along, but he wasn't happy about it. He kept looking back at the house we'd just left. "I don't know how you can turn a blind eye to other people's suffering."

"He's not suffering," I said.

"I am," Monk said.

After hearing Joyner's story, and those of his neighbors, I was beginning to wonder if I was being too hard on Neal and Kate Finney. It appeared that Esther Stoval didn't do much to encourage warmth and understanding from the people around her. I wondered how I'd feel about Esther if I had to live on the same street with her year after year. Maybe I'd be dancing with glee over her death, too.

There was one last neighbor whom Monk wanted to question, if only because there were six houses on each side of the block and he couldn't bear to leave on an odd number.

Lizzie Draper lived in the Victorian on the corner—her house also doubled as her art studio. It was a bright, open, and airy space, filled with colorful bouquets of flowers, one of which she was using as model for the still life she was painting. I could see why. The bouquet was a stunning mix of green orchids, blue hydrangeas, red and yellow lilies, orange roses, coral peonies, purple trachelium, yellow celosia, and red amaryllis.

The sad thing was she didn't have the talent to capture the vibrant colors or the natural beauty of the bouquet. Samples of her other paintings, sketches, and sculptures were everywhere, and, I have to say, I've seen better artwork at Julie's middle school open house.

The only sculptures worth studying were her breasts, enormous implants like two basketballs tucked into her loose-fitting denim shirt. She had three buttons opened to reveal a provocative glimpse of her deep cleavage.

"I'm Adrian Monk, and this is Natalie Teeger," he said. "We're assisting the police in their investigation of Esther Stoval's murder."

Monk stared at her chest. She was clearly flattered, but I knew it wasn't her bosom that enthralled him. It was the three buttons. If she didn't open one more button, or button one up, he might have a stroke.

"I'd like to ask you three some questions," he said.

"Three?" she said.

"I think he means three questions," I said. "Don't you, Mr. Monk?"

"Did you see or hear anything unusual Friday night?" Monk said to her buttons.

"I wasn't home," she said. "I was at work. I'm a bartender at Flaxx."

I knew the place. It's a hot club on Market Street. It's where the beautiful, young, rich people go to admire how beautiful, young, and rich they are. I tried to get a job there once, but I didn't have the right qualifications. Monk was staring at hers.

"You're not an artist?" I said.

"It's who I am, but it's not what I do. It's what sustains me, but not what I live on. It's—"

"I think I get it," I said, interrupting her.

She looked back at Monk, who was still fixated on her buttons.

"When did you get back from work?" It was getting increasingly difficult for him to concentrate. Or breathe.

"After midnight," Lizzie said. "The whole street was closed off. There were firemen everywhere. I couldn't believe what had happened."

His unwavering attention to her chest finally became too much even for her. She bent her knees to look him in the eye, but he matched her move, crouching to stay focused on her buttons.

"Mr. Monk, you haven't looked me in the eye once since you came into my house."

"I'm sorry; it's your buttons," Monk said. "They are very distracting."

"My buttons, how sweet." Lizzie straightened up and smiled with false modesty. "I didn't mean to make you uncomfortable. They're new, and I guess I like showing them off."

"You should have two," Monk said.

"That's what God intended."

"Or four," Monk said.

"Four?"

"But this isn't natural," Monk said, pointing at her cleavage. "You should really fix those."

"What did you just say to me?" Her smile morphed into an angry sneer. It wasn't pretty.

"I think there's been a misunderstanding," I said, which was like trying to stop a runaway train after it had already jumped the tracks and plowed into an orphanage. "He doesn't mean what you think he means."

"There's no reason to get upset; it's very easy to correct," Monk said. "You can do it yourself."

She marched to the door and held it open. "Get out. Now."

Monk held up his hands in surrender, gave me a look, and left. I tried to apologize, but she hustled me out and slammed the door behind me.

"Can you believe some people?" He shook his head in disbelief. "They get so worked up over nothing."

8

Mr. Monk Straightens Up

Julie sat on the rim of the bathtub watching me while I stood at the mirror, fixing my hair and putting on a little makeup for my date with Firefighter Joe. The bathroom door was closed, so I knew there was no chance of Monk invading our privacy. Julie knew it, too.

"You're not really going to leave me alone with him, are you?" Julie said.

"Mr. Monk is a very sweet man," I said.

"He's strange."

"Stranger than Mrs. Throphamner?" I said, referring to her usual babysitter. "At least Mr. Monk won't take his teeth out and put them in a glass while he watches television."

"Mom, he wouldn't let me tie my shoes this morning because the two ends of my shoelaces weren't even. And then after I relaced the shoes, he *measured* the laces to be sure they were right."

"That's his way of showing how much he cares about you."

"That's not all. He insisted on tying my shoes because the bows I make aren't 'symmetrical.'"

"Things will be just fine tonight if you follow a couple of simple rules. Don't ask him to make choices. Don't create disorganization of any kind. And whatever you do, don't make popcorn."

"Why not?"

"No two kernels are the same. It makes him crazy."

"Gee, how can you tell?" she said. She'd recently discovered sarcasm, the perfect tool to express her growing frustration, common among all kids her age, with having to tolerate parental authority.

"He likes Wheat Thins. They're squares. There's an unopened box in the pantry."

"Why can't I come with you?"

"It's a date," I said.

"Who says you can't bring your daughter on a date?"

"You don't see me inviting myself to your sleepovers with your friends, do you?"

"You're going to *sleep* with him tonight?"

"No, of course not," I said. "That wasn't what I meant. I'm just saying that sometimes I need a little time to myself. Would you like me to come along on your dates?"

"I don't date," she said. "You won't let me yet."

"Well, if you did, would you want me there?"

"Fine." She sighed, and it came out more like an anguished groan. "What are we supposed to do while you're out having fun?"

I started to clean up the mess I'd made at the sink. "Do what you always do. Watch a movie. Read a book. IM your friends."

"What about Mr. Monk?"

I looked at the wet towels draped over the shower curtain rod, at the razor I had used to shave my legs, and at all the cotton balls on the floor that had missed the garbage can . . . and I hatched an evil, insidious plot: I decided to leave them.

"Don't worry about Mr. Monk," I said, giving her a kiss on the cheek. "He'll be busy getting an early start on tomorrow's shower."

I gave myself one last critical appraisal in the mirror, decided there was nothing left I could do without expensive cosmetic surgery, and left the bathroom. It was perfect timing because Firefighter Joe was already knocking at the door.

Monk opened it with a handkerchief, perhaps in case someone infected with bubonic plague had touched the doorknob while we weren't looking.

Firefighter Joe looked just as good in a leather bomber jacket, polo shirt, and brown corduroy pants as he did in uniform. I had a hunch he looked good in everything. He held a nice bouquet of roses, carnations, and morning glories in one hand and a tiny gift box in the other.

"You're right on time." Monk tapped his watch. "To the second. That's very impressive."

"Mr. Monk?" Joe said, brow furrowed with confusion. "I didn't realize that you and Natalie were—"

"We're not," I interrupted. "Mr. Monk is staying with us while his apartment building is being fumigated. You look great, by the way. Not that it's an afterthought. I mean, I noticed it right away, which isn't to say—"

"Mom," Julie said. She knows I tend to babble when I'm nervous and does her best to stop me, mostly to save herself, rather than me, from embarrassment.

"These are for you," Joe said as he offered me the flowers and Julie the gift box.

"What is this for?" Julie asked.

"Open it and see," he said.

Julie let out a little gasp when she saw what was in the box. She took out a tiny red badge, similar to the one that Captain Mantooth gave Monk, only this one had a dog-bone emblem.

"It's Sparky's fire dog badge," Julie said. "I can't take this."

"I want you to have it," Joe said. "For caring about Sparky so much that you hired the best detective in San Francisco to find his killer."

It didn't matter what Joe might say or do on the date; he'd won me over already. Julie, too. She gave Joe a hug.

"Mom said I could come with you."

"No, I didn't," I said quickly, before Joe could reply. "You're staying here with Mr. Monk."

"It's going to be fun," Monk said. "We can play with LEGOs."

"I'm twelve," Julie said indignantly. "I don't have any LEGOs."

"Then it's a good thing I brought mine," Monk said.

"You play with LEGOs?" Julie said, astonished.

"Are you joking? I'm a red-hot LEGO demon. I've got the building-block fever."

Julie gave me a pleading look, as if I were abandoning her to wolves. "Mom, please. The man has LEGOs."

"It can get pretty intense," Monk said. "But we'll start with some simple structures before we increase the excitement."

"Don't get her *too* excited," I said to Monk. "She's got school tomorrow."

I gave her a kiss and got Joe out of there as fast as I could.

This isn't a story about me or my love life; it's a story about Adrian Monk and how he solved two puzzling murders, so I won't bore you with a lot of details about my date with Firefighter Joe. Oh, who am I kidding? It's my book and I'm going to talk about whatever I feel like. If you don't like it, flip ahead a couple of pages.

Some guys try to impress you on a first date by taking you to either a fancy restaurant or a trendy one or on some creative excursion. But I think a date is all about introducing a person to who you are, what matters to you, and what your approach to life is. I guess, in some ways, you're getting that when a guy tries to wow you with extravagance or cleverness. He's telling me he's not the guy for me.

Joe took me to his favorite restaurant in Chinatown, a ten-table, family-owned place with dead ducks hanging in the window as an enticement to come in and sample the menu. Monk would have run away screaming.

Everyone knew Joe there, so it was almost like going to dinner with his family. The food was good, and it was cheap. Another woman might have walked away with the impression that Joe was a cheapskate. Not me. It showed me that Joe was a confident, easygoing guy who was well liked by others and comfortable with his life. Besides, as a single mother on a limited income, I'm always looking for affordable places to eat. It also told me that he was stable and reliable—a guy who runs from relationships and commitments doesn't go to the same restaurant for years and make friends with the staff.

We talked about the usual first-date stuff. We told each other abbreviated versions of our life stories. I tried to tell mine without dwelling too much on Mitch's death so as not to depress myself or Joe. I learned that he was raised in Berkeley, that his father was a poet and his mother was a park ranger, and that he'd never been married.

The conversation then turned to firefighting. He told some exciting stories about fires and the colorful history of his firehouse, which was built after the 1906 quake on the site of a rooming house that was the final hideout of desperado Roderick

Turlock, the notorious train robber who bedeviled the Pinkertons with his daring gold thefts.

Talking about the firehouse, of course, brought up the investigation into Sparky's death. I filled Joe in on what we'd learned, that on the night of Sparky's murder Gregorio Dumas claimed he saw a fireman leave the station a half hour after the rest of the company went to put out the fire at Esther Stoval's house.

Joe said Gregorio had to be lying, since all the firemen on duty were at the fire. Nobody was left behind at the station or sent back for any reason later.

I could see that talking about Sparky was bringing him down, so I told him some stories about Monk, who amazes me because he can untangle the most perplexing, complicated murder mysteries but is afraid to step into a telephone booth.

We left the restaurant and walked aimlessly around Chinatown for a while, then stopped in at City Lights Bookstore at Broadway and Columbus to browse. I liked that we could enjoy each other's company even when we weren't saying anything, but were just standing near each other looking at books.

The clock was inching toward midnight by the time he drove me home. We were only a few blocks away when he pulled over at Dolores Park, at the corner of Church and Twentieth. The park was a scary place at night, full of vagrants and drug dealers.

"Why are we stopping?" I asked.

"I'd like to pay my respects," he said.

Joe pulled over, got out of the car, and went over to a fire hydrant, which was painted gold. I got out and joined him, looking around to make sure no killers, rapists, or junkies were heading our way.

"What are we doing here?" I asked.

"This was the little fire hydrant that saved San Francisco after the 1906 quake," he said, gazing at it thoughtfully.

I glanced at the hydrant. It never struck me as special, though I'd certainly noticed it over the years, usually when some dog was peeing on it.

"This one?" I said. "It seems so far away from downtown."

"The quake knocked out all the other hydrants. But it was water from this one that finally tamed the firestorm. Every year after that, at five A.M. on April eighteenth, survivors of the quake would show up here and give it another coat of gold paint. Some still do, but mostly it's up to members of the St. Francis Hook and Ladder Society to carry on the tradition. I've missed the last couple of anniversaries."

I thought he might salute the hydrant or something, but he just gave it a nod and we got back in the car. I wondered if every fireman was as into the lore and legend of San Francisco firefighters as Joe was.

He got me from the park to my doorstep in about two minutes and walked me to my door. I wanted to avoid any awkward moments, so I took the initiative and gave him a friendly kiss on the lips.

"I had a great time," I said. "A really, really great night."

"So did I," Joe replied. "I hope we can do this again sometime soon."

I wasn't going to leave him hanging. Or myself. "When are you off duty again?"

He gave me a big smile. "Wednesday."

"It's a date," I said. "Same time?"

"Same time." He gave me a kiss, a little friendlier than the one I had given him.

I unlocked the door and went inside. I immediately froze. Something wasn't right. I mean, I was definitely in my house—these were my things— but there was something wrong. Off-kilter. Weird. Like I'd stepped through the door into an alternate universe. It was as if I weren't standing in my house, but in a brilliant re-creation, like a movie set.

I blinked hard and looked around again. What was it that was giving me that feeling of being in another dimension?

Monk came out of the kitchen with a glass of milk. "Did you enjoy your date?"

"He's a very sweet man," I said.

I told Monk the story about the firehouse and the train robber and the reasons Joe thought Gregorio Dumas was lying about seeing a fireman at the station. Monk mulled all of that for a moment, working out that nonexistent kink in his neck.

"How did things go tonight with you and Julie?" I asked.

"We worked the LEGOs for a while."

Monk gestured to the kitchen. I looked past him and saw a massive and elaborate LEGO castle, complete with drawbridge, turrets, and a moat, erected on our table. It would have taken me a year to build that.

"She's got the touch," he said proudly.

"Really?"

"With the right training and lots of practice, I think she could become a LEGO master."

"Like yourself."

"I don't like to brag."

"So what did you do with the rest of your evening?" I asked, still feeling unsettled and off balance.

Monk shrugged. "I straightened up a little bit."

So *that* was it.

I looked around the room again and saw what I'd only registered unconsciously before. Monk had done exactly what he said: He'd literally straightened the place. He must have taken a T square and a level to everything in the house. All my stuff was still there, only it had been adjusted. Aligned. The furniture was centered and each piece was repositioned at uniform, measured distances from the others. All the pictures on the wall had been rehung, so that the spaces between them were consistent. The knickknacks and framed photos on the tables and shelves were grouped by height and shape and spaced evenly apart. The magazines were arranged by name and stacked chronologically. He'd reorganized my books alphabetically, by size, and, for all I knew, by copyright date as well.

The living room—and I assumed the entire house—was clean, organized, and utterly sterile. It looked like a model home. I hated it.

"Mr. Monk, everything in here is level and centered and perfectly organized."

"Thank you." He beamed with pride, which only frustrated and infuriated me more.

"No, it's wrong. Don't you see? You've taken all the personality and charm out of my house."

"Everything is still here," Monk said. "Except the dirt, the dust, and half a grilled cheese sandwich I found under the couch."

"But there's no more clutter," I said. "It looks like robots live here."

"And that's a bad thing?"

"*People* live here, Mr. Monk. Eight years of marriage, twelve years of parenting, a mother and daughter living together; that all leaves a trail. I like that trail. It comforts me. It's the muddled arrangement of photos on the shelf, the half-read book left open on the arm of a chair, and yes, even the forgotten grilled cheese sandwich. Clutter and disorganization, those are signs of life. It *is* life."

"Not mine," he said.

Those two words carried an infinite sadness that made me ache and, for a moment, forget my own frustration and think about his.

Monk's life was a constant pursuit of order. I'm sure that's why he became a detective and why he's so good at solving murders. He notices all the things that don't fit as they should and puts them into their proper places, creating a solution. Restoring order.

The only mystery he hasn't been able to solve is the one at the heart of his own personal disorder.

The murder of his wife.

Everything else he did, like organizing my house or making sure my daughter's shoelaces were even, was a poor substitute for the perfect order he lost with Trudy. That could never be restored.

But I couldn't say all that to him. Instead I took his hand in mine.

"Your life is a lot messier than you think. I'm a big mess and I'm part of it, aren't I?"

"You and Julie," Monk said. "And I'm glad you are."

"Me, too, Mr. Monk."

"Actually, I've loosened up quite a bit."

"You have?"

"I haven't always been the easygoing guy you know today," Monk said. "There was a time when I was very uptight."

"I can't imagine that." I gave his hand a squeeze and let go. "Please don't straighten up my house anymore."

He nodded.

"Good night, Mr. Monk."

"Good night, Natalie."

I went to my room. It wasn't until I was in bed, and nearly asleep, that I realized that I'd held his hand and he didn't ask for a wipe. Even if he sanitized his hands later, at least he didn't do it in front of me. That had to mean something, and whatever it was, I think it was something good.

9

Mr. Monk and the
Thirtieth Floor

Straightening up the house must have exhausted
Monk because on Monday morning Julie woke up
before he did and managed to beat him to the
bathroom by a few seconds. They nearly collided
at the door at six o'clock.

"I need to use the bathroom first," Monk said.

"Is it number one or number two?"

"I think I have a constitutional right not to have
to answer that question."

"I need to know how long you're going to be,"
Julie said, holding the door possessively with one
hand, her school clothes draped over her arm.

"No longer than usual."

"I can't wait that long," Julie said. "School starts
at eight fifteen, not noon."

She closed the door on him. He stared at the
door for a moment, then looked at me. I was

standing outside my bedroom, not bothering to hide my amusement.

"Does she have to use the bathroom so often?" Monk said.

"Would you prefer she didn't bathe at all?"

"But it was ready for me. I cleaned it last night."

"You cleaned *everything* last night," I said, and padded past him into the kitchen.

The LEGO castle was gone. Monk must have dismantled it and put all the pieces back in their proper boxes before he went to bed. No wonder he'd overslept. I opened the pantry to get myself a bagel and noticed that Monk had rearranged all the boxed and canned goods by food group and expiration date.

Monk came in and reached past me for his box of Chex. The cereal was made up of almost perfect squares of shredded wheat. The imperfect squares would be sorted out of his bowl before he poured in the milk.

I opened the cupboard to get him a bowl and was shocked to find it empty. There wasn't a single bowl, plate, or dish inside, just barren shelves.

I turned to look at Monk, who was sitting at the table carefully selecting Chex one at a time from the box and eating them.

"What happened to all my dishes?"

He wouldn't look up at me, pretending instead to concentrate on the difficult task of selecting Chex. "It's a little complicated."

"I don't see the complication, Mr. Monk. I had

dishes last night and now I don't. Where are they?"

"You had seven bowls, which isn't right. You should have six or eight, but not seven. So one bowl obviously needed to go. But you had eight plates. You can see the problem."

"I can see that I don't have any dishes; *that's* the problem."

"Everyone knows you can't have six bowls and eight plates, so two plates had to go. But then I noticed that some of the bowls and plates were chipped, and not all of them in the same places. You had a matching set of dishes that didn't match at all. I was faced with a situation that was spiraling out of control into total chaos. The only reasonable thing to do was to get rid of them all."

Monk looked up at me then, clearly expecting sympathy and understanding. He sure as hell wasn't going to get it from me.

"Reasonable? You call throwing out all of my dishes *reasonable*?"

" 'Thoughtful,' 'conscientious,' and 'responsible' also came to mind," Monk said. "But I thought 'reasonable' said it best."

"Here's what we're going to do today before you solve any murders or catch any bad guys," I said. "As soon as you are showered and dressed, we're going to Pottery Barn and you're going to buy me a new set of dishes, or you can eat your next meal in this house off the floor."

I reached for the silverware drawer for a knife to cut my bagel, but I stopped before opening it.

"Do I want to open this drawer?" I asked.

"It depends what you're looking for."

"A knife would be nice," I said. "Actually, how about any silverware at all?"

Monk shifted in his chair. "You don't want to open the drawer."

"You can add silverware to the list of things you're buying me today," I said, and went to the refrigerator. I picked up the carton of orange juice and took a drink from it.

Monk cringed, as I knew he would. "You really shouldn't drink from the carton."

"Fine." I turned and pinned him with the coldest, cruelest, most accusatory glare I could muster. "Do I still own a glass I can drink from instead?"

He shifted in his seat.

"I didn't think so." I took the carton with me and slammed the refrigerator door shut. "I hope your credit card is paid up, Mr. Monk, because it's going to get a real workout today."

I stomped back to my bedroom with my bagel and orange juice and left Monk alone in my dishless, knifeless, cupless kitchen.

The streets were damp, and fog completely obscured the skyline on that Monday morning, but the city was bustling. The downtown sidewalks were jammed with young professionals wearing the latest fashion accessory—something electronic in the ear.

There wasn't a naked ear in sight.

Everyone except us seemed to be wearing either a pair of white iPod earphones or one of those Bluetooth cell phone units that looked like the radio Q-tip that stuck out of Lieutenant Uhura's ear on the original *Star Trek*.

It was after twelve by the time we finished shopping for dishes, silverware, and glasses at Pottery Barn.

I'll never admit this to Monk, but once I got past my initial anger, I was glad he threw my stuff out. I'd been ashamed to have people over to eat because we had chipped dishes and silverware that had been mangled in the disposal. But I couldn't afford to replace any of it. Now Monk was buying me new kitchenware, and I was thrilled. (It wasn't until he suggested we browse the cookware that I discovered he'd thrown out my pots and pans, too.) Here's how awful I am: I actually began to toy with the idea of "accidentally" letting him see the mess in my closet so he'd buy me a new wardrobe, too.

To make shopping as painless as possible for both of us, I picked solid colors for the dishes and let him open all the boxes in the store to inspect each piece for imperfections. Every so often while this was going on, I'd feel a pang of guilt, like I was taking advantage of him or something. But then I'd remind myself that *he* was the one who went into *my* kitchen and threw out all of *my* dishes. And then my anger would come back and beat the crap out of my guilt and I was fine with myself all over again.

We'd just finished loading up the back of my Cherokee with all my goodies when Stottlemeyer called. The captain was on his way to interview Lucas Breen, the developer who planned to demolish Esther Stoval's block, and asked if we wanted to join him. We did.

Breen Development Corporation was in a thirty-five-story Rubik's Cube that had shouldered its way between two other buildings in the Financial District for a view of the bay. The lobby was a glass atrium that had its own florist, chocolatier, and a small outpost of the Boudin Bakery, which makes the best sourdough bread in the city, maybe even the world.

Stottlemeyer, sipping a cup of coffee from Boudin, was waiting for us in front of Flo's Floral Designs. The smell of fresh sourdough was making me swoon.

"Morning, Natalie. Monk. I heard you talked to everybody in Esther's neighborhood. You come up with any clues we missed?"

"No," Monk said.

"That's depressing," Stottlemeyer said. "What about your other case, the one with the dog; how's that going?"

"I think I'm on to something," Monk asked.

That was news to me. But Monk doesn't always share with me what's going on in his mind, and, I have to say, most of time I'm deeply thankful for that.

"Want to trade cases?" Stottlemeyer said.

"I don't think so," Monk said. "Though you could do me a favor. Could you ask Lieutenant Disher to find out everything he can about a notorious robber named Roderick Turlock?"

"It's the least I can do. What's Turlock notorious for?"

"Robbing trains," I said.

"Do people still do that?"

I didn't think it would help our cause to mention that Turlock was captured in 1906. Apparently Monk agreed with me, since we both treated Stottlemeyer's question as a rhetorical one. We must have been right, because Stottlemeyer didn't wait for an answer.

"So, Monk, you ready for this?" Stottlemeyer tipped his head up.

Monk looked up, searching for whatever it was the captain was talking about. "For what?"

"To see Breen," Stottlemeyer said. "He's a rich, powerful man. He's not going to appreciate either one of us suggesting he might have been involved in Esther Stoval's murder."

"He's up there?"

"Thirtieth floor," he said. "Rich guys love to look down on everybody."

Stottlemeyer approached the security guard, a beefy guy with a boxer's nose who manned a marble-topped counter in front of the elevators. Stottlemeyer flashed his badge, introduced us, and said we were there to see Lucas Breen. The guard called up to Breen's office, then nodded to the captain.

"Mr. Breen will see you now," the guard said.

"Great," Monk said. "When's he coming down?"

"He's not," Stottlemeyer said. "We're going up."

"It would be better if he came down."

Stottlemeyer groaned and turned to the guard.

"Could you ask Mr. Breen if he'd mind meeting us for a cup of coffee in the lobby? My treat."

The guard made the call, spoke for a moment, then hung up. "Mr. Breen is very busy and can't leave the office at this time. If you want to see him, you need to go to his office."

"I tried, Monk," Stottlemeyer said. "So let's go."

We headed for the elevators, but Monk dragged behind. "I have an idea. Let's take the stairs."

"Thirty floors?" I said.

"It'll be fun."

"It'll be fatal," Stottlemeyer said. "I can talk to Breen without you. You really don't need to be there."

"I want to be there," Monk said.

"I'm taking the elevator," Stottlemeyer said. "Are you coming or not?"

I looked at Monk. He looked at the elevator, took a deep breath, and nodded.

"Okay," he said.

The three of us got into the elevator. Stottlemeyer hit the button for the thirtieth floor. The doors closed. Monk covered his finger with his sleeve and hit the button for the second floor. And then the fourth. And then the sixth. He hit the button for every other floor all the way up to the thirtieth.

Stottlemeyer rolled his eyes and sighed.

The instant the doors opened on the second floor, Monk stepped out, took several deep breaths, then came back in.

"I think this is going very well," he said.

On the fourth floor he burst out with a cry, startling the people in the waiting room at the Crocker Advertising Agency.

"It's a living hell," he told them.

Monk took several hungry breaths of air and then leaped back into the elevator as if he were plunging into deep water.

The instant the elevator reached the sixth floor, he threw himself out into the lobby of Ernst, Throck, and Fillburton, Attorneys at Law, and screamed something about the "injustice and inhumanity" of it all.

By the eighth, Stottlemeyer and I were resigned to our fate, leaning against the handrails and doing our best to relax. We played Tetris on Stottlemeyer's cell phone screen while Monk paced, and groaned, and cried, and pulled at the imaginary leeches in his hair.

Stopping at every other floor, it took us forty minutes to reach Breen's office on the thirtieth. I won six games and Stottlemeyer won eight, but he's had a lot more practice, working on his technique during stakeouts. When the elevator doors opened, Monk staggered out, gasping for air, his face drenched with sweat, and collapsed onto the black leather couch in the waiting room.

"Sweet Mother of God," he whined. "It's finally over."

I gave him a bottle of Sierra Springs water from my purse—which, by the way, is about the size of the baby bag I lugged around when Julie was an infant. It's full of water, Wet Ones, Baggies, even some Wheat Thins in case he gets hungry.

The only thing I'm not carrying with me that I carried then are diapers.

Stottlemeyer went up to the receptionist, a disarmingly attractive Asian woman who sat behind a sweeping desk that made her look like the anchorwoman on the eleven-o'clock news. Except that the breathtaking view of the city behind her wasn't a backdrop; it was the real thing.

"Captain Stottlemeyer, Adrian Monk, and Natalie Teeger to see Mr. Breen," he said.

"We were expecting you to be here almost an hour ago," she said.

"So were we," he said.

Monk guzzled the water and tossed the empty bottle over his shoulder. The color was beginning to return to his cheeks. He mopped his forehead with his handkerchief and then tossed that, too.

"Going down will be much easier," I said reassuringly.

"Yeah, because I'll be taking the stairs."

The receptionist spoke up. "Mr. Breen will see you now."

She gestured toward a massive set of double doors that reminded me of the gates to the Emerald City of Oz, only without the munchkin guard. Breen had an Asian supermodel instead, which I'm pretty sure the wizard also would have preferred.

The doors slid open on their own as we approached, which was intimidating. Sure, the doors at Wal-Mart do the same thing, but somehow it's different when you aren't pushing a shopping cart.

And there, in a cavernous office of glass and mahogany and stainless steel, stood real-estate developer Lucas Breen, his arms outstretched, a welcoming smile on his face, his capped teeth gleaming like polished ivory.

10

Mr. Monk Buys Some Flowers

Everything about Lucas Breen's office screamed money and power. His floor-to-ceiling windows offered a commanding view of the city and the bay. The intricately detailed models of his most architecturally daring office towers were dramatically lit and displayed on marble stands. The designer furniture was arranged like sculptures. There were pictures on the wall of him and his gorgeous, bejeweled wife shaking hands with presidents, kings, movie stars, and local politicians.

And even if Breen's office didn't scream money and power, his handmade jacket, monogrammed shirt, elegant watch, and expensive shoes certainly did. I'd wow you with the brand names, but my fashion and jewelry expertise doesn't extend beyond what you can find at Mervyn's, JCPenney, and Target.

Breen was in his forties, remarkably fit, and

naturally tanned—the kind of body and rich tan
that comes from playing tennis on your Marin
County estate, lazing around on yachts in the Ca-
ribbean, and having tantric sex.

Okay, I don't know about the tantric sex part,
but he looked like the type who would brag that
he was having it even if he weren't.

"Thank you for making the time to see us, Mr.
Breen," Stottlemeyer said, shaking the developer's
hand.

"My pleasure, Captain. I'm pleased to do anything I can to assist the San Francisco Police Department," Breen said. "That's why I'm so honored to
be a member of the Police Commission."

You've got to admire how Breen got that in
there so quickly, as if Stottlemeyer didn't already
know that the chief of police and the department
answer to Breen's oversight committee.

"You must be Adrian Monk. I've been an ad-
mirer of yours for some time." Breen offered his
hand to Monk, who shook it, then immediately
turned to me for a wipe. "Please, Mr. Monk, allow
me."

Breen took a disinfectant wipe from his pocket
and gave it to Monk, who scrutinized the package.
It was a Magic Fresh.

"No, thank you," Monk said.

"It's a moist towelette," Breen said.

"It's a Magic Fresh."

"They're all the same."

"That's like saying all corn flakes are the same,"
Monk said.

"They are."

"I prefer Wet Ones," Monk said, and held his hand out to me. I gave him a package. "I don't trust anything with magic in it."

Breen forced a smile and tossed the package on his desk. Somebody was going to be fired for not providing Breen with the correct wipe for Monk.

"We're investigating the murder of Esther Stoval," Stottlemeyer said. "And, for obvious reasons, your name came up."

"You realize, of course, that I never actually met Esther Stoval or set foot in her home. Other members of my company interacted with her and tried to address her concerns," Breen said. "But from what I heard, she was a very difficult individual."

"Is this the project?" Stottlemeyer asked, tipping his head toward a model.

"Yes, that's it," Breen said, leading us over to a scale model of Esther's block.

The three-story building was a clever amalgamation of styles—Victorian, Spanish Renaissance, French château, and a dozen others—that made it seem at once both vintage and new. But there was something calculated, commercial, and Disneyesque about the building's charm. I knew I was being manipulated with subliminal design cues meant to evoke cable cars and foggy streets, Fisherman's Wharf, and the Golden Gate, and I hated that it was working. Maybe Esther Stoval hated it, too.

While Stottlemeyer and I admired the model, Monk looked at all the pictures on the wall of Breen and his wife with celebrities and politicians.

"What's the selling price of the condos?" I

asked, not that I was in the market or anything like that.

"Six hundred thousand and up, which, without getting into specific numbers, is what we paid the homeowners for their properties. But they weren't the only ones who benefited. Once you revitalize one corner of a neighborhood, it creates a domino effect of beautification that enhances the whole community. Everyone wins. Unfortunately, there's an Esther Stoval in every neighborhood."

"Do they all end up dead?" Monk asked.

Stottlemeyer shot him a look. "What Mr. Monk means to say is that—"

Breen interrupted him. "I know what he means. No matter how beneficial my projects are to a community, Mr. Monk, there is *always* opposition. Environmental groups, historical societies, homeowners associations, and an occasional recalcitrant individual. Most of my day is spent working on compromises that unify people and invigorate neighborhoods."

"You didn't reach one with Esther," Monk said.

"We offered her a premium for her property, as well as a lifetime lease on the condominium of her choice in the project," Breen said. "You can't get more amenable than that. She refused to even negotiate. But in the end, her opposition became irrelevant."

"Because she's dead," Monk said.

"Because we were planning to move ahead without her."

"How could you?" I asked. "Her house was right in the middle of the block."

"I didn't get this far in the real-estate business, Ms. Teeger, without being creative." Breen went to his desk and unfurled an architect's rendering of a building that was very similar to the model. "We were going to build around her."

The revised plans showed the building encircling Esther's house on three sides, shrouding it in almost complete darkness and robbing her of any privacy at all. With the way the building was designed, however, Esther's house didn't look out of place at all, but instead like a quirky, intentionally amusing design element. It was a nasty way of dealing with Esther, though I suppose it was a lot nicer than murder.

"She never would have gone for this," I said.

"She wouldn't have had a choice," Breen said. "The planning commission was scheduled to vote on the project next week, and she was the lone voice of opposition. I have it on good authority that we were likely to win unanimous approval from the commission. The project would have been built with or without her."

"You were going to drive her out by making her life absolutely miserable," Monk said.

"On the contrary, we would have been friendly neighbors, I assure you," Breen said. "She and her cats could have stayed there as long as they liked. That said, we designed the building so that when she eventually passed away, we would have the choice of either letting her home stand or tearing it down for a plaza."

"So you're saying that Esther Stoval's murder didn't change a thing for you," Stottlemeyer said.

"Not as far as the project is concerned," Breen said. "However, as a San Franciscan, and a human being, I'm truly horrified about what happened to that poor old woman. I don't think her murder had anything to do with our building. She was probably killed by some crazed junkie looking to steal something to finance his next fix."

I couldn't recall seeing any junkies, crazed or otherwise, on the street when Monk interviewed the neighbors, but at least that theory made more sense than Disher's theory of crazed cats smothering the old lady and setting the house on fire.

"Well," Stottlemeyer said. "I think that covers everything, don't you, Monk?"

"Where were you Friday night between nine and ten P.M.?" Monk said.

"I thought we just established that I had nothing to gain, either directly or indirectly, from her death," Breen said. "What difference does it make where I was when she was killed?"

"Actually, Monk is right; it's one of those procedural questions we're always supposed to ask," Stottlemeyer said. "I'd hate for someone like you, on the Police Commission and all, to think I wasn't doing my job."

"Very well," Breen said. "I was at the 'Save the Bay' fund-raiser at the Excelsior Tower Hotel from eight P.M. until midnight."

"With your wife?" Monk pointed to the pictures on the wall. "This is your wife, isn't it?"

"Yes, I was there with my wife, and the mayor, and the governor, and about five hundred other concerned citizens," Breen said. "Now, if there are no other questions, I have a very busy day."

He took a key-fob-size remote out of his pocket, aimed it at his office doors, and they slid open again—a real subtle hint that our meeting was over.

"Thanks for your help," Stottlemeyer said as we left the office. Monk trailed behind, taking one last glance back at Breen.

"There's a *big* difference between Raisin Brans," Monk said. "Trust me on that."

It wasn't until we were at the elevators, out of earshot of the receptionist or anyone else, that Stottlemeyer turned to Monk, who was heading for the stairwell door.

"You want to tell me why you were needling Breen?" Stottlemeyer punched the call button for the elevator as if it were someone's face. "And it'd better not be because he uses the wrong brand of disinfectant wipe or wouldn't come down to the lobby to meet you."

"He's the guy." Monk covered his hand with his sleeve and opened the door to the stairs.

"What guy?"

"The guy who killed Esther Stoval," he said. "It was him."

And with that, our elevator arrived and Monk disappeared into the stairwell. Stottlemeyer started to go after him, but I gently tugged his sleeve to stop him.

"Do you really want to chase him down thirty floors?" I said. "It can wait."

He looked at me, sighed with resignation, and stepped into the elevator.

"Sometimes I could kill him," he said. "And it would be justifiable homicide."

After Stottlemeyer called the office to get Disher started on confirming Breen's alibi and exhuming the background on train robber Roderick Turlock, the two of us enjoyed a leisurely lunch at the Boudin Bakery in the lobby.

We both ordered Boston clam chowder in fresh sourdough bread bowls and took a table by the window, where we could watch all the accountants, stockbrokers, bankers, and homeless people go by.

We talked about our children and the schools they were going to, and how kids don't go outside and play anymore; they schedule playdates instead. I know; it sounds like awfully mundane, boring stuff to talk about, which is why I'm sparing you the actual conversation.

But here's why I even mention it at all: It was the first time the two of us had ever really talked, and while it wasn't what you'd call a particularly scintillating or intimate conversation, at least it wasn't about Monk or murders or law enforcement. It was about life.

I believe that it was sitting there, eating our soup and picking at our bread bowls, that I saw Leland Stottlemeyer as a person instead of a homicide cop for the first time.

We sat at a table where Monk would be sure to see us when he finally got to the lobby, which ended up being about a half hour after we'd left him on the thirtieth floor.

Monk staggered out of the stairwell looking as if he'd just trekked on foot across the Mojave Desert. He undid the top two buttons at his collar and, without even acknowledging us, shuffled into Flo's Floral Designs.

"You think he saw us?" Stottlemeyer said.

"I don't know," I said.

Neither one of us got up to check. We weren't finished with our soup and we both knew Monk had to pass us if he wanted to leave the building. But the incident was a conversation killer. We were both silent, watching the florist shop, waiting to see what would happen next.

After a few minutes he came out holding a beautiful bouquet of flowers and collapsed into a seat at our table.

"Water," he croaked.

I took a Sierra Springs bottle out of my bag and passed it to him. He guzzled it down and sagged into his seat.

"How was your walk?" I asked.

"Invigorating," Monk replied.

"Who are the flowers for?" Stottlemeyer said.

"You."

Monk handed them to the captain, who took them, a befuddled look on his face. I doubt he appreciated the beautiful mix of lilies, roses, orchids, and hydrangeas. It was a stunning bouquet.

"Is this some kind of apology?"

"It's evidence that Lucas Breen is guilty of murder."

Stottlemeyer looked at the flowers, then back at Monk. "I don't get it. What do the flowers have to do with anything?"

That's when I recognized them. I'd seen them before and I remembered where.

"I talked to Flo." Monk gestured to the florist shop. "This bouquet is one of her original designs. She's very proud of it."

"Good for Flo," Stottlemeyer said.

"Lucas Breen bought one just like it from Flo on Thursday," Monk said.

"So?"

"They were for his mistress, Lizzie Draper," Monk said. "I saw the same bouquet in her house yesterday."

I don't know how Monk noticed the bouquet, since his gaze was locked on Lizzie Draper's cleavage the whole time we were there. Monk must have astonishing peripheral vision. It was the same extraordinary bouquet Lizzie was using as a model for the painting she was working on.

"Even if that's true," Stottlemeyer said, "what does that have to do with Esther Stoval's murder?"

"Esther Stoval spied on her neighbors. She used binoculars to look into her neighbors' homes and took pictures," Monk said. "She once turned a neighbor in to the cable company for watching ESPN with an illegal converter box."

"I'm surprised she lived as long as she did," Stottlemeyer said. "You don't come between a man and his sports."

"I think Esther had incriminating photos of Lucas Breen and Lizzie Draper and threatened to show them to his wife if he didn't halt the condominium project. A divorce could have cost him tens of millions of dollars. That's why Breen killed Esther."

Stottlemeyer shook his head. "That's a mighty big leap, even for you, Monk."

"That's what happened," Monk said.

I was sure he was right. Stottlemeyer was sure, too. Because if there is one thing Monk is always right about, it's murder. And Monk knew that we knew. Which made the situation all the more frustrating for the captain.

Stottlemeyer held up the bouquet. "And *this* is all you've got?"

"We also have her buttons," Monk said.

"Her buttons?"

"I couldn't help noticing them," he said.

That was probably the biggest understatement of the day.

"The letters 'LB' were written on them," Monk said. "At the time I thought it was a brand name, but it wasn't. It was a monogram. The shirt she was wearing was handmade for Lucas Breen."

11

Mr. Monk and the
Suspect Smell

We reconvened in Stottlemeyer's office, where he put the bouquet in an empty Big Gulp cup and filled it with water. Vases aren't easy to come by in the homicide department of the SFPD.

Disher came in and stared at Monk with dismay. "What's wrong? Are you feeling all right?"

"I feel fine," Monk said.

"Are you sure?"

"Positive," Monk said. "Why do you ask?"

"It's just that I've never seen you so, so . . ." Disher searched for the right word. "Unbuttoned."

"Unbuttoned?" Monk said.

Disher motioned to his collar. "Your top two buttons are unbuttoned."

"Oh, my God." Monk immediately flushed with embarrassment and buttoned his collar up. "How long have I been naked? Why didn't you say something?"

"It was two buttons, Mr. Monk," I said.

"Word is probably spreading all over the department right now!" Monk said.

"I'm sure nobody noticed," Stottlemeyer said.

"I strolled in here half-naked. They aren't blind." He buried his face in his hands. "I'm so ashamed."

"You're among friends, Monk." Stottlemeyer came around his desk and squeezed Monk's shoulder reassuringly. "Nobody is going to say anything. You have my word."

Monk looked up, stricken. "Could you talk to them for me?"

"Sure," Stottlemeyer said. "Who?"

"Everyone," Monk said. "Every officer in the building."

"Okay, I can do that," Stottlemeyer said. "But could I wait until after we discuss how we're going to prove that Lucas Breen killed Esther Stoval?"

"That's not going to be easy," Disher said. "There's no physical evidence that puts him in that house when Esther was killed."

"Or anybody else," Stottlemeyer said.

"He did it," Monk said. "If we work backward from there, we'll find something."

"He's got a rock-solid alibi." Disher went to Stottlemeyer's computer and clicked a few keys. "I've pulled dozens of press photos off the net of Breen and his wife arriving at eight P.M. and departing at midnight. I talked to the photographers and got the approximate times the photos were taken from them."

"Good work," Stottlemeyer said.

Disher angled Stottlemeyer's monitor so we could see the pictures on the screen. Sure enough, there were photos from various angles from different photographers of Breen and his wife in their rain-coats, huddled under an umbrella and rushing into the lobby from the rain. There were also photos of the Breens leaving at midnight with the governor and his wife.

"There were five hundred guests at that event. I doubt anybody can account for his movements the whole night," Monk said. "The Excelsior has dozens of exits. He could have left the hotel and come back and no one would have noticed."

"Pull the security-camera footage from the hotel," Stottlemeyer told Disher. "Maybe there's something. And talk to some of the guests and hotel staff, see if anybody noticed he was gone."

"Breen built the Excelsior. I'm sure he knows how to get in and out without being seen," Disher said. "Besides, leaving the hotel doesn't put him in Esther's house, holding a pillow to her face."

"One step at a time," Stottlemeyer said.

"Okay," Disher said. "So what does a train rob-ber who died in 1906 have to do with all this?"

"Nothing," Monk said. "That has to do with the murder of a firehouse dog."

"You're trying to solve a one-hundred-year-old murder of a dog?"

"Sparky was murdered Friday night," I said.

"By a ghost?" Disher said.

"Whoa." Stottlemeyer raised a hand. "Could somebody please tell me what's going on?"

"In the late eighteen hundreds, Roderick Turlock and his gang robbed trains that were carrying bank cars filled with gold coins," Disher said. "The Pinkertons finally tracked him down to a boardinghouse in San Francisco, where he was killed in a shoot-out, taking his secret with him."

"What secret?" Monk asked.

"What he did with the stolen gold," Disher said. "Most of it was never found. Legend has it that he buried it somewhere."

"That's real interesting, but can we discuss San Francisco's rich and colorful history another time?" Stottlemeyer said. "We've got a murder to solve here and no evidence whatsoever."

"You're forgetting about the buttons," Monk said. "And the flowers."

"Right, of course. The flowers." Stottlemeyer snatched the bouquet out of the Big Gulp cup. "Tell you what, Randy, I'll take these over to the DA right now while you and Monk go arrest Breen."

Stottlemeyer marched to his door. Disher stood in place, not sure what to do.

"You want me to . . . I mean, should I . . . ?" Disher looked at Monk. "Is he serious?"

"No, I'm not serious." Stottlemeyer pivoted on his heels and waved the bouquet as he spoke, shaking off some of the petals. "Lucas Breen is on the Police Commission, for God's sake. What we need is his DNA all over the crime scene, twenty-two eyewitnesses who saw him there, and a video of him smothering the old hag. And then maybe, *maybe*, we've got something to go on."

Stottlemeyer shoved Disher out of the way, slammed the bouquet back into the Big Gulp cup, and took a seat behind his desk. He took a deep breath, then glanced at Monk.

"Tell me how you think he did it."

"I think he left the hotel, killed Esther, set fire to her house, then went back to the party."

"That's not a very cunning plan," Disher said.

"It worked, didn't it?" Stottlemeyer said. "Did you check out Lizzie Draper's alibi?"

Disher nodded. "They have some kind of *Coyote Ugly* thing going at Flaxx. There are a hundred guys who saw her dancing in a wet T-shirt on the bar, pouring drinks and juggling bottles until midnight."

That, by the way, was the other reason I didn't get the job at Flaxx. I don't jiggle or juggle.

"Assuming you're right, Mr. Monk," I began, then paused when I saw the chastising look he was giving me. "Excuse me, *knowing* you're right, Breen couldn't have taken his car, not without the valet and the press seeing him go. And he wouldn't have hailed a taxi and taken the risk that a cabbie might remember him. So how did Breen get to Esther's house and back again?"

Stottlemeyer nodded at me. "You're getting the hang of this, Natalie."

"He must have walked," Monk said.

"Is that possible?" I wondered. "I mean, could he do all that in an hour on foot?"

Monk shrugged. "There's only one way to find out."

*   *   *

As we left the police station, Monk apologized to every officer we passed for his "earlier nakedness," which he blamed on disorientation caused by his sinus medication, not that anyone asked or cared.

"Allergies," he said to them. "It's the monkey on my back."

We drove to the Excelsior, which was on Montgomery Street, a few blocks northeast of Union Square. Although it was a relatively new building, constructed in the last decade, it was crafted in the Beaux Arts style favored by San Francisco's elite in the early 1900s. The big-ticket touches that advertised wealth were all there: the grand arched doorways, the monumental stone columns, the sculpted balustrades, and the arched windows adorned with carved-leaf crowns and ornamented keystones.

I reluctantly left my Cherokee in the Excelsior's underground garage, where it costs more to park a car per day than it does to rent one. As Disher predicted, even a casual inspection revealed dozens of ways out of the building, including doors on each floor of the parking structure and a service exit that opened into a dark alley.

The service exit into the alley was also conveniently blocked from view from the street by several large Dumpsters. If Breen used this door to slip out of the building, he could have taken the alley a full block before having to emerge onto the street, putting him at a safe distance from the hotel and any press gathered out front. Monk assumed that was the likeliest route for Breen to have taken, so we followed it, too. But from that point, there were any number of routes he might have taken. Monk chose the most direct one, going straight up Montgomery, to start with.

It was nearly dark as we began our walk, and it began to drizzle. Our trek took us past the towers of the Financial District, where business-people and clerical workers were already streaming out, eager to get a head start on the rush-hour traffic. And the night shift of homeless people was beginning to move in, seeking shelter in the al-coves and doorways, scrounging in the trash bins, and hitting up passersby for money.

Monk wouldn't give them money, but he handed out individual packages of Wet Ones from my purse to every indigent we passed. They didn't seem to appreciate the gesture, particularly one guy, who slept on a piece of cardboard and wore an ill-fitting, tattered overcoat over several layers of filthy shirts.

When Monk tossed him a Wet One packet, the homeless man rose up from his mat.

"What the hell am I supposed to do with this?" he said indignantly, holding the Wet One in dis-gust. His hair and beard were matted, his skin deeply tanned and caked with dirt. He smelled of body odor and rot, like he'd been sleeping in a Dumpster. The stench was an invisible force field that kept Monk a good three feet away from him.

"You're right," Monk said to the man. "It wasn't very thoughtful of me."

Monk reached into my bag, took out two handfuls of wipes, and dumped them at the man's feet.

"One isn't nearly enough," Monk said, and hurried away, sneezing, the homeless man shouting profanities in our wake.

I handed Monk a Kleenex. Monk blew his nose, then put the used tissue into a Ziploc bag, which he sealed and stowed in his pocket.

"That man sleeps with cats," Monk said.

"I think that's the least of his problems."

I looked over my shoulder and saw the homeless man gathering up the wipes and putting them into the pocket of his overcoat. He saw me looking at him and flipped me off. *Have a nice day to you, too,* I thought.

We walked north, following Montgomery as it crossed Columbus Avenue and rose up toward Telegraph Hill. The office buildings and restaurants soon gave way to upscale galleries and residences. We zigzagged along side streets into the residential triangle of Victorian homes and garden apartments roughly bordered by Columbus Avenue, Montgomery Street, and Filbert Street. It was a steep climb—not nearly as steep as the one I took to Delores Park each Sunday, but we were still breathing pretty hard when we reached the crest of the hill and found ourselves, much to my surprise, facing Firefighter Joe's station house.

"Do you mind if we stop in and say hello to Joe?" I asked. Breen would have needed a rest about now, I thought, even if he had been in a hurry. We were eight or ten serious blocks from the Excelsior, and we'd been walking for about twenty minutes.

"That's a good idea," Monk said. He looked like he could use the rest, too.

It was also a chance to dry off a bit. Drizzle isn't so bad until it accumulates and you suddenly realize you're soaked, which we both were.

Besides, we'd more or less proven that Breen could have walked from the Excelsior to Esther's place, which was only a few blocks from the fire station, in a half hour.

Everything in the station was gleaming, of course. Even the turnouts, the firefighting rigs hanging in the open racks, were all clean, the latches and zippers shining.

The firemen were all in the kitchen eating pizza. I couldn't help noticing that Sparky's bed basket and rubber hot-dog squeak toy were still there. Monk also noticed it. I guess Joe wasn't willing to accept that Sparky was gone quite yet. I knew the feeling. I kept Mitch's clothes hanging in the closet for almost a year after he died. And I know Monk still has the pillow his wife slept on. It's in a plastic bag in his closet.

Joe broke into a big smile the minute he saw me, jumped out of his seat, and rushed over to greet us. But once he got to me, he wasn't quite sure what he should do. Kiss me? Hug me? Shake my hand? We settled on a friendly hug.

"Natalie, Mr. Monk, what a nice surprise. You're just in time to join us for some pizza." Joe glanced back to Captain Mantooth, who held out a slice to Monk on a napkin.

"No, thank you," Monk said. "We just stopped by to ask you some questions."

Once again I was out of the loop. I thought it was a happy coincidence that we ended up in front of the firehouse.

"Captain Mantooth, did you notice any towels missing before Friday night?"

"Sure, they're always disappearing," Mantooth said. "They're like socks. You know how that is, Mr. Monk."

"No, I don't." Monk looked genuinely perplexed.

"Everybody loses socks," Mantooth said. All the men around him nodded in agreement. So did I. "You've never lost a sock?"

"How could I? They're either on my feet or they're being carried in the basket back and forth between the hamper, the laundry room, and the sock drawer," Monk said. "I don't see how it's humanly possible to lose a sock."

"It's one of the great mysteries of life," Joe said. "Where do all those socks go?"

"The same place as our towels." Mantooth laughed.

"And my panties," I added. Mantooth's smiled faded. I looked around. Everybody was staring at me. "C'mon, guys, *everybody* loses underwear."

The men shared glances, shook their heads, and looked at me with bewilderment, especially Monk and Joe.

"I know this for a fact," I said.

"I want you to think about something, Captain," Monk said, saving me from further embarrassment, though I'm sure that wasn't the reason he spoke up. "In general, were you more likely to notice a towel or two missing after you returned from responding to a fire?"

Mantooth mulled that over for a moment. "Now that you mention it, yeah, maybe you're right. But to be sure I'd have to check my records."

"You keep a record of missing towels?" I asked, incredulous.

"I keep track to justify the expense of buying new ones," Mantooth said. "I have to account for every penny that I spend."

I had a feeling he would whether he had to or not. No wonder Monk wanted to be a fireman. Mantooth was almost as anal as he was, which gave me reason to wonder what Joe's dark side might be like. Joe had been amazingly punctual when he came to pick me up for our date. Was punctuality a thing with him? What would happen the first time I was late to meet him somewhere?

Monk turned to Joe. "Did Sparky run around the neighborhood only when the company was on call to a fire?"

"Yeah," Joe said.

"How come you didn't tie him up?"

"Sparky always came back," Joe said. "I didn't want to restrict his freedom."

"When he came back," Monk asked, "what did he smell like?"

Joe seemed bewildered by the question. I certainly was. "Like crap. I don't know what he got himself into."

"How bad was the smell?"

"I usually had to give him a bath as soon as he got back or Cap would give me hell."

"I like a clean station," Mantooth said. "Cleanliness is the outward expression of order."

"Amen, brother," Monk said, and then he smiled at me. I've seen that smile before, usually just before somebody gets arrested and sent to prison for a very long time. "Let's go have a talk with Mr. Dumas."

I followed Monk across the street to Gregorio Dumas's house and knocked on the door. Monk stood directly behind me, using me as a shield, his hands poised to protect his groin from canine attack. How gallant.

Gregorio opened the door wearing a red smoking jacket, pajama pants, and so much bling that he made Mr. T, Sammy Davis Jr., and Liberace look under-accessorized by comparison. I know those celebrity references are dated, but somewhere between the time I graduated college and the day I became a mother, my cultural needle got stuck. I don't want to think about how out of touch I am with American popular culture. It makes me feel like I've become my mother, and that's scary.

Anyway, back to Gregorio. Monk asked if the dog was out back and, if she was, if we could come in and talk to him for a moment.

Gregorio reluctantly invited us in. We took a seat on the couch and he sat in a chair across from us. He didn't look too happy about our being there.

"Can we make this quick? *Jeopardy* is on," Gregorio said.

"That's the game where they give you the answers and you have to come up with the questions," Monk said.

"Yes, it is."

"Oh, great," Monk said, "let's play."

"What do you mean?" Gregorio said. "You want to watch TV with me?"

"Let's have our own game. I'll give you the answers and you can give me the questions. Ready? Here's the answer: *Roderick Turlock's gold.*"

Gregorio flinched as if he'd been slapped.

"C'mon, Mr. Dumas," Monk said, "take a guess."

Gregorio didn't say anything, but he began to sweat under his pompadour. Monk mimed the sound of a buzzer.

"Time's up. The question is: Why have you been tunneling from your house to the sewer and from the sewer to the fire station? That was fun, wasn't it? Here's another answer: *To wipe your footprints off the firehouse floor.* Can you tell me the question?"

Gregorio licked his lips and wiped his brow.

"You aren't even trying, Mr. Dumas," Monk said.

"I am," he said. "I just don't know the question. The answer makes no sense."

"I know, I know," I said, raising my hand and waving it enthusiastically.

Monk smiled and pointed to me. "Yes, Natalie, what's your guess?"

"Why did Mr. Dumas steal the towels?" I said.

"Correct!" Monk said. "He tunneled under the firehouse searching for the gold whenever the firemen left the station. But he didn't want Sparky barking and attracting attention to his digging, so he'd lure him out of the station with a rubber hotdog squeak toy. It's Sparky's favorite. There's one on Mr. Dumas's porch that's identical to the toy in Sparky's basket."

All the disparate facts, all the things we'd seen and heard, suddenly fell into place for me. It was an exhilarating feeling, and for a moment I understood why detectives want to be detectives.

"Sparky got to this house by way of the tunnel and the sewer," I said. "That's how Sparky got past the razor-wire fence and impregnated Letitia. And that's why Sparky always came back to the station smelling like he was covered with crap. It *was* crap."

Gregorio broke into a deep sweat.

"Natalie is winning this round, Mr. Dumas," Monk said. "You're going to have to guess the right question to this answer to stay in the game. Here it is: *Fifteen years in prison.*"

"What the hell are you talking about?" Gregorio screeched.

Monk shook his head. "No, I'm sorry, the correct question is: What's the combined jail term for filing a fraudulent lawsuit and committing an extreme act of animal cruelty?"

"I treat Letitia like royalty!" Gregorio said.

"But you murdered Sparky," I said.

"You've got it all wrong," Gregorio said. "Yeah, I've been digging for Turlock's gold, and I was in the firehouse Friday night, but I didn't kill Sparky."

"Convince us," I said.

"The truth is, Letitia is over-the-hill, past her prime. The only reason she won her last show two years ago was because I spent twenty-two thousand dollars on an extreme makeover."

"She had plastic surgery?" Monk said.

"It bought us another year on the dog show circuit, but that was it," Gregorio said. "The judges have sharp eyes, and no amount of cosmetic surgery can prevent the inevitable decline of beauty. We've been living on the gold coins I've been able to dig up under the firehouse. My plan was that once the coins ran out, we'd live off a settlement from the fire department on our lawsuit."

"Your fraudulent lawsuit," I said. "You were using Letitia to keep Sparky occupied while you hunted for gold."

"Tell us what really happened on Friday night, Mr. Dumas," Monk asked.

Gregoria sighed heavily. "It started out like usual. As soon as the fire trucks left, I took the tunnel to the firehouse basement. I could hear Sparky barking. But when I came out in the basement I didn't hear anything. So I took two towels, wiped off my feet, and went upstairs to look around. That's when I saw Sparky lying there and the fireman leaving."

I snorted in disgust. "You're sticking to your story that a fireman did it? It's laughable. Why

don't you just go all the way and admit what
you did?"

"Because I'm telling the truth," Gregorio said,
his eyes welling with tears. "I couldn't have killed
Sparky."

"Why not?" I asked with as much sarcasm and
disgust as I could put behind the two words.

"It would have broken Letitia's heart." He
wiped a tear from his cheek. "And mine, too. I
loved that damn dog."

Monk tilted his head from side to side and
shrugged his shoulders. "Yes, that makes perfect
sense."

And with that, Monk abruptly got up and
walked out the door without so much as a good-
bye. I had to hurry to catch up with him outside.

"You're not going to nail him?" I said.

"I just did," Monk said, setting off in the direction of the Excelsior.

"For stealing towels and filing a fraudulent lawsuit, but what about killing Sparky?"

"He didn't kill Sparky," Monk said.

"Then who did?"

"It's obvious," Monk said. "Lucas Breen did."

12

Mr. Monk Makes His Move

It was dark now, and we were retracing our steps back downhill to the Excelsior, where I'd have to skip a car payment to pay the attendant for parking. That was a compelling motive for murder right there. I was surprised the parking lot attendants weren't wearing Kevlar and sitting in bulletproof cages.

"Why would Lucas Breen want to murder a firehouse dog?" I asked.

"He didn't want to," Monk said. "He had to. Breen didn't know the dog was there when he sneaked into the firehouse."

"What was Breen doing there?" I asked. As we got closer to the Financial District, the number of people around us thinned out and the streets seemed to get darker and colder.

"He came to steal a firefighter's coat and helmet," Monk said. "Breen was the fireman whom Mr. Dumas saw leaving the firehouse."

"I don't understand this at all," I said. "What makes you think that was Breen?"

"Means, motive, and opportunity," Monk said, then explained to me his theory of what happened on Friday night.

Lucas Breen slipped out of the Excelsior around nine fifteen, walked to Esther's house, and smothered the woman with a pillow. He made it look like she fell asleep smoking, and then he hid outside until he was sure the living room was consumed with flames. Breen was rushing back to the hotel when he discovered he'd left something incriminating behind.

But it was too late to run back inside the house; it was already ablaze and the firefighters were on their way. And he couldn't take the chance that whatever belonged to him would burn in the fire. As luck would have it, the firehouse was nearby. He decided to steal a firefighter's gear, go back to Esther's house, retrieve whatever he'd left behind from the inferno, then return the outfit to the station on his way to the hotel.

"But he didn't know about Sparky," Monk concluded. "The dog charged him, so Breen grabbed the pickax to defend himself."

That would mean it happened just as Monk described the first time we visited the firehouse.

We were so busy talking, I hadn't paid much attention to our surroundings, but that changed as we passed between two buildings and a blast of icy wind slapped me awake.

The forest of skyscrapers blocked out what little moonlight there was. The wind whistled between the building, tossing fast-food wrappers and other loose trash, the tumbleweeds of a modern city.

I clutched my jacket tightly around myself. The chill wasn't the only thing making me shiver. Monk and I seemed to be the only people on the street. It was amazing how fast the Financial District buildings had emptied out. With the exception of the occasional passing car or bus, it felt like we were the last two people on earth.

"What was it that made you realize Breen came to steal firefighting gear?" I asked.

"When we visited the firehouse the first time, I saw a firefighter's coat on a hanger that was facing the wrong direction," Monk said. "I fixed it, but it's bothered me ever since."

Only Monk would be bothered by something like that. I once made the mistake of accepting a baker's dozen at Winchell's, and Monk has been haunted by that thirteenth doughnut ever since.

"Captain Mantooth likes order," Monk said. "The firefighters know better than to hang a coat on a hanger that's facing the wrong way. But Breen didn't. The coat I rehung was the one he stole the night he murdered Esther Stoval."

"Then his fingerprints will be all over it," I said.

Monk shook his head. "The coats and helmets are cleaned shortly after every fire to remove the toxins from the smoke."

If the firemen weren't so anxious to clean and shine everything, we might have had the evidence we needed to nail Lucas Breen. But now we had nothing, unless Monk had figured out something he wasn't telling me yet.

"So how are you going to prove that Lucas Breen was in the firehouse?"

Before Monk could answer, someone grabbed me from behind, yanked me into an alley, and put the edge of a very sharp knife to my throat.

"Drop your purse," a raspy voice hissed into my ear.

Monk turned and his eyes widened in shock. "Let her go."

"Shut up and get over here or I'll slit her throat right now."

Monk did as he was told. We backed deeper into the dark alley. I was afraid to breathe, or even to tremble, for fear the movement would make the blade slice me.

"You," the attacker said to Monk. "Give me your wallet and your watch."

Monk took out his wallet, opened it, and began to carefully examine the contents.

"What the hell are you doing?" the mugger said. I was thinking the same thing. Didn't Monk see the knife to my throat?

"Sorting through my wallet for you," Monk said.

"I can do that myself," the mugger said. I could smell the alcohol on his breath and the desperation in his sweat. Or maybe that was my desperation I was smelling.

"But if I do it," Monk said to the mugger, "I can keep what you'd otherwise throw away."

"Give me the damn wallet!"

"Obviously you want the money and the credit cards, but I'd like to keep the photo of my wife." Monk showed him the tiny photo of Trudy.

"Fine, keep it. Give me the rest. Now. Or I'll slit her throat. I will."

I felt him shaking with nervous frustration right through the sharp edge of the knife pressed against my skin. All it would take was the slightest increase in pressure and I'd be bleeding.

"Please do as he says, Mr. Monk."

Monk ignored me and took out a green-and-gold card, holding it up for the mugger to see. "What good is my Barnes and Noble Reader's Advantage Card to you? You don't strike me as a big reader. Do you really need a ten percent discount on books? I think not."

"I'm going to cut her, Goddamn it!" the mugger said. I believed him. He was getting edgier by the second.

"And what about my Ralphs Club Card? What good is it to you? You probably get your discount on groceries by stealing them."

All of the mugger's attention was focused on Monk now. I felt the pressure on my neck slacken and his hold on my waist loosen. Without thinking, I grabbed his wrist with one hand, smacked him in the face with the back of my other hand, and stomped on his foot as hard as I could. I felt the bones crack under my heel.

The mugger yelped and released me, dropping his knife. I kicked the knife away, spun around, and drove my knee deep into his crotch. He doubled over and I shoved him headfirst into the wall.

The mugger bounced off the wall and dropped flat on his back to the ground. I planted my knee in his crotch, pinned down his arms with my hands, and looked up at Monk.

He was still standing there, absorbed with putting everything back in the right place in his wallet. My heart was pounding and I was breathing hard as the adrenaline surged through me.

"Thanks," I said. "You were a big help."

"I was distracting him until you could make your move."

"*My* move? What about *your* move?"

"That was my move." Monk put his wallet back in his pocket. "Where did you learn to do that?"

"I'd like to know, too." The mugger groaned.

"Watching my daughter in her tae kwon do class." I glanced at Monk and jerked my head toward my purse. "You can use my cell phone to call the police."

"Not yet." Monk came over and crouched beside me. "Excuse me, Mr. Mugger. Do you work this street a lot? Is this your mugging turf?"

The mugger didn't answer. I ground my knee into his testicles until he whimpered. I am woman; hear me roar.

"Answer the question," I said.

The mugger nodded. "Yeah, it's my patch."

"Were you working on Friday night?" Monk asked.

"I don't get a lot of vacation days in my profession," the mugger said.

"Did one of your victims Friday night include a man named Lucas Breen?"

"Screw you."

I increased the pressure on his privates. "You'll have a hard time screwing anything ever again if you aren't more forthcoming."

I knew I sounded like a character in a bad cop movie, but I was still riding on adrenaline and pissed off about having a knife to my throat. The tougher I talked, the better I felt and the more the fear began to fade away.

"Yeah, I robbed Breen," he croaked. His eyes were bulging so much I was afraid they might pop out and bounce away. I eased the pressure I was exerting on him.

"What time did you mug him?" Monk asked.

"I don't have a watch."

"You must have stolen hundreds of watches in your career. You never considered keeping one?"

"I don't have lots of appointments."

"Was Breen missing anything?"

"He was after I met him," the mugger said.

"But not before," Monk said.

"I took his wallet and his watch. I let him keep his wedding ring."

"Why?" I said.

"Because people are real touchy and stupid about 'em. They'll risk their lives for their wedding rings." He looked at Monk. "I've never seen anyone do it for a Ralphs Club Card."

"The savings really add up," Monk said. "Did you notice anything unusual about Breen?"

"He was in a big hurry, couldn't wait to give me his stuff," the mugger said. "And he smelled like smoke, like he just ran out of a burning building or something.''

Monk called Stottlemeyer and, while he was filling him in, a black-and-white the captain sent showed up and two officers jumped out to take care of the mugger. I took the phone from Monk, called my neighbor Mrs. Throphamner, and begged her to take care of Julie for a couple hours while we followed up on what the mugger told us. Ever since I started working for Monk, Mrs. Throphamner has become used to my frantic calls for emergency babysitting.

We were just finishing up giving our report to the officers when Stottlemeyer showed up and motioned us into his car.

"Where are we going?" I asked.

"I think it's time to have another chat with Lucas Breen," Stottlemeyer said. He made some calls and found out that Breen was still at his office, just a few blocks away.

When we got to the building, Stottlemeyer used the guard's phone to call up to Breen's office. He spoke to the secretary and asked if Breen would come down to the lobby to meet with us. When the secretary said that Breen refused, Stottlemeyer smiled.

"Fine," he said. "Tell him we can have the conversation about Lizzie Draper at his house in front of his wife."

Stottlemeyer hung up, then motioned to the Boudin Bakery. "Can I buy you a cup of coffee while we're waiting for Breen to come down?"

Lee Goldberg

I took Stottlemeyer up on his offer and convinced him to sweeten the deal with a fresh sourdough baguette. Monk settled for a warm bottle of Sierra Springs water from my bag.

Five minutes later Lucas Breen emerged from the elevator alone and joined us at our table.

"What's so important you had to drag me out of my office?" Breen said.

"You didn't have to come down," Stottlemeyer said. "But I guess you didn't want the missus hearing about your affair with Lizzie Draper."

"I've never heard of her."

"She's your mistress," Stottlemeyer said.

Breen grinned with smug self-confidence and tugged at the cuffs of his monogrammed shirt. "Is that what she says?"

Stottlemeyer shook his head.

"I didn't think so," Breen said.

"We know you bought her a bouquet of flowers from the florist in this lobby," Stottlemeyer said.

"Do you? I buy lots of flowers from Flo. I buy them for my wife, my secretary, my clients, and to beautify my office. How do you know her bouquet came from me? It could have come from anybody in this building. The woman could even have bought the bouquet here herself."

"You bought it for her," Monk said. "Probably the same time you left her your shirt. She was wearing it when we met her. The buttons are monogrammed with your initials."

"My wife donated some old clothes to Goodwill," Breen said. "She always hated that denim shirt. Perhaps this woman you talked to enjoys shopping for bargains at secondhand clothing stores."

"How did you know it was denim?" Monk asked. "We didn't tell you what kind of shirt she was wearing."

"The buttons," Breen said quickly. "Only my denim shirts and short-sleeved sportswear have my initials on the buttons instead of the cuffs."

"How do you know we weren't talking about one of your short-sleeved shirts?"

"I'm a happily married man and faithful to my wife, but even if I weren't, adultery isn't a crime."

"But murder is," Monk said. "You killed Esther Stoval."

"That's laughable," Breen said. "I had no reason to want her dead."

"Esther knew about your affair and was blackmailing you," Monk said. "On Friday night you slipped away from the fund-raiser, smothered Esther, and set fire to her house."

"You're forgetting that I didn't leave the Excelsior hotel until midnight," Breen said.

"Yes, you did, and we can prove it," Stottlemeyer said. "You were mugged on the street a block away from the hotel. We have the mugger, and we know you reported your stolen credit cards to your bank. But here's the odd thing: You didn't report the mugging to the police. Gee, I wonder why."

Breen sighed wearily. "I briefly stepped out of the hotel for a smoke, and that's when I was mugged. It hardly qualifies as 'leaving.' "

"Then why didn't you tell anybody about it?" Stottlemeyer said.

"Because I promised my wife I'd quit smoking. If she knew I was still smoking cigars, she'd have my head."

"*That's* why you didn't report the mugging? Because you were afraid your wife would find out that you were still smoking?" Stottlemeyer said, incredulity dripping from every word.

Breen absently tugged again at the cuffs of his handmade shirt. I don't know if it was a nervous habit, or if he just wanted us all to admire his cuff links.

"I don't appreciate your tone, Captain. I didn't tell the police because I knew the press would pick up on it and the mugging would be all over the news. The last thing I want to do is create the impression that the neighborhood is a hotbed of crime. I have an ownership interest in the Excelsior. We'd lose room bookings, weddings, and convention business. But it's more than that. I love San Francisco. I don't want to do anything that might hurt the city's image or cause a decline in tourism."

"That's a good story, and we're all moved by your civic pride," Monk said. "But here's what really happened. You left something behind in Esther's house. So you stole a firefighter's coat and helmet in order to go back into the house and get it. But you didn't know the firehouse had a dog, and when he came at you barking and growling, you killed him with a pickax."

"Now you're accusing me of murdering a dog,

too?" Breen said. "This is outrageous. Do you have any proof to back up this fantasy of yours?"

"The mugger said you reeked of smoke," I said.

"*Reeked?* He sounds like my wife. My God, everybody is antismoking now, even the muggers. Like I said before, I was having a cigar. That's what he smelled. The wonderful aroma of a Partagas Salamones."

Breen looked past me, something outside catching his eye. I glanced over my shoulder and saw a bum walking past the window. It was the same bum whom Monk had gifted with a couple dozen Wet Ones, shuffling by in his overcoat, pushing a rickety grocery cart overflowing with garbage. He saw me watching him and flipped me off.

Breen turned to Stottlemeyer, and when he spoke, his tone was much harder than before. "You've taxed my patience long enough with this inane inquiry. Make your point and get it over with."

"Monk is right. You killed the lady and the dog, and you're going down for it. All four of us sitting here know that," Stottlemeyer said. "The thing is, since you're such a booster of the police department and all, I thought I'd give you the chance to cut a deal before we both spend a lot of needless time and expense on this."

"I heard you were a rising star in the department, Captain, and that you, Mr. Monk, were a brilliant detective. Obviously I was misinformed. I'm deeply disappointed in both of you. We're done here."

Breen rose from his seat, acknowledged me with a tip of his head, and walked back to the elevator.

"He's disappointed in us, Monk." Stottlemeyer finished his coffee. "I'm crushed; how about you?"

"He's going to make life hard for you, Captain," Monk said.

"Not as hard as I'm going to make it for him," Stottlemeyer said. "I'll get search warrants tonight, and we'll ransack his home and office for that little item he went back to Esther's house to get—just as soon as you tell me what that little item is."

"Something very, very incriminating."

"Which is . . . ?" Stottlemeyer said.

"Something that points directly, irrefutably, and conclusively to him as the killer."

"Yes, I get the concept of incriminating," Stottlemeyer said. "But what is it, exactly, that I should tell the judge that we're looking for?"

Monk shrugged.

Stottlemeyer looked at Monk, then at me, then back to Monk. "You don't know?"

"Something so unbelievably damaging to him that he'd literally walk through the red-hot flames of hell to get it back."

"Well, there go my search warrants," Stottlemeyer said. "So what you're basically saying is, we've got bupkis."

"Actually," Monk said. "It's probably less than that."

13

Mr. Monk Does His Homework

Stottlemeyer drove us back to the Excelsior and used his badge to get my car out of the parking lot for free. It must be nice to have a badge and be able to park wherever you want without worrying about fees or tickets.

I made Monk promise not to say anything to Julie about the attempted mugging. She'd lost her father, and I didn't want her worrying every time I left the house with Monk that she might lose me next. If Monk had a problem with my lie of omission, he didn't say anything.

When we got home, lugging in our Pottery Barn purchases, Julie was at the table working on her homework, and Mrs. Throphamner was on the couch watching TV. Mrs. Throphamner's dentures were on a napkin on the coffee table, facing the TV so they, too, could enjoy *Diagnosis Murder*.

I introduced Monk to Mrs. Throphamner. "He's staying with us for a few days."

She popped her teeth back into her mouth and offered her hand to Monk. "It's a pleasure to finally meet you."

Monk took one look at her hand, which was covered with blisters, and shook the air between them instead.

"Yes, it certainly is," Monk said, shaking the air enthusiastically. "What happened to your hands?"

"I've been tending my roses," she said. "It's hard work, but I love it."

I paid Mrs. Throphamner twelve dollars for babysitting. She stuffed the bills in her cleavage, blew a kiss to Julie, and went home in a hurry so she wouldn't miss a second of Dick Van Dyke's sleuthing.

"Mrs. Throphamner's such a sweet woman," I said after she left.

"She's a witch," Monk said. "Did you see those gnarled hands and her puckered, toothless face?"

Julie giggled happily. She happened to share Monk's opinion. I thought they were both being cruel.

"She's old and lonely; that's all. Her husband spends most of his time lately at their fishing cabin up near Sacramento. She's had nothing to do the last few months except tend her garden and watch TV."

Of course, that was also very good for me, because it coincided with my newfound employment with Monk and made her available almost anytime for babysitting. I liked to believe that Mrs. Throphamner and I were doing each other a favor.

I heated up a frozen pizza for dinner, set the table with paper plates, and talked to Julie about her day at school while Monk disposed of the napkin Mrs. Throphamner had rested her teeth on. He put on rubber dish gloves and used a pair of barbecue tongs to pick up the napkin and take it to the fireplace, where he incinerated it. Then he disinfected the coffee table and the air around it with enough Lysol to eradicate every germ within a square mile. I had to open the window in the kitchen so we wouldn't be eradicated, too. Julie watched him closely, amused and fascinated at the same time.

"I can still smell her," Monk said.

"It's her flowers you're smelling," I said. "I opened the kitchen window. She spends so much time tending her garden that she picks up the fragrance of her roses."

He studied me, trying to discern whether I was telling the truth or not, then decided to believe me and put away the Lysol and threw out the gloves. I would have washed the gloves and used them again, but I'm not Adrian Monk.

As soon as the pizza was ready, Monk cut it into eight even slices. We sat down to eat, and I gave Julie an edited account of our day, leaving out the mugging and the identity of Sparky's killer, but said we were close to getting the culprit. I know that was being overly optimistic, but I had a lot of faith in Monk.

After dinner, Julie went back to her homework while I unpacked and washed all the new dishes and silverware. I know Monk would have been glad to do the washing for me, but Julie had other plans. She asked him if he'd help her with her homework.

"That's very nice of you," Monk said. "But I don't want to intrude on your fun."

"You think homework is fun?" Julie said.

"Homework was my second favorite thing about school."

"What was your favorite?" Julie asked.

"The tests, of course. You know what was almost as much fun? Deducing days in advance exactly when the next surprise 'pop' quiz was coming up. The teachers pretended like this irritated them, but it was really their clever way of encouraging me to challenge myself. Boy, does this bring back memories. I used to love aligning the rows of desks each day. Do you ever do that?"

"No," Julie said.

"You aren't being aggressive enough," Monk said.

"I don't think that's what it is."

"The trick is getting to school an hour early, before some other enterprising student beats you to it. Not that anyone ever beat me to it."

"Are you sure anyone wanted to?"

"Yeah, right. Next thing you'll tell me nobody competes to get an even-numbered locker. You're such a kidder." Monk turned to me. "Isn't she a kidder?"

"She's a kidder," I said. "And a josher."

"So," Monk asked her, "what are you studying tonight?"

"A bunch of stuff. But there's something I thought you might know a few things about," Julie said. "In Life Sciences, we're learning about infectious diseases."

"You're talking to the right man," Monk said, reaching for her Life Sciences textbook. "When I was in junior high, I taught the teacher a few things about the subject."

"I'm not surprised." She opened the book and pointed to a page. "We're doing this project tomorrow."

Monk read it aloud. " 'Everyone in class should shake hands with two people and record their names—' " He stopped midsentence. "How can they put children through this? Don't they realize how dangerous it is? Didn't they send home permission slips for this?"

"Uh, no," Julie said. "Why should they?"

"Why? *Why?*" Monk turned to me. "Tell her."

"It sounds innocent enough to me," I said.

"It does? Well, you won't think so after you hear this." Monk read again from the textbook: " 'Now shake hands with two different people, take their names, then shake hands with two more.' What kind of teachers are these? Are they insane? I suppose they tell the kids to run around the classroom with scissors, too."

"It's just a practical exercise that teaches kids how diseases are spread," I said.

"By having them spread diseases themselves?" Monk said. "What's next? Having the kids drink cyanide-laced fruit juice to see how poison works? I can't imagine how they teach sex education."

"I have an idea." Julie took the book from Monk and closed it. "How about if you quiz me for the test instead? Here are some of the questions."

She handed Monk a piece of paper.

"I hope you plan on bringing extra gloves and disinfectant wipes to school tomorrow," Monk said.

"Extra?" she said.

"You *do* take gloves and disinfectant wipes to school, don't you?"

Behind Monk's back, I nodded vigorously to Julie, and she got the message.

"Yes, of course, who doesn't?" she said. "I just thought what I usually bring would be more than enough. So are you going to quiz me?"

Monk sighed with relief, nodded, and glanced at the paper. "Okay, here goes. What are pathogens?"

"Organisms that cause disease," Julie answered, a confident smile on her face.

"Wrong," Monk said.

Her smile faded. "That's the right answer. I know it is."

"The correct answer is everything."

"Everything?"

"All organisms cause disease. Name four sources of pathogens."

Julie bit her lip, thought for a moment, then ticked off the answers one by one on her fingers. "Another person, a contaminated object, an animal bite, and the environment."

"Wrong," Monk said. "The correct answer is everything."

"Everything?"

"The entire world is a pathogen. Next question: What are the four major groups of pathogens?"

Julie tapped her fingers on the table. "Um, viruses, bacteria, fungi, and protists."

"Wrong," Monk said. "The correct answer is—"

"Everything," Julie interrupted.

"Correct." Monk smiled and handed the paper back to her. "You're going to ace this test."

"But what about the other study questions?"

"There's only one answer for all of them."

"Everything?"

Monk nodded. "Life is simpler than you think."

Julie finished her homework and went to her room to IM her friends. I put away everything, expecting Monk to join me at any moment to lecture me on the proper arrangement of pots and pans or something, but he didn't show.

The phone rang. It was Joe.

"We didn't get a chance to talk when you came by," Joe said. "And then you went across the street and didn't come back. I kept waiting for you to come back."

"Oh," I said. Brilliant answer, huh?

There was an awkward silence, the likes of which I hadn't experienced since high school.

"You missed all the excitement," Joe said. "A bunch of people from the city engineer's office and the Public Utilities department were here. Turns out Dumas has a tunnel under his house to the sewer and another one from the sewer into our basement."

"I know; Mr. Monk was the one who figured it out," I said. "Dumas has been digging up Roderick Turlock's treasure of stolen gold coins."

"Did he kill Sparky?"

"Afraid not," I said. "Mr. Monk is still working on that one."

"What about the mystery of your disappearing panties? Are you having any luck with that one?"

I almost said he could help me solve that mystery himself, but caught myself in time. Instead I said, "I'm really looking forward to seeing you Wednesday night."

I supposed that could have been interpreted as conveying almost the same thought as what I didn't say, but not so brazenly.

I don't know how he interpreted it, because suddenly I heard the fire alarm bell go off at the station.

"Me, too, Natalie. I've got to run," Joe said.

"Be careful," I said, and we hung up.

My heart was racing, but for a whole lot of different reasons. One, I was excited. Two, I was nervous. And three, I was terrified, and not about our date. It was that alarm. It meant Joe was going to be rushing off to some fire. I knew that was what he did for a living—he was Firefighter Joe, after all—but the thought of him charging into some inferno made me queasy. I hadn't felt that kind of queasiness since Mitch used to go off on his tours of duty. I felt it every time until the one mission when he didn't return.

I went down the hall on my way to my room and walked past the open door of the guest room. I saw Monk lying on his bed, staring at the ceiling, his arms folded across his chest as if he were resting in a coffin.

I went into his room and sat on the edge of the bed. "Are you okay, Mr. Monk?"

"Yeah."

"What are you doing?"

"Waiting," he said.

"For what?"

"The facts to fall into place."

"Is that what they do?"

"Generally," he said, sighing.

"And you just wait."

He sat up and leaned back against the headboard. "What's frustrating about these murders is how simple they are. We know how they were done and we even know who did them. The challenge is finding evidence where none appears to exist."

"You've had bigger challenges than this before," I said. "You'll figure it out."

"This is different," Monk said. "I usually have a lot more space to think."

"Space?"

"I start and end my day in an empty house. There aren't any people or distractions. Everything is in its place. Everything is in order. All that's left is just me and my thoughts, and sometimes my LEGOs. And that's when the facts of a case fall naturally into place, and the ones that don't point me to the solution of the mystery."

"And that's not happening now," I said.

"I'm still waiting."

In other words, our messy house and our messier lives were too much for him. He longed for the peace, solitude, and sterility of his house. He was homesick. And my house was about as unlike his as it was possible to get.

"Would you like me to find you a hotel room, Mr. Monk?" I tried to make the offer as nicely as possible, so he wouldn't think I was angry or offended, which I wasn't.

"No, of course not," he said. "This is great."

At first I thought he was being dishonest, but then I wondered if, compared to the alternatives, staying with us really wasn't so bad.

A hotel could be even worse. Maybe he'd hear the TV next door, or a couple making love upstairs, or kids playing in the room below. Even if he didn't hear anything, maybe just knowing so many people were in the building would be enough to distract him. Or, worse, what if he couldn't stop thinking of the hundreds of people who'd stayed in his room, slept in his bed, and used the bathroom? And if that wasn't enough stuff to distract him, what about the horror of mismatched wallpaper?

Compared to all of that, our guest room must have felt like a padded cell—in a good way, if there is such a thing.

So what he was really talking about was me and Julie. *We* were the ones creating all the distraction.

I got up from the bed. "I'll leave you alone to your thinking."

"No, no, I'll go with you," he said, getting up.

"But what about all those facts that need to fall into place?"

"They'll fall later," Monk said. "The problem with having so much space is that I never get a chance to help someone with their homework."

I smiled to myself. As afraid as he was of human contact, it was nice to know that even Adrian Monk still needed it.

14

Mr. Monk and the Rainy Day

When I got up at six on Tuesday, Monk was already showered, shaved, and dressed, and the bathroom tub was clean enough to perform surgery in. I wouldn't have been surprised if he spent the night in the bathroom just to make sure he got to it first. If so, it's a good thing neither Julie nor I got up in the middle of the night to pee.

The three of us had Chex cereal for breakfast in our brand-new bowls and swapped sections of the *Chronicle* among ourselves. There was an article on a back page about a warehouse fire last night, and how the roof caved in and sent two firefighters to the hospital. My throat went dry. Could that have been the fire Joe was called to? What if he was one of the firefighters who was hurt?

It was seven thirty, too early to call the fire station, unless I wanted to wake everyone up. I'd call later. Or maybe it would be better, I thought, to call now.

I was yanked out of my worries by the sound of a car horn outside, signaling that Julie's ride to school had arrived.

Julie shoved all her books into her backpack, grabbed her sack lunch, and was heading out the door when I stopped her.

"Don't forget your raincoat," I said, taking it off the coat tree by the door.

She hated wearing her raincoat. She would rather get soaked from head to toe. The thing is, just a year earlier she had needed that raincoat more than anything else on earth. It was what everyone was wearing, and without it she would have been shamed out of adolescent society. The raincoat cost $100 at Nordstrom, but I found one for less than half that much on eBay. It was probably stolen, or a knockoff, but it saved Julie from disgrace, and she wore it every day, whether there were clouds in the sky or not. And then something happened, some great cosmic shift in society and culture. Raincoats were out; getting drenched was in.

"Mom," she whined. "Do I have to?"

"There's a sixty percent chance of rain," I said. "Just take it with you. It's better to be prepared."

"So I get wet," she said. "Big deal."

"Take it," I said.

"It's only water," she said. "It's not like it's acid."

I didn't have the time or patience to argue. I unzipped her backpack, rolled her raincoat into a ball, and shoved the raincoat inside.

"You'll thank me later," I said.

"You sound like *him*." She motioned to Monk. It wasn't meant as a compliment.

I was about to scold her for her rudeness, but he didn't notice her disrespectful behavior. He was sitting straight up in his chair, lost in thought, and shrugging his shoulders as if neither one fit in its socket quite right.

Julie marched off and slammed the door behind her, but by that point her drama was wasted on me. I was watching Monk. I knew what all that shifting around in the chair meant—the facts were falling into place.

He knew what Breen left behind.

And I couldn't help noticing that his break-through didn't happen in some blissfully sterile environment of solitude, cleanliness, and order. It happened in my messy kitchen in the midst of a typical breakfast-table squabble between a sane, reasonable, rational mother and her deranged, un-reasonable, irrational daughter.

"Do you have a computer with an Internet connection?" Monk said.

"Sure," I said. "It's not like we live in a cave."

I regretted the comment right away, because I knew he'd take it as a dig. I didn't mean it to be one; I just forgot for a moment that Monk doesn't have an Internet connection at his house. He's afraid of catching a computer virus, which is also why he doesn't have a computer.

I went back to my room, got my laptop, and brought it to the kitchen table. I have a technogeek neighbor who designs Web sites for a living out of his apartment. He took pity on us and let us piggyback on his wireless network to use his high-speed connection. I was up and running and surfing the Net in seconds.

"What do you need?" I asked Monk.

"Can you get me detailed information on what the weather in San Francisco was like on Friday night?"

That was too easy. I was hoping for something a little more challenging so I could show off my Web-surfing prowess.

I quickly Googled my way to a site that tracked weather patterns, zeroed in on Friday night in San Francisco, and showed Monk his options. He could check out the temperature, rainfall, humidity, dew point, wind speed, direction, and chill. He could peruse satellite photos, Doppler radar, and 3-D animated views of the fog patterns and the movement of the jet stream.

"Can you show me when it was raining, hour by hour?" Monk said.

It wasn't as impressive as watching the fog roll in and out in 3-D, but sure, I said, I could show him the rainfall, which was tracked in a straight-forward graph. Bor-ing. The least they could have done was jazz it up with a few animated raindrops rolling down the screen.

"Look," he said excitedly. "There was intermittent drizzle and rain until about nine thirty, then it let up until about two A.M."

How thrilling, I thought. But what I said instead was something along the lines of, "What does it mean?"

"I'll show you," Monk said. "Could you search the Web and bring up the photos of Lucas Breen taken at the 'Save the Bay' fund-raiser that Disher showed us?"

I did a quick Google search that gathered about a dozen photos from the "Save the Bay" home page, various newspaper Web sites, and a couple of snarky gossip blogs (one of which speculated that Mrs. Breen's trip to Europe the morning after the party was for "another facial refreshening" at a plastic surgery resort in Switzerland).

The photos were the same ones we had seen before of Breen arriving at the Excelsior in the rain with his wife and then the two of them leaving at midnight with the governor.

Monk pointed to the screen. "When Breen arrived, it was raining. You can see that he's huddled under his umbrella and wearing an overcoat."

Then Monk pointed to the picture of the Breens leaving the party. "But here, his umbrella is closed under his arm and he's not wearing his overcoat."

"Because it's not raining anymore."

"So where's his coat? Why isn't he carrying it?"

Good question. In light of everything that happened, I could think only of one answer.

"He left it in Esther Stoval's house," I said.

"According to the weather report, we know it didn't stop raining until nine thirty, so he must have been wearing his overcoat when he slipped out of the hotel to see Esther," Monk said. "She probably asked him to take it off and hang it up when he came in. Then they talked for a minute or two."

"How do you know that?"

"Because of where her body was found. She was sitting on the far corner of the coach, facing the chair where he sat," Monk said. "She said or did something that provoked him. He flew out of the chair and smothered her with the pillow. After that, all that was on Breen's mind was covering up the crime, staging the fire, and getting out of that house as fast as possible. It wasn't raining when he left, so he probably didn't realize he'd forgotten his overcoat until he was halfway back to the hotel."

Which would have put him right smack in front of the empty fire station.

"Breen couldn't risk the possibility that any part of his coat might survive the fire," Monk said. "If it was like the rest of his wardrobe, it was handmade and had monogrammed buttons. It would point right back to him. He had to go back and get it."

I bet it was while Breen was standing in front of the fire station, staring in panic at the empty garage, that he came up with the bright idea of how to save himself. When he ran in to get the gear, I'm sure the last thing he expected was that some barking, snarling dog would come charging at him. Wasn't it enough that he left his coat behind? Did fate have to add a dog to his misery, too?

But Breen survived unscathed, and things went much smoother after that. He slipped into the burning house in his firefighting gear unnoticed by the other firemen, snatched his overcoat, and got out again. He returned the firefighting gear to the station without being seen and without having to fight off any more ferocious animals.

He must have thought the worst was over. And then he got mugged.

Unbelievable. His luck was so bad, I might have felt sorry for him if he hadn't killed a woman and a dog and if he weren't such a pompous jerk. Despite all his incredible misfortune, he made it back to the party without being missed. I'm sure he went straight to the bar and knocked back a few. I would have.

It was hardly the perfect murder, but I doubt anybody would ever have known what he did if it weren't for a twelve-year-old kid hiring a detective to find out who killed a dog.

But I was getting ahead of myself. Breen wasn't caught yet. We didn't have enough evidence. We didn't have the coat.

"So assuming he got his overcoat back," I said, "what did he do with it?"

"We have to assume the overcoat was burned or damaged by the smoke and that he ditched it somewhere between Esther's house and the hotel."

"What about Lizzie Draper's house?"

Monk shook his head. "Too risky. What if she stumbled on the overcoat before he had a chance to get rid of it? He wouldn't want her, or anybody else, to be able to connect him to the fire. He ditched it somewhere else, somewhere between the fire station and the hotel."

Then I knew where we should start looking.

* * *

I had an ulterior motive for wanting to start at the fire station. For one thing, I didn't want to pay for parking at the Excelsior. For another, I wanted an excuse to drop by and see if Joe was okay.

But when we got to the station, it was empty. They were out responding to a call.

"I'm sure he's okay," Monk said. We were standing outside the firehouse.

"Who?"

"Firefighter Joe. That's why we're here, isn't it?"

"No, we're here to retrace Breen's steps and look for places where he might have ditched the overcoat."

"That would be the hard way," Monk said. "I called Disher before we left the house and asked him to see if the mugger remembers whether Breen was carrying an overcoat or not."

"Then we didn't have to come all the way down here," I said. "We could have waited at home to hear from Disher."

Monk nodded. "But you wanted to check on Firefighter Joe ever since you read about the warehouse fire in the paper this morning."

"How did you know?"

"You never read past that article," Monk said. "And the whole time we were talking, you kept looking furtively at the phone, debating with yourself whether it was still too early to call."

Sometimes I forget that Monk is a detective. I also forget that when he's not being the single most irritating person on the planet, he can be a very sweet man.

"Thank you," I said.

My cell phone rang. It was Disher.

"We had to make a deal with Marlon Tolliver to get Monk the information he wanted," he said.

"Who is Marlon Tolliver?"

"Your mugger. He got himself a pretty good public defender. We had to agree to drop the assault-with-a-deadly-weapon charge against him in return for his testimony about his dealings with Lucas Breen."

"So he gets away with putting a knife to my throat?"

"To get him to talk, we had to give him something, and that was all we had," Disher said. "It was the best we could do without you here crushing his *cojones*."

"I'll be glad to come down and do it," I said.

"The deal is done, and here's what he told us," Disher said. "Breen was holding his overcoat when Tolliver mugged him."

"Thanks," I said. "Could you do me a favor?"

"Of course; that's why I'm here, to do all of Monk's legwork for him."

"This is a favor for me," I said.

"You want me to knee Tolliver in the *cojones* for you?"

"There was a warehouse fire last night and some firefighters were hurt. Is there some way you could find out if one of them was Joe Cochran?"

"No problem," Disher said. "I'll call you back as soon as I know something."

I thanked Disher and told Monk the news. "Breen still had the coat when he was in the alley outside the hotel."

"Then that's where he ditched it," Monk said. "Somewhere in the alley."

We walked to the hotel. It was faster than finding another parking spot and cheaper, too. We passed a few homeless people who, after seeing us the other day, knew better than to ask Monk for a handout. I was glad we didn't run into the guy who had flipped me off.

The streets were crowded with people, but I still approached the alley cautiously, just in case there was another mugger hiding in the darkness. Monk was also being cautious, only for different reasons. He was trying very hard not to step in anything dirty, which isn't easy in a filthy, smelly alley.

We walked slowly, looking for places where Breen might have disposed of the overcoat. It soon became obvious to both of us that there was really only one place he could have stashed it out of sight—in one of the trash bins near the hotel service exit.

Without saying anything to Monk first, I climbed up on one of the Dumpsters. Monk freaked out.

"Step away from the Dumpster," Monk said. "Very slowly."

I stayed where I was. "It's a Dumpster, Mr. Monk. Not a bomb."

"Don't be a hero, Natalie. Leave it for the professionals."

"I'm not an expert in police procedure, but I don't think Captain Stottlemeyer is going to be able to get a forensics team down here to search this Dumpster based only on your hunch."

"I'm not talking about the crime-scene investigators; they aren't equipped to handle a situation like this," Monk said. "This requires professionals who deal with garbage every day."

"You want me to call a garbage man?"

"That's a pejorative and sexist term. They really prefer 'sanitation technician.' "

"How do you know?"

"I talk to them," Monk said.

"You do? Why?"

"They're people, too, you know."

"Who hang around with garbage," I said. "I'd think you'd want to be as far away from them as possible when they show up."

"I take precautions," Monk said. "Gloves, surgical mask, goggles. But I have to be there to supervise."

"You supervise your trash collection? Why?"

"I have special needs."

"Believe me, I know, but what does that have to do with your trash?"

"I have to make sure my trash isn't being mixed with the other trash," Monk said.

"Why? What terrible thing could possibly happen?"

"It could get dirty."

"It's trash, Mr. Monk. It's all dirty, even yours."

"No, mine is clean dirty," Monk said.

"Clean dirty," I said. "What is that?"

"For one thing, each of my discarded items is placed in an individual airtight bag before being put in the mother bag."

"So it won't get the other trash in the 'mother bag' dirty."

"Not everyone is as conscientious as I am," Monk said. "It's the sad truth."

"But your bags get tossed in the back of the truck with everybody else's trash anyway."

Monk shook his head. "My bags ride up front with the drivers."

"It doesn't make a lot of difference in the end," I said. "It still goes to the dump."

"My garbage goes in zone nine."

"Your trash has its own zone?"

"All the really clean trash goes there."

I groaned, handed him my purse, and climbed up the rest of the way onto the trash bin.

"Wait, wait," Monk protested. "You're exposing yourself."

I stopped. "Are my pants riding down on my butt?"

"Hell, no," Monk said.

"Then what am I exposing?"

"You're exposing your body to deadly toxins," Monk said. "You haven't had your shots. You aren't wearing gloves. You aren't using a respirator. It's suicidal."

"Mr. Monk, I'm only going to lift the lid," I said.

"And God only knows what you'll release into the atmosphere," Monk said. "If you're not going to think about yourself, think of humanity, think of your daughter, but most of all, think of me."

I lifted the lid. Monk screamed and leaped away

as if he expected the Dumpster to explode, spraying its shrapnel of decaying food, broken glass, old shoes, and soiled diapers all over him. It didn't.

I looked inside. The bin was nearly empty, with only a few bulging "mother bags" of trash at the bottom. I knew that couldn't have been all the garbage the hotel had tossed since Friday. I slid along to the end of the bin and climbed over to the next one. I lifted the lid. It was empty. So was the next one.

If the overcoat had been in one of the bins, it was gone now, along with any hope we had of proving Lucas Breen was guilty of murder.

I looked over my shoulder for Monk, but he wasn't behind me anymore. He was standing on the street twenty yards away, holding a handkerchief over his nose and mouth.

I had to yell the bad news to him.

"We're too late," I said.

15

Mr. Monk Visits His Trash

It took me thirty minutes to convince Monk it wasn't necessary for him to call a hazardous materials emergency response team to come and decontaminate me, the alley, and the rest of the block.

But to do that, I had to assure him I was clean, which meant I had to wipe my hands and face with Wet Ones about fifty times, and use the hotel restroom to brush my teeth, wash out my eyes with Visine, and clean my sinuses with nose spray.

Even then, as we drove to the city dump, Monk sat as far away from me in the car as he could without riding outside on the luggage rack.

All of the city's nonrecyclable garbage is taken to the San Francisco Solid Waste Transfer Center, which is a fancy way of saying "a garbage dump with a roof over it." The trash is collected there until it can be transported by bigger trucks to the

Altamont Landfill in Livermore, about sixty miles east of San Francisco.

The transfer center is an enormous hangar-like building next door to Candlestick Park, which these days is called Monster Park, and not because it's an amusement park full of dinosaurs. It's also not named after the killer winds that swoop in off the bay—the winds that blew Giants pitcher Stu Miller off the mound during the 1961 All-star game and that tossed the entire batting cage into center field during a New York Mets practice. Nor is the stadium named for the fact that it's upwind from an enclosed garbage dump.

It's named for Monster Cable, some company that makes computer cables and paid the city millions of dollars for the right to plaster their name on the stadium. I think the city should have also let the cable company put their name on the transfer station at no charge. They could've called it "Monster Dump," since that's what it smelled like and since the name is a lot catchier than "San Francisco Solid Waste Transfer Center."

It's a testament to Monk's determination to get Breen that we were there at all. You know what his reaction was when I merely lifted the lid of a trash bin, and now here he was at the heart of darkness itself—the city dump.

Monk didn't want to get out of the car. He just sat in his seat, staring in horror at the enormous warehouse and the line of trash trucks going in and out of the building. So I had to call Chad Grimsley, the facility supervisor, and ask him to come out and meet us.

Ten minutes later, Grimsley scooted out of the warehouse in a golf cart. He was a thin, little man with a trim goatee, and he wore a yellow hard hat that seemed five sizes too big for his head.

Grimsley pulled the golf cart right up to the passenger's side of the car. Monk rolled down the window a quarter of an inch and held a handkerchief to his face.

"I'm Adrian Monk and this is my assistant, Natalie Teeger." Monk motioned to me in the driver's seat. I waved at Grimsley. "We're working with the police on a murder investigation. I'd like to talk to you about a trash pickup outside of the Excelsior hotel."

"Your assistant mentioned that on the phone," Grimsley said. "Why don't you come up to my office and we can discuss it?"

"I'd rather not," Monk said.

"I can assure you it's perfectly safe to step out of your car," Grimsley said. "You don't even notice the smell after a few minutes."

"You don't notice radiation either," Monk said. "But it's still killing you."

Grimsley looked past Monk to me. I shrugged.

"The trash in the neighborhood around the Excelsior was picked up at approximately seven this morning," Grimsley said.

"Where would it be now?" Monk asked.

Grimsley pointed to the warehouse. "In there. It was dumped about two hours ago."

Monk showed Grimsley one of the pictures of Breen wearing his overcoat that we'd printed out before we left the house.

"We're looking for this overcoat. If you could grab it for us, put it in an airtight bag, and bring it out here, we'd appreciate it."

"I'm afraid it's not that simple. It really would be better if I could show you." Grimsley pointed to the office building adjacent to the transfer station. "Those are the executive offices. You could drive right up to the lobby door and run inside. It's only about five feet from the curb to the door so you can hold your breath the whole way."

Monk closed his eyes and nodded to me. I drove up as close to the lobby doors as I could get. He took a deep breath, opened the door, and ran into the lobby.

I got out, met Grimsley at the door, and walked in. We took the stairs up to Grimsley's office on the fifth floor. One entire wall of his office was a window that allowed him to look over the transfer station floor.

The warehouse was the size of several airplane hangars and was dominated by a mountain of trash that dwarfed the trucks emptying their loads and continuously adding to its bulk. Tractors loaded the trash into a complex maze of conveyor belts that sorted and fed the garbage out to larger, long-haul trucks that lined the far end of the facility.

"Twenty-one hundred tons of solid waste pass through this station every day," Grimsley said. "It takes one hundred ten trips per day to move it all from here to the Altamont Landfill."

"I see," Monk said weakly, putting his hands against the window to steady himself. The sight of so much garbage was making him dizzy. "And where is zone nine?"

"Zone nine?"

"Where you keep the special trash."

"Recyclables go to a separate facility; so does construction and demolition debris."

"I'm talking about the zone for the really clean trash. Like mine," Monk said. "I'd like to visit my trash."

Grimsley motioned to the mountain of garbage. "That's the only zone we've got. Be my guest."

Monk blanched. He looked like a child who'd just found out there was no such thing as Santa Claus, the Easter Bunny, and the Tooth Fairy all at once.

"You mix all the trash together?" Monk said in disbelief.

"As it comes in, we just dump the new on top of the old," Grimsley said.

"My God," Monk muttered.

"So where could we find the trash that was picked up from the Excelsior?" I asked.

"On the leading edge of the pile, right in front here," he said. "It's still early, so your overcoat may only be under twenty or thirty tons of solid waste at the moment."

"Twenty or thirty *tons*?" Monk said.

"You're very lucky," Grimsley said.

I asked Grimsley if he could reroute the rest of the trash deliveries to another end of the facility and essentially lock off the twenty or thirty tons where the overcoat might be buried until they could be searched. He said he could.

We left Grimsley's office and went downstairs in silence. Monk was in a daze, so much so that he didn't ask for a single wipe after leaving the office. He didn't say a word on the way to the police station, either. It was a nice break and gave me a chance to worry about Joe without any distractions.

I don't know what unsettled Monk the most; the discovery that his trash was mixed with everybody else's, or the realization that the key piece of evidence he needed was buried somewhere under tons of garbage.

I tried to reach the captain at the station, but was told that he and Disher were at the scene of a homicide on Mount Sutro. The officer manning the phones knew Monk and me, so he gave us an address on Lawton Street and that's where we headed.

The rows of tightly packed apartments clung to the wooded slopes of Mount Sutro like mussels on a wharf piling, a tide of thick fog lapping up against them. As we wound up Lawton, the street curved and I glimpsed the massive base of Sutro Tower above the roofline in a shadowy blur that could just as easily have been a mirage.

The three-story apartment buildings climbed the mountain in steps, forming a stucco corridor through the trees, with the forest on one side and the cliff on the other. A dozen police vehicles were parked in front of one of the buildings, creating a bottleneck on the narrow street, not that it really mattered. We were the only traffic on the road, if you don't count the squirrel that leisurely crossed in front of us.

I found a space two blocks up from the crush of police cars and we walked downhill to the apartment building where Stottlemeyer and Disher were working a murder investigation.

The building was a charmless, architecturally featureless block of human cubbyholes constructed in the seventies to provide basic shelter and a view of the asphalt flatlands of the Sunset District and, on the rare clear day, the Pacific Ocean beyond.

The activity was in a spartan, ground-floor apartment with a view of the building across the street. I couldn't see the point of living way out here, away from everything, for the opportunity to look out the window at another generic apartment.

The interior was every bit as bland and unremarkable as the exterior. A subdivided, eight-hundred-square-foot box. Off-white walls. Off-white countertops in the kitchen. Off-white linoleum on the floors. Brown carpet. White popcorn ceilings.

The victim was a man in his forties, who was now lying faceup on the entry-hall floor with a neat little bullet hole through the Ralph Lauren logo on his blue dress shirt. He went into the afterlife in a state of astonishment at his demise, his dead eyes still wide-open in permanent surprise.

I'm not a detective by any stretch, but even I could tell by where the body had fallen that he was shot by whoever was behind the door when he answered it. There was a crocheted pillow discarded beside his body with a hole blasted through the center, the cotton stuffing frosting the dead man like snow.

Simply walking into the crime scene seemed to revive Monk, snapping him out of his garbage-induced stupor. Seeing the corpse had the opposite effect on me. I didn't shut down, but I felt awkward and depressed. Awkward because I didn't really belong there and I didn't have anything to contribute and I was always in the way. Depressed because there was a dead body in front of me and, even though I didn't know him, anytime I see a corpse I can't help thinking that whoever he was and whatever he did, someone loved him. The dead always reminded me of Mitch and of the suffering I felt when I lost him.

But I felt something else this time, too. Fear. It was like a barely audible hum, but it was there. It was irrational, of course. The killer was long gone and I was surrounded by armed police officers. But the atmosphere in the room was still electrified by the recent violence.

Maybe my fear was a visceral, instinctive reaction to the smell of blood, to the scent of cordite. Murder was in the air, and every one of my receptors, physical and psychological, was picking up on it.

Between my awkwardness, my sadness, and my fear, I was feeling pretty uncomfortable. I wanted to run right back to the car, lock the doors, and turn up the radio until the music drowned out what I was feeling.

But I didn't. I soldiered on. Brave and stalwart, that's me.

The officer at the door told us that Stottlemeyer and Disher were in the bedroom. As we made our way through the apartment, Monk stopped to study the body, examine the matching living room and dining room sets, and squint at the framed prints on the wall. I felt like I was in a hotel room instead of someone's apartment.

Stottlemeyer was standing in front of the open closet, where four perfectly pressed pairs of slacks and four matching Ralph Lauren shirts were hanging.

Disher was in the bathroom looking at the medicine cabinet, which was filled with wrapped bars of soap, shaving cream, cologne, and razors.

"Hey, Monk, what brings you down here?" Stottlemeyer said.

"I think we may have a breakthrough in the Breen case," Monk said.

"That's great; tell me about it later," Stottlemeyer said. "I'm busy here."

"What do you think happened?" I asked him. Now that we were away from the body, I was feeling a little better. I could almost forget someone was murdered here. Almost.

"Looks to me like a professional hit," Stottlemeyer said. "The dead man is Arthur Lemkin, a stockbroker. Maybe he was skimming funds or somebody didn't like the way he invested their money. There's a knock at the door; Lemkin opens it and gets popped. Nobody heard a thing. The hit man used a small-caliber gun and a pillow to muffle the shot. Very slick, very simple."

"We need your help," Monk said.

"Monk, can't you see I'm working a crime scene here? One murder at a time, okay?"

Monk shook his head. "This really can't wait."

"This was a guy you would have liked, Monk," Disher said, emerging from the bathroom and leaving the medicine cabinet open behind him. "He kept himself real clean and wore identical shirts every day. And have you seen the rest of his apartment? Everything matches, all nice and symmetrical."

"Not really. The paintings on the wall aren't quite the same size." Monk turned to Stottlemeyer. "Captain, please, all I need is for you to take a few minutes to listen to what I have to say and then a few more minutes to make a phone call or two."

"I need to gather the evidence here while it's fresh," Stottlemeyer said. "You know how important the first few hours in an investigation are. Give me a couple of hours and then we can talk, but not now."

"His wife killed him," Monk said. "Now can we move on?"

Stottlemeyer froze. We all did.

"You've just solved the murder," said Stottlemeyer in such a way that it managed to be a statement and question at the same time.

"I know I should have solved it five minutes ago, but I'm a little off my game. I've had a rough morning," Monk said. "You know how it is."

"No, Monk, I don't," he said wearily. "I wish I did, but I don't."

"How do you know his wife did it?" Disher

asked. "How do you even know Lemkin *has* a wife?"

"Because he wouldn't need this love nest if he didn't," Monk said.

"Love nest?" Stottlemeyer said.

"It's a place used only for having affairs with women who are not your wife."

"I know what a love nest is, Monk. What I don't know is how you figured out that's what this is."

I didn't know, either.

"All the furniture is rented—that's why they are matching sets—plus I saw the tags underneath the pieces."

"You looked underneath the furniture?" Disher said.

"He does that everywhere he goes," Stottlemeyer said.

I knew that was true. In fact, I'd even seen him do it at my house. There might be something under there and he can't stand not knowing. What if there is lint building up? The thought was too much for Monk to bear.

"The big clues are the clothes and the toiletries," Monk said. "Lemkin kept four matching pairs of pants and four shirts in the same color so he could change into fresh, clean clothes after each illicit rendezvous without his wife knowing he'd ever changed clothes. He stocked up on soap and cologne because he was careful to take every precaution to make sure that she'd never smell another woman on him."

I should learn to trust my own instincts, or at least how to interpret them. From the moment I walked into the apartment, it felt like a hotel room to me. But I hadn't bothered to think about what had given me that impression. Monk did. He was acutely aware of the things that we took for granted, that we saw without seeing. That was one of the differences between Monk and me. Here's another: I don't have to disinfect a water fountain before taking a drink and he does.

"Okay, so he was having affairs," Stottlemeyer said to Monk. "How do you know it was his wife who shot him and not some outraged husband or spurned lover or a hired killer?"

"All you have to do is look at the body," Monk said, and headed for the living room.

We all followed him. As soon as I saw the corpse, all my trepidation and discomfort came rushing back, hitting me with a wallop. That low hum of fear increased in volume.

But Monk, Stottlemeyer, and Disher crouched beside the corpse as if it were nothing more significant than another piece of furniture. Whatever I was feeling, they were immune to it.

"Lemkin was shot once in the heart," Monk said. "Why not the face or the head? He was shot in the heart because of the heart he broke. You can't ignore the symbolic implications."

"This isn't a high school English class," Disher said. "This symbolism stuff is a stretch even for you."

"Not when you notice the killer also took Lemkin's wedding ring," Monk said, pointing to the band of pale flesh around the victim's ring finger. "It was obviously for the sentimental value."

"Or the cash value," Disher said.

"Then why didn't the killer take the Rolex, too?" Monk said, motioning to the big gold watch on the victim's wrist. "There's more. The killer used a small-caliber gun, traditionally a 'woman's weapon.' And look at what the killer used for a silencer—a crocheted pillow. Something she knitted during all those hours he left her alone to be with other women. The unintended symbolism is practically a confession."

I was suddenly aware that I was crouching, too. All the awkwardness and discomfort I felt before was gone. In trying to understand Monk's reasoning, I'd begun to see Lemkin's corpse the same way that they did: not as a human being, but as a book to be read, a puzzle to be reassembled, a problem to be solved.

"My freshman English teacher was right: The C I got in his class did come back to haunt me." Stottlemeyer stood up and looked at Disher. "Find Lemkin's wife, Randy. Charge her with murder one and bring her in."

"Yes, sir," Disher said, and hurried out.

Stottlemeyer turned back to Monk and smiled. "So, Monk, what was it you wanted?"

We stepped outside, and Monk spent the next ten minutes explaining to Stottlemeyer how he figured out that we needed to find Lucas Breen's overcoat and where he thought it might be now.

"You want to search thirty tons of trash for an overcoat that *may* have been tossed in one of the Excelsior garbage bins," Stottlemeyer said.

"I'm sure that it was," Monk said. "If we don't

recover it now, before more trash is added to the pile and it's all hauled to the landfill, we never will."

"A search like that is going to require a lot of people and a lot of man-hours. I don't have the authority to approve that kind of expense. I've got to take the request directly to the deputy chief and make a case for it."

"Can you do that now?" Monk said.

"Sure, it's not like I've got anything on my plate at the moment," Stottlemeyer said. "You took care of that in the apartment."

"It was nothing," Monk said.

"I know," Stottlemeyer said. "I can't tell you how inadequate that makes me feel. Sometimes I'm not sure whether to thank you or shoot you."

"Did you know they don't have a zone nine?"

Stottlemeyer shot a quick glance at me, then looked at Monk and tried to appear genuinely surprised. "You've got to be kidding."

"I was shocked, too. All the trash just gets mixed together; can you believe it?"

"That's difficult to imagine," Stottlemeyer said.

"It's a breach of the public trust," Monk said. "There should be an investigation."

"I'll be sure to bring that up in my discussion with the deputy chief," Stottlemeyer said. "Wait for me at the station. I'll meet you there as soon as I'm done with him."

16

Mr. Monk Shakes His Groove Thing

We waited in Stottlemeyer's office. I browsed through a well-thumbed old copy of the *Sports Illustrated* swimsuit issue that came with 3-D glasses. It was either that or last month's *Guns and Ammo*. Monk busied himself reading the open case files on the captain's desk.

I put on the 3-D glasses and opened the magazine. Dozens of supermodel breasts burst out of the pages at me like cannonballs. It was startling. I tried to imagine what my breasts would look like in 3-D instead of 1-D. I doubt anybody could tell the difference. There's nothing remotely D about my bosom.

Disher came into the squad room escorting a handcuffed woman I assumed was Mrs. Lemkin, even though she didn't look anything like I imagined she would. Since her husband was stepping out on her, and she was spending her time crocheting, I pictured her as a homely, pale woman in a plain dress with her hair pulled back tightly in a bun. But Mrs. Lemkin wasn't like that at all. She must get out a lot for jogging and aerobics, and she knew how to wear makeup (a skill I'd never mastered). She was clearly proud of her trim body and showed it off in a sleeveless T-shirt and tight jeans, her long black hair tied back in a pony-tail that she looped through the back of a pink Von Dutch baseball cap.

Our eyes met for a moment, and what I saw in hers was pride, anger, and not a hint of remorse.

Disher handed her off to a uniformed officer for booking, then motioned for me to come out to talk with him.

"Was that Mrs. Lemkin?" I asked.

"Uh-huh," Disher said. "We found her sitting at her kitchen table, in front of her laptop, going on an eBay buying binge."

"What was she bidding on?"

"Porcelain dolls," Disher said. "Nothing like shopping to ease the pain of gunning down your husband."

"She didn't look like she was in much pain to me."

"Maybe it's because of the glasses," he said, motioning to my face.

I had forgotten I was still wearing them. I took them off and grinned to hide my embarrassment. "I was just reading some of the articles in *Sports Illustrated*."

"Those glasses certainly help the words spring off the page, don't they?"

"And a lot of other things too," I said. "If these glasses worked on all magazines, I bet men would read a lot more."

"I certainly would," Disher said. "I meant to tell you back at the crime scene that I did that favor for you. Joe Cochran *was* one of the firemen who got hurt last night."

I know this is a cliché, but it felt like my heart dropped down to the floor. I guess people use that expression a lot because that's the only way to describe what bad news feels like. Tears started to well up in my eyes. Disher must have noticed, because he quickly spoke up again.

"He's fine, he's fine," Disher said. "It was just a mild concussion and a few bruises. They sent him home this morning."

I was relieved and wiped the unspilled tears from my eyes, but I still felt a tremor of worry. What would happen the next time he ran into a burning building? Would he be so lucky? That was his job, and if I kept seeing him, I would have to get used to it.

"Thank you," I said. "I really appreciate it."

"By the way," Disher said, lowering his voice to a whisper and opening his notebook, "his record is clean, no arrests or outstanding warrants, but he does have three unpaid parking tickets. He's never been married, at least not in this country, but he lived with a woman three years ago. Her name was—"

I interrupted him. "You ran a background check on Joe?"

Disher nodded proudly. "I figured as long as I

was checking his health, I'd check out everything else."

"I don't want to know about everything else."

"But everything else is who he is."

"Which is why he should be the one to tell me about it," I said. "Or I should discover it for myself."

"That's taking a big risk, Natalie. I've been burned too many times," Disher said. "I never go out on a date anymore without knowing everything about a woman."

"That's why you don't go out on dates anymore," I said. "Every relationship needs a little mystery. Discovery is half of romance."

"That's the half I don't like," Disher said.

I made him rip out the pages that contained the details of Joe's past from his notebook and tear them up. Disher wasn't pleased but I didn't care. Even though I wasn't the one who snooped into Joe's past, I felt guilty for violating his privacy.

Disher looked past me and noticed, for the first time, what Monk was reading. He rushed in and snatched the case files from Monk.

"What do you think you're doing?" Disher said.

"Passing the time," Monk said.

"By reading confidential case files of open homicide investigations?"

"You didn't have the latest issue of *Highlights for Children*," Monk said. "You really should renew your subscription."

"We never had one," Disher said.

"I love to spot the hidden objects in the drawings," Monk said to me. "It keeps me sharp."

Disher started to put the files back on the desk one by one.

"Wait," Monk said and pointed at the file in Disher's hand. "The gardener."

"What?" Disher said.

"The gardener is the killer," Monk said. "Trust me on this."

"Okay, we'll keep that in mind," Disher said dismissively, set the file down and started to put down the next one.

"The mother-in-law," Monk said.

"You read the file just once and you know that for a fact?"

"Definitely the mother-in-law," Monk said. "It's a no-brainer."

Disher set another file on the desk.

"The twin brother," Monk said.

And another.

"The shoe-shine man."

And another.

"The bike messenger."

Disher plunked down the rest of the stack on the desk all at once.

"The beekeeper, the long-lost aunt, and the po-diatrist," Monk said in a rush. "You dropped a file."

Disher bent down and picked it up.

"The nearsighted jogger," Monk said. "He couldn't possibly have seen the woman in the window. He wasn't wearing his glasses."

"I hope you were taking notes," Stottlemeyer said as he entered the office with a scowl on his face.

"Didn't have to," Disher said, tapping his forehead. "It's all right here."

"Write it down," Stottlemeyer said.

Disher nodded, took out his notebook, and started writing.

"How did it go with the deputy chief?" Monk asked.

"It didn't," Stottlemeyer said. "He won't let me authorize the search."

"Why not?" Monk asked.

"Because he doesn't think we have a case," Stottlemeyer said. "In fact, I've been ordered to stop harassing Breen, a respected member of the Police Commission, with baseless and offensive accusations. I've been told to start looking in other directions."

"He got to them," Monk said.

"Big-time," Stottlemeyer agreed, then looked up at Disher. "Randy, have the crime lab go down to the firehouse and check the firefighting gear on the off chance they might find Breen's fingerprints or DNA remaining on whatever coat, helmet, boots, or gloves he borrowed."

"Sir, we don't even know which ones Breen used."

"I'm aware of that," Stottlemeyer said. "But we can at least eliminate the ones that the on-duty firemen were wearing the night of the fire."

"But another shift has come on since then, so there's a good chance that all the gear has been used and cleaned more than once since the murder."

"I didn't say it was going to be easy. It's a long

shot and a hell of a lot of work, but that's how you, and me, and everybody who isn't Adrian Monk break cases. It takes sweat and dogged determination."

Monk stood up. "Lucas Breen killed Esther Stoval and Sparky the dog. If we don't find that overcoat, Breen will get away with murder. Captain, we have to search that garbage."

"I can't," Stottlemeyer said. "But there's nothing stopping you from searching the trash."

"Yes, there is," Monk said. "There's me."

"My hands are tied. Of course, all of that could change if you were to stumble on, say, a scorched overcoat that belongs to Lucas Breen."

"It could take us weeks to go through all that garbage," I said.

"I'd really like to help; you know that. But I can't," Stottlemeyer said. "You're on your own."

Before we left Stottlemeyer's office, I shamed the captain into calling Grimsley at the dump and asking him to hold the thirty tons of trash for a couple of days so we'd have a chance to search it. Stottlemeyer was careful, though, to say it wasn't an official request but more along the lines of a personal favor.

Grimsley said he was he was glad to do whatever he could to help the police in their investigation.

But we weren't ready to go out to the dump that afternoon. Monk had an appointment with his shrink, Dr. Kroger. Facing the likelihood of having to dig around in a mountain of trash, Monk really needed some help with his anxieties, so canceling the session was out of the question.

I had some anxieties of my own. I don't have Monk's aversion to germs, but I certainly wasn't looking forward to spending a day wading in other people's garbage.

I called Chad Grimsley and told him we'd be out in the morning.

While Monk was having his session, I waited outside the building and gave Joe a call at home. He answered on the first ring, his voice full of energy and good cheer.

"How can you sound so peppy after a burning warehouse collapsed on your head?"

"It's just another day at the office," he said.

"Is there anything I can do for you?"

"You're doing it," he said. "How's your investigation going?"

I told him the broad strokes, but I left out Lucas Breen's name and occupation. I didn't want Joe doing something stupid like beating the crap out of Breen.

My subtle omission of key details wasn't lost on Joe. "You've neglected to mention the name of the guy who killed Sparky and who belongs to that overcoat."

"I did," I said.

"You don't trust me?"

"Nope," I said. "But I mean that in the nicest possible way."

"What happens if you don't find that overcoat?"

"The killer gets away with killing Sparky and the old lady."

"If that happens," Joe said, "will you tell me his name then?"

"I don't think so," I said.

"You're a smart lady," he said. "And pretty, too. Are we still on for tomorrow night?"

"I am if you are," I said, "And if you don't mind being with someone who has spent the day in thirty tons of garbage."

"Stop," Joe said. "You're getting me all excited."

I laughed and so did he. It had been a long time since I'd met a man who made me laugh with him instead of at him. Even so, I felt a tickle of anxiety in my chest as I flashed on the image of him charging into a fire.

It's just another day at the office.

We agreed to meet at my house the next night for our date, and then we said our good-byes.

I parked the Jeep in the driveway. Monk and I got out and saw Mrs. Throphamner on the other side of my low fence. She was in her backyard, kneeling on a rubber pad in the wet mud, toiling over her patch of vibrant roses. They were blooming, and the fragrance was overwhelming.

"Your roses are beautiful," I told her.

"It's hard work, but it's worth it," she said, holding a little shovel in her hand.

"They smell wonderful."

"Those are the Bourbons," she said and pointed her shovel at the large, raspberry-purple flowers.

"The Madame Isaac Pereire variety. They're the most fragrant rose there is."

I opened up the trunk, we got out the groceries we bought on the way home, and we carried them into the house.

"Do roses bloom all year?" Monk asked me.

"They do in her yard," I said. "Mrs. Throphamner constantly switches them out since she started her garden a few months ago. She likes lots of color all the time."

While I unpacked the groceries, Monk got the water boiling and insisted on making dinner for the three of us. I didn't argue. It's not often I get a night off, and besides, I knew he wasn't going to leave a mess for me to clean up.

When Julie got home, I helped her with her homework at the kitchen table while Monk prepared what he called his "famous" spaghetti and meatballs. Pretty soon, though, Julie and I were too captivated by Monk's unusual preparations to pay any attention to textbooks.

The sauce was out of a jar from Chef Boyardee ("Why bother competing with the master?" Monk said), but he made his meatballs by hand (gloved, of course, as if performing surgery), carefully measuring and weighing them to ensure that they were perfectly round and identical.

He boiled the spaghetti noodles, poured them into a strainer, and then selected individual noodles, laying them out on our plates to make sure they were equal in length and that we had exactly forty-six noodles apiece.

When we sat down to dinner, Monk served us

our spaghetti on three separate plates: one for the noodles, one for the sauce, and one for our four meatballs each. We barely had room on the table for all the plates.

"Aren't the noodles, sauce, and meatballs supposed to be mixed all together?" Julie asked.

Monk laughed and shook his head at me. "Kids—aren't they precious?"

And then he took a noodle on his fork, wound it around the prongs, stabbed a meatball, then dipped it all in the sauce and put it in his mouth.

"Mmmm," Monk said. "That's cooking."

After dinner, we each relaxed in our own way. Julie went to the living room to watch TV. I sat at the kitchen table, sipping a glass of wine and leafing through an issue of *Vanity Fair*. And Monk did the dishes.

I like reading *Vanity Fair*, but I'm thinking of canceling my subscription anyway. There are fifty pages of ads before you even get to the table of contents, it sheds an endless number of subscription postcards all over the house, and the magazine smells like a cheap hooker. Not that I've ever smelled a hooker, cheap or otherwise, but I imagine they're drenched in perfume.

"The night is young," Monk said. "Let's party."

I was sure I'd misunderstood him, dazed as I was by the wine and perfume.

"Did you just say you wanted to party?"

"Call Mrs. Throphamner; ask her to come over and watch Julie." Monk pulled off his apron and tossed it on the counter in a show of devil-may-care abandon. "We're going clubbing. I mean that in the party sense, not the baby-seals sense."

I set down my magazine. I couldn't imagine why Monk would want to go somewhere filled with loud music and writhing people pressing their sweaty bodies against one another.

"You want to go dancing?"

"I want to go to Flaxx and talk to Lizzie Draper, Breen's mistress," Monk said.

"You sure you don't just want another look at her enormous buttons?"

"I think I can turn her," Monk said.

"You really believe Lizzie is going to help us get her super-rich lover?" I said.

"It's worth a try," Monk said.

I knew what was really going on, and I told him so. "You're desperate to try anything that could help you avoid rummaging through mountains of trash tomorrow."

Monk gave me a look. "Hell, yes."

The interior of Flaxx was industrial chic—lots of exposed beams, air ducts, and water pipes against sheets of brushed aluminum, corrugated metal, and scored steel. The spinning, multicolored lights in the ceiling reflected wildly off the silver surfaces, creating a kind of retro psychedelic effect.

Lots of twentysomething men and women, trying their best to look disaffected and cool, lounged on deeply cushioned, brightly colored divans the size of king-size beds. They'd come here straight from their offices and cubicles, dressed for success but with their garments loosened to show off the cleavage, piercings, or tattoos that proved they were still bad boys and girls. They came to escape one grind by indulging in another; that much was clear by the way some of them danced and made energetic use of the divans.

Monk tried to avert his gaze from the grinders and the gropers, but it wasn't easy. If he looked away from the dance floor, he saw the divans. If he looked away from the divans, he saw the flat-screen monitors on the walls, which showed music videos that featured a lot of coy, soft-core, girl-girl action. I didn't find it very shocking. Lesbian sexuality has become a very stylish and hip marketing tool to sell everything from lingerie to underarm deodorant. In the process, it has lost its shock value and edgy eroticism. Well, at least to me. Certainly not to Monk.

The music was loud and percussive and pummeled my body and ears. I liked it and found myself swaying instinctively with the rhythm, but Monk winced as if each beat were a beating.

"This is a bad, bad place," Monk said.

"It seems pretty tame to me," I said.

"Oh, yeah? Take a look at that." He motioned to a bowl in the middle of one of the tables.

"What?"

"Mixed nuts," he said gravely, implying all manner of danger.

"So?"

"Cashews, walnuts, peanuts, almonds, all in one bowl. It's a crime against nature."

"We can call the Sierra Club on our way out."

"That's bad enough, but to put them out in a

bowl for people to share . . ." He shivered. "Think how many hands have been in that bowl, *strange* hands that have been"—that's when his gaze fell on one of the couples on a divan—"God knows where."

Monk quickly looked away from that shocking sight and back to the bowl. He gasped and staggered back.

"What?" I said.

He couldn't bring himself to gaze again at whatever had offended him. All he could do was jerk his head in the general direction of the table.

"The bowl," he said, whispering as if it might hear him and take offense.

"I know, mixed nuts," I said. "A crime against nature."

He shook his head. "Look again. Tell me I didn't see crackers and pretzels in that bowl," he said, adding with dire significance, "*with* the mixed nuts."

I glanced at the bowl, knowing even before I did that he was right. Nut and crackers cohabitating.

"It's a trick of the light," I said.

He started to look again but I stopped him. "Don't torture yourself. Remember what we're here for. Focus."

Monk nodded. "Right. Focus. Wet Ones."

I handed him several packets of wipes, and we made our way toward the bar, which snaked along the back of the room and looked more like a stripper's catwalk than a place to elbow up for a brew. The gleaming poles at either end of the curving bar, and the men pressed up against it, tongues barely in their mouths, added to the effect.

We managed to find a space at the bar, though it meant we were shoulder-to-shoulder with the people beside us. Monk squirmed and crossed his hands in front of his chest so they didn't touch anything or anyone.

I didn't have his phobias, but I did the same thing. The way the guy beside me was bumping into me, his arm brushing against my breast, I was certain he was doing it on purpose to cop a quasi-feel. One more time, and he was going to feel my elbow in his kidney.

Three bartenders, all women, all enormously endowed, all wearing bikini tops and short skirts, danced to and fro as they prepared drinks. One of the bartenders was Lizzie. At least Monk wouldn't have any buttons to fixate on this time. Name tags on the other two women identified them as La-Tisha and Cindy.

Lizzie stopped in front of us, still swaying to the beat. "You again," she said to Monk. "The button man."

"I need to talk to you about Esther Stoval's murder," Monk said.

"I already told you," she said. "I don't know anything about it."

"You know the murderer," Monk said.

LaTisha rang a big bell on the wall, jacked up the volume on the music, and suddenly jumped up on the bar. The crowd of men roared with approval. All except for Monk.

"Does she have any idea how unsanitary that is?" Monk yelled into my ear. "People eat and drink on the bar."

"They don't seem to care," I said, gesturing to the men around us, who were whooping and hollering.

"What do they know?" Monk said. "They eat mixed nuts."

Lizzie jumped on the bar right in front of us and, along with LaTisha, began dancing, thrusting her pelvis into Monk's face.

"It's Lucas Breen," Monk said to her feet.

"Can't you see I'm working?" she said.

"I'm trying not to," Monk said.

Cindy tossed a long-necked bottle of tequila up to Lizzie, who caught it and spun it around like a baton. LaTisha also caught a bottle and matched her move for move. This number was choreographed and was probably repeated a dozen times every night.

"We know you're having an affair with him," Monk said.

"If you want to talk to me, get up here," Lizzie said.

"What?" Monk said.

"You heard me." She gyrated in front of him a few more times, her huge breasts swaying. The men around us scrambled forward to shove dollars under the waistband of her skirt, jamming us against the bar.

"Do that again," a guy yelled to her. He was on the other side of the man who kept brushing against me.

She put a foot on the yeller's shoulder, leaned down, and poured tequila on his head. He lifted his face up to her and opened his mouth to receive the liquor like a chick in a nest eager to be fed.

Faced with the prospect of getting splashed with tequila, Monk quickly climbed up on the bar and then stood there stock-still, with Lizzie dancing in front of him and LaTisha dancing behind him.

"Shake your groove thing," Lizzie said.

"I don't have one," Monk said.

"Everybody has a groove thing," LaTisha said.

"Then I'm fairly certain mine was removed at birth," Monk said. "Or when I had my tonsils taken out."

The bartenders started flinging their bottles to each other on either side of Monk. He drew his arms in against himself and closed his eyes. I don't know whether he was afraid of getting hit with a bottle or a drop of tequila.

"Dance or I won't talk to you," Lizzie said as she juggled the bottles back and forth to LaTisha. "Do you know how much any of those guys would pay to be up here instead of you with me?"

"I'd pay them."

"Dance," she said.

Monk tapped a foot and snapped his fingers and rolled his shoulders.

"That's dancing?" Lizzie said.

"If it's too hot for you, get out of the kitchen," Monk said. "We know Esther Stoval was black-mailing Lucas Breen about your relationship. That's why he killed her."

"I didn't say we had a relationship." She tossed

her bottle down to Cindy, who caught it and expertly flipped it back on the shelf.

"You were wearing his monogrammed shirt when we met."

"I got it at Goodwill," she said. "Maybe I have one of yours, too."

"A man who has killed once to protect his secret could kill again," Monk said. "You could be next."

Lizzie grabbed the pole and began to slide up and down it lasciviously, her back to Monk. The crowd cheered and whistled with glee. Even the women seemed to be into it.

"You're supposed to put money under my skirt," she said.

Monk reached into his pocket, pulled out a Wet One packet, and, with his eyes squinted nearly shut, tried to put it in the waistband of her skirt. But she kept moving, wiggling her butt to tease the audience and make his task more difficult.

"What do you want from me?" she asked.

"To do the right thing and help bring a murderer to justice. Wear a wire," Monk said, finally slipping the Wet One packet into her skirt and backing away. "Get him to incriminate himself."

"Never," she said. "I don't wear wires."

"You don't wear much of anything," Monk said.

She turned now and danced in front of Monk. The other bartender came up behind him, and the two women squeezed in close, sandwiching him between them as they danced.

"If I were sleeping with a man like Lucas Breen, I wouldn't betray him," she said. "I'd die to protect him."

"Then your wish might come true," Monk squeaked, doing some gyrating himself, but only to scrupulously avoid any physical contact with the women on either side of him.

"You'll never beat Lucas Breen," Lizzie said. "You're no match for him, button man. You're out of your league."

"What about you?" Monk said. "You think you're in his league? You're dancing on a bar. How long do you think it will be until he discards you like one of his monogrammed shirts?"

She and her partner each did a split, spun around, and slipped off the bar on the other side, leaving Monk dancing there alone.

The show was over.

The women went back to filling drinks and dancing behind the bar. Lizzie made a conscious effort to pretend Monk wasn't there, which wasn't easy. It's hard to ignore a man standing on the bar.

Monk looked for a way to climb down without touching the countertop, but it wasn't possible.

I elbowed the guy beside me. He yelped. "What was that for?"

"You know what it was for," I said. "Move back, perv. He needs room to jump off."

The guy and his tequila-soaked buddy moved aside. Monk jumped off the bar and landed soundly on his feet.

"I think I found my groove thing," he said.

"I'm glad to know the night wasn't a complete waste," I said as we left.

17

Mr. Monk and the Mountain

The next morning Monk sat at the kitchen table and ate his bowl of Chex as if it were his last meal before his execution. And that was exactly what I said to him.

"At least an execution is quick," Monk said. "I feel like a man condemned to a life sentence of hard labor in raw sewage."

"This isn't going to take the rest of your life."

"It's just going to feel like it."

"I'm glad you're going into this with a positive attitude," I said. "What advice did Dr. Kroger give you?"

"He admires my dedication and sense of purpose. He said if I concentrate on the goal I hope to achieve, I won't notice my surroundings."

"That's good advice. What did you say?"

"What if the goal I want to achieve is to get the hell out of my surroundings?"

Before we went to the dump, Monk made me stop at a medical supply store on O'Farrell that carried the kind of outfits those NIH doctors wear when they're dropped into an African village to stop something like an Ebola outbreak or the Andromeda strain.

They outfitted Monk in a hard helmet with a large, clear face mask, and a bright orange jumpsuit with matching heavy-duty gloves and boots. The outbreak suit, as they called it, also came with a self-contained breathing apparatus like firefighters and haz-mat people wear. By the time he was all suited up, Monk looked like the brightly colored offspring of an astronaut and a scuba diver.

I declined Monk's offer to buy me the same getup. I figured whatever Grimsley had for me would be enough. Monk nagged me some more, but I told him if he wanted to give me something, he could give me the money he was going to spend on another silly suit. That shut him up.

When we got to the transfer station, Grimsley was waiting with jumpsuits, gloves, boots, hard hats, goggles, and air-filter masks for us to wear. His mouth dropped open when he saw Monk step out of the car in that outbreak suit.

"All of that really isn't necessary, Mr. Monk."

"Have you seen that mountain of garbage?" Monk said, his voice coming out of a speaker on his helmet.

"What I have here is really all the protection

you'll need," Grimsley said. "We have an elaborate air-purification system, and we control airborne particulate matter by regularly wetting down the waste."

"So we're going to be soaked in garbage," Monk said. "This nightmare gets worse every second."

Grimsley handed me my stuff, and while I put it on over my tank top and sweats, he gathered together some paperwork he wanted us to sign. They were release forms absolving the sanitation company from liability for any injuries we might sustain, or illnesses we might suffer, from going through all that rotting waste.

Monk signed the papers and looked at me. "I bet you wish you were in one of these now."

The truth was that I did, but I certainly wasn't going to admit it to him. Once the papers were signed, Grimsley pointed to some shovels, picks, and rakes in the back of his cart.

"Feel free to use whatever tools you need," Grimsley said. "Good hunting, Ms. Teeger."

He actually tipped his hard hat. I was half tempted to curtsey.

"Thank you, Mr. Grimsley." I plucked a rake out of his cart, handed it to Monk, then took one for myself.

I watched as Monk hesitantly lumbered toward the garbage. He stepped on a dirty diaper and screamed.

One small step for man, one major step for mankind.

I covered my nose and mouth with the mask,

adjusted my goggles, and plunged into the garbage.

The first hour or two went slowly. I tried not to think too much about what I was doing or listen to Monk's sobs. Things went a lot smoother for me once I decided to approach my work as a sociological exercise—to make something of a game out of it.

Instead of focusing on all the mundane, gross, and dangerous things I encountered (dead rats and other animals, junk mail, broken glass, decaying food, America Online CDs, soiled sheets, used razor blades, snot-covered Kleenex, curdled milk, etc.), I amused myself with all the interesting stuff people threw out: broken toys, porno tapes, vinyl records, love letters, magazines, scrap paper doodles, utility bills, canceled checks, well-read paperback books, yellowed family photos, business cards, empty prescription drug bottles, magazines, broken pottery, baby clothes, cracked snow globes, birthday cards, office files, shower curtains, those kinds of things.

If I found an unusual pair of shoes or a loud Hawaiian shirt, I tried to imagine the person who owned them. I read some of the discarded letters, skimmed some family photos, and examined a few credit card bills to see what other people were buying.

Every now and then I'd check on Monk, who'd be raking trash and whimpering, sounding like a depressed Darth Vader. One of those times, I looked up and saw Monk reaching for a big blue trash bag in the pile above him. He tugged at it, trying to pull it free. I saw right away what would happen if he succeeded.

I yelled to him to stop, but he couldn't hear me through that damned helmet of his. I started toward him, but I was too late. He pulled the bag, fell on his butt, and an avalanche of garbage spilled on top of him, burying him in an instant.

I hurried over to him and clawed away the trash as fast as I could. I wasn't worried about him smothering. I knew he had his own air supply. I was worried about him losing his mind.

I was frantically digging when I was joined by a half-dozen firemen in full fire gear, who started dragging away as much trash as they could. I glanced at the firefighter closest to me and saw the smiling face of Joe Cochran, a bandage on his forehead underneath his helmet.

"What are you doing here?" I said. I was never more relieved to see anyone.

"Making sure whoever killed Sparky doesn't get away with it," Joe said. "The rest of these guys are off-duty firemen who volunteered to help. We came in just as Mr. Monk pulled the trash down on himself."

"You're supposed to be recuperating," I said.

"This is how I recuperate," he said.

"Suiting up and slogging through garbage?"

"Hey, it was either do this or rescue cats from trees, chase purse snatchers, and make the world safe for democracy."

"You're wonderful," I said. I could have kissed him right there, if my mouth weren't covered with a mask and my hands weren't full of rotten Chinese food.

"You've got that backward," Joe said. "You're the one standing hip-deep in gunk to get justice for a dog you never met. You're the one who is wonderful."

"Help! Help!" Monk's muffled voice came from beneath the trash just a few feet away. The firefighters and I converged on the spot, and within a few moments we exposed Monk, who was clutching the blue trash bag like a life preserver.

Joe and another firefighter pulled Monk out, but he refused to let go of the blue bag.

"Are you okay?" I asked, wiping away eggs and chow mein and barbecue sauce from his helmet so I could see his face.

"I haven't been okay since we got here," Monk said.

"Is the overcoat in there?" Joe asked, motioning to the bag.

"No," Monk said.

"Then what's so important about that bag?"

"It's my trash," Monk said.

Joe looked at me. I shook my head and silently mouthed, *Don't ask.*

He didn't, and we got back to work.

Monk put his blue bag in the back of the electric cart, took a few minutes to recover, and then, much to my surprise, joined us again in the trash.

Over the next few hours Joe and his men recovered a couple more of Monk's blue bags and thoughtfully placed them in the cart with the other one.

I stopped only for bathroom breaks. I'd lost my appetite for lunch. Monk felt the same way.

But the firemen must have been accustomed to ugly tasks like this, because they had no problem taking a break to eat. They enjoyed their fast-food meals, undeterred by the stench of garbage all around them, and plunged right back into the city's rotting waste afterward without any trouble digesting.

Joe worked the hardest of all. He was doing it for me, and for Monk, but mostly for Sparky.

I was glad he was there. But as happy as I was to have Joe's company, his presence brought back that twinge of anxiety in my chest. I tried to dismiss it as simply the fear of beginning a relationship, but I knew it was more than that. I tried to ignore the feeling the same way I was ignoring the uglier aspects of our search.

It wasn't working. I wondered if that was how Monk felt when he tried to ignore all the things in a case, or in life, that didn't fit.

It was late afternoon when Monk called out, "Over here! Over here!"

We scrambled over to see what he'd found.

He lifted up an Excelsior napkin, pinched between two fingers and held at arm's length from his body.

It meant we'd finally reached the trash from the bins outside the hotel. We all began digging with renewed energy and hope.

We dug up a lot more items that clearly came

from the hotel—billing statements, broken dishes, banquet menus, pounds of table scraps, damaged linens, tons of those tiny little liquor bottles, even some clothes, but by five o'clock we still hadn't found an overcoat.

Monk decided to call it quits for the day, and I was thankful. I was tired and I wanted to clean up before my date with Joe. And, let's face it, our morale was pretty low.

We thanked the firefighters again for their help. I told Joe that I'd meet him at my house in a couple of hours.

As Monk and I were on our way out, Chad Grimsley came down to the floor from his office and asked if he could have a word with the two of us.

We got into his cart, the one with Monk's trash bags in the back, and Grimsley drove us to the other end of the transfer station. He stopped at a roped-off corner of the facility with a sign mounted above it that read, ZONE NINE. RESERVED FOR THE CLEANEST TRASH ONLY.

Grimsley turned to Monk. "I believe your trash belongs here, sir."

Monk stared at the roped-off area for a long moment and then did something incredible. He took off his gloves and offered his hand to Grimsley.

"Thank you," Monk said.

"You can come and check on it anytime you like." Grimsley shook his hand.

Monk put his gloves back on and, with a happy smile on his face, began unloading his bags and placing them behind the ropes.

"That was a really nice thing to do," I said to Grimsley.

He shook his head. "Mr. Monk is a very special man. I have an inkling of the kind of demons he had to overcome to spend the day in tons of garbage. That's worth something, Ms. Teeger, and it demands acknowledgment and respect."

Grimsley motioned to the blue bags in the center of the newly christened zone nine. "That's the least I can do."

When Monk climbed back into the car, I could see contentment on his face. We hadn't found the piece of evidence we needed to convict Lucas Breen, but at least some small measure of order had been restored.

18

Mr. Monk Stays Home

Monk let me shower first, because he anticipated being in the bathroom for hours. In fact, he suggested that Julie might want to make arrangements with Mrs. Throphamner to use her facilities if the need arose.

When Monk went in to shower, I sat Julie down in the living room and gave her detailed instructions for the night. I wanted her to keep a close watch on Monk to make sure he didn't remodel our house while I was gone and to call me if things got out of control.

"So you want me to babysit him," she said.

"I wouldn't put it like that," I said. "I'm asking you to guard our house, our belongings, and our privacy."

"In other words, you want me to perform babysitting *and* security services."

"What are you getting at?"

"I have better things to do than watch Mr. Monk all night while you hang out with Firefighter Joe," Julie said. "If I'm going to babysit, I expect to be paid. Six dollars an hour, plus expenses."

"What expenses?"

"Things could come up," she said.

"If you're doing your job, nothing is supposed to come up."

"Okay, six dollars an hour plus you kick in for a chicken delivery from the take-out place," she said. "Unless you'd rather have Mr. Monk cook a meal in our kitchen without you here to supervise. Who knows what he might discover, rearrange, or throw out?"

She had a good point. When did Julie become so observant? I wondered. And when did she learn how to negotiate like that? She was growing up way too fast.

"You've got a deal," I said.

We shook on it, and then I pulled her into a hug. When I let her go, she looked at me with a furrowed brow.

"What was that for?" she asked.

"Growing up," I said. "Being adorable. Surprising me. Being you. Do I need to go on?"

"No, you're making me nauseous as it is."

There was a knock at the door. Julie leaped off the couch and opened it. Joe Cochran stood there with another bouquet of flowers.

"You didn't have to bring me more flowers," I said.

"I didn't bring them for you. They're mostly for

me in case I didn't do a good enough job show-
ering after our day in the dump," he said with a
grin. "They're very fragrant. Mind if I carry them
the rest of the evening?"

"I'll take my chances."

I took the flowers from him and put them in
the vase. I told Julie not to wait up, gave her a
kiss, and we left.

Joe took me to dinner at Audiffred, a French
bistro that was, appropriately enough, located on
the street level of the historic Audiffred Building
at One Market Street down at the waterfront. It
was constructed in the late 1800s by a homesick
Frenchman, so the building had such typical Pari-
sian architectural motifs as a mansard roof, decorative brick battlements, and tall, round-topped
windows.

Audiffred was a fancier place than I'd dressed
for, but the San Francisco dining scene had adopted
the L.A. philosophy that you can go anywhere in
jeans and running shoes as long as you have the
attitude to pull it off.

Well, if there's one thing I've got plenty of, it's
attitude. It's a shame that won't pay the mortgage.

Joe ordered a steak, well-done, with fingerling
potatoes and sautéed spinach. The menu noted
that the cow who sacrificed himself for Joe's meal
was a vegan and never consumed hormones. I'd
never seen a cow's diet mentioned on a menu
before.

I ordered rack of lamb, but when I asked the
superficially perky waitress whether my sheep was
a vegan or not, she just gave me a blank look. She

didn't even crack a smile when I asked what the fish liked to eat before they ended up on the plate. Joe was amused, though, and that's what counted.

"They take themselves way too seriously here," he said. "And the food isn't good enough for them to be so snooty."

"Then why do you come here?"

"The food is fair, the decor is nice, and the place has been a friend to the fire department for over one hundred years."

"You mean they donate money?"

"Better than that," Joe said. "They donate booze."

He explained that the Audiffred Building was one of very few in the city that survived the devastating 1906 earthquake and the fires in the aftermath.

"The owner of the saloon that was here offered the firefighters a barrel of whiskey each if they saved the building from the flames," Joe said. "They did, and to this day firefighters drink here for free."

"Maybe the waiters are just snooty to you because they know you're not paying for the drinks," I said. "I'm not a nurse or anything, but should you be having alcohol after what happened to you the other night?"

Joe touched the bandage. "This? Ah, it's nothing. I've been hurt worse."

"You have?"

"I've got a nasty burn on my back from a fire a couple of years ago," he said. "It's not a pretty sight, which is why I wore a shirt to dinner."

"I wondered why you did that," I said.

He went on to tell me the story of how he got burned. To be honest, I don't remember a lot of the details, except that it involved a blazing tenement, a staircase that gave way, and a narrow escape. As he told the story, his whole face lit up, and he got more and more animated, the words spilling out in an excited rush. It was a memory he didn't mind reliving and a story he liked to tell, even though it was an experience that left him physically scarred for life.

I know that's part of what you do on your first couple of dates: You tell stories about yourself that show you in a really great light, or that illustrate aspects of your life and your character that are important to you. But sometimes you reveal things about yourself that you didn't intend.

The story certainly proved Joe was caring, brave, and heroic, but that's not the message I took from it. What I got was that he liked fighting fires. No, he *loved* fighting fires. The risks meant nothing to him. The accident that happened years ago and the one that happened the other night were near-misses he was bound to experience again.

Just another day at the office.

He loved battling fires the way Mitch loved flying fighter jets. The reasons why I was attracted to Joe weren't a surprise to me. He was great-looking, with a body I wanted to devour, and had a personality that reminded me of Mitch's.

But the more he talked, and the more attracted I became to him, the more my anxiety intensified.

Was it fear of a new relationship? Or was it something else?

Our dinner was served, and Joe asked me about how I balanced single motherhood and working for Monk. I think he asked me because he wanted to eat his steak before it got cold, and he couldn't do that and tell another rousing firefighting anecdote.

So now it was my turn to tell a story about myself that would show what a clever, funny, caring, strong, terrific person I was. My vague anxiety turned into a very clear and definable panic. What story could I possibly tell that would accomplish all that? I didn't think I had one.

"I don't think of it as balancing single motherhood with anything else. Julie comes first, before me, before anything. I just try to make it through each day without screwing up too badly."

"How did you end up working for Monk?"

Okay, that was a good story. But unlike Joe's stories of his harrowing brushes with death, it wasn't one I enjoyed telling. I was much better at telling funny anecdotes about Mr Monk's bizarre, obsessive-compulsive behavior, though I always felt guilty afterward, as if I were breaching a trust.

"Someone broke into my house late one night. I walked in on him and he tried to kill me. I killed him instead. The police couldn't figure out why the intruder was in my house, so they called in Mr. Monk to help them investigate."

Joe set down his fork. "You killed a man?"

I nodded. "I didn't mean to; I was defending myself. I still can't believe I did it. When you're in a situation like that, I suppose instinct takes over. I did what I had to do to survive. I was lucky; there happened to be a pair of scissors within reach. If there hadn't been, I'd be dead."

I never thought of myself as capable of violence, certainly not of killing someone. It was a memory I tried to avoid. It scared me. It wasn't so much the attacker himself, the fight, or the fact that I almost died that terrified me. The nightmare was imagining what would have happened to Julie if I were killed.

What would he have done to her? And if she escaped, what would her life have been like after losing both of her parents to violent deaths?

Maybe it was that fear that gave me the ability to fight back so hard, to kill rather than be killed. It gave me an edge I wouldn't have had otherwise.

After that experience, I immediately enrolled Julie in tae kwon do class, despite her protests. I wanted to be sure that if she were ever attacked, her instincts would take over, and that her instincts would kick ass.

I could see that Joe wanted more details about the killing, but he was kind and perceptive enough not to ask. So he moved past that.

"Why was the intruder in your house?"

"Mr. Monk figured out he was after a rock in my daughter's goldfish aquarium," I said. "A rock from the moon."

"From the *moon* moon?" Joe pointed up.

"Yeah, that moon," I said. "It's a long story."

"You're full of long stories." He reached across the table for my hand. "I'd like to hear them all."

His hand was big and warm and strong, and I couldn't help imagining what it would feel like against my cheek, my back, my legs.

I became achingly aware of just how many long months it had been since I'd spent time with a man, if you catch my drift. And yet, the anxiety I felt was even stronger than my desire.

I'm a normal woman, healthy and still relatively young, and I'm not ashamed of or embarrassed about my needs, so that wasn't what it was. Nor was it the prospect of bringing another man into my life. There had been other men since Mitch, and I hadn't felt this same kind of apprehension then. And it wasn't because of any reservations about the kind of man Joe was or how Julie would feel about him.

But the apprehension was there, and it wasn't going away.

I was spared having to tell Joe another story by the trill of my cell phone. I reluctantly, and self-consciously, took my hand from his to answer the call.

I was certain the caller was Julie and that Monk had done something terrible, like reorganizing the drawers in my bedroom. I shuddered to think what he—and Julie too, for that matter—might have stumbled upon.

But it wasn't Julie, and my bedroom secrets were safe. It was Captain Stottlemeyer calling.

"Are you with Monk?" he asked.

"Not at the moment," I said. "Why?"

"I've got a murder, and I'd like Monk's perspective on it. Can you get him down here?"

It wasn't unusual for Stottlemeyer to ask for Monk's help on a particularly puzzling homicide. Monk regularly consulted with the SFPD on a per-case basis, though nobody told me how much he got paid.

Stottlemeyer gave me directions to the crime scene. It wasn't far from the restaurant, but I had to go back home and pick up Monk first.

"We'll be there in an hour," I said, and flipped the phone shut. "I'm sorry, Joe, but we have to go. There's been a homicide, and the police want Mr. Monk's help."

"It can't wait until dessert?"

"Think of that call as my fire alarm," I said.

"Gotcha." He waved to the waitress for the check.

On the way home, I explained my working relationship with Monk to Joe, who didn't understand exactly what I did for a living. I told him my job was mostly helping Monk manage the everyday demands of life and smoothing his interactions with other people so he could concentrate on solving murders. And that I also handed out a lot of wipes and kept him hydrated with Sierra Springs, the only water he'll drink.

"I don't know how you do it," Joe said as he walked me to my door.

"Most days, I don't know either."

He kissed me. A real, deep, passionate, toe-curling kiss. And I gave it right back to him. The kiss lasted only a minute or so, but when we unclinched my heart was racing as if I'd just run a mile. It was a kiss that promised so much more, born of the urgency of our forced parting. For me, there was also a hint of melancholy. For some reason it felt to me like a kiss good-bye, even though we'd be seeing each other at the dump the next morning.

But I didn't have the time to sort out my feelings; I was in too big a hurry. I banged on the bathroom door to get Monk out of the shower. I told him Stottlemeyer needed him pronto at a crime scene. Then I called Mrs. Throphamner, who agreed to come over and watch Julie.

"I still expect to be paid for the hours I worked," Julie said.

"But Mr. Monk never even left the shower," I said. "You didn't have to do anything."

"Not my problem," she said with a shrug.

I dug into my wallet and gave her a twenty because I didn't have any tens or singles, just what the ATM spit out on my last visit. "Here. Credit my account with the balance for next time."

Monk emerged from the bathroom perfectly coiffed and in a fresh set of clothes, as if he were starting a new day. Behind him the bathroom looked as if it had never been used. He shifted uncomfortably in his clothes.

"What's wrong?" I asked.

"I still feel dirty," he said.

"I'm sure that will pass."

"So am I," Monk said. "In a few years."

"Years?"

"No more than twenty," he said. "Or thirty. But I'm being conservative."

I figured that worked out to roughly one year for each ton of garbage we had to sort through.

Monk spotted the flowers in the vase. "Who brought those?"

"Joe. Actually, he brought them for himself. He was afraid he might still smell from the dump," I said. "Maybe you'd like them."

Monk leaned down and sniffed the flowers, then stood up straight and started working that kink out of his neck, the one caused by a fact that doesn't fit.

I was about to ask him what it was about the flowers that set him off when Mrs. Throphamner arrived and hurried to the TV.

"Forgive me, *Murder, She Wrote* is starting on channel forty-four," she said. "I don't want to miss the murder."

"It's okay," Monk said, heading for the door. "We're a little late for a murder ourselves."

19

Mr. Monk and the Wet Ones

Captain Stottlemeyer was waiting for us on Harrison Street, where the 80 Freeway emptied into the city center in a tangle of off-ramps and overpasses. The wail of the cold wind and the roar of traffic overhead created a loud, bone-rattling shriek. It sounded as if the earth itself were screaming in pain.

The freeway passed over a weed-covered lot that was ringed by a corroded cyclone fence that had been peeled back in places. Stottlemeyer stood in front of one of the openings, with his hands deep in the pockets of his coat and his collar turned up against the biting wind. Behind him, forensic techs in blue windbreakers moved slowly through the lot, looking for clues.

The lot was strewn with discarded couches, soiled mattresses, and crude structures of scrap plywood, corrugated metal sheets, and cardboard boxes erected atop wooden shipping pallets. Shopping carts overflowing with bulging trash bags were parked in front of some of the makeshift shelters like cars in driveways.

"Sorry to drag you down here, Monk," Stottlemeyer said.

"Where are all the people?" Monk asked.

"What people?" Stottlemeyer asked.

"The ones who live here." He motioned to the neighborhood of cardboard tract homes.

"They scurried away like frightened rats after somebody discovered the corpse," Stottlemeyer said. "A couple officers in a patrol car happened to be driving by when the mass exodus occurred. It piqued their curiosity, so they investigated. It's a good thing the officers were around or it could've been weeks before we found the body, if ever."

"Why's that?"

"We don't get in here much," Stottlemeyer said. "And even if we did, the body is kind of out of the way."

The captain beckoned us through the hole in the fence while he held open the flap. Monk hesitated a moment, then turned to me.

"I'm going to need the suit," Monk said.

"What suit?" I said.

"The one I wore today," Monk said. "I need it."

"We returned the outbreak suit on the way home," I said. "You insisted that it had to be incinerated."

"I know," Monk said. "I need another."

"They're closed," I said.

"It's okay," Monk said. "We can wait."

"They're closed permanently, at least to you," I said. "The owner was quite clear about that."

"I'll stay in the car while you go in."

Stottlemeyer groaned. "Monk, it's late. I've been working a sixteen-hour day. This is my third murder. I'm hungry, I'm cold, and I just want to go home."

"Fine," Monk said. "We'll meet back here in the morning."

He started to go, but Stottlemeyer grabbed his arm. "What I'm saying is that you can step through the fence on your own or I can throw you. It's your choice."

"I'd prefer a third option."

"There is no third option."

"How about a fourth? Because three isn't really a very good number anyway."

"How about I throw you in there now?"

"That's a third option, and before you said there were only two," Monk said. "How can we have a reasonable conversation if you're incoherent?"

Stottlemeyer took a menacing step toward Monk.

"Okay, okay," Monk said, waving Stottlemeyer away. "Give me a minute."

Monk looked at the hole, looked at the lot, then looked at me. Then he looked at everything again.

"You have five seconds," Stottlemeyer said in a tone full of violent intent.

Monk held out his hand to me and snapped his fingers. "Wipes."

I gave him four. He used two to wipe down the

pieces of the cyclone fence he intended to touch while stepping through. He used the others to protect his fingers as he touched the bits of the fence he'd just cleaned.

Monk took a deep breath and stepped through, then immediately jumped away from something on the ground with a yelp.

"What?" I asked.

"Bottle cap."

He said it breathlessly, as if he'd narrowly avoided stepping on a land mine.

I climbed through the opening and Stottlemeyer followed, glaring at Monk.

"This way," the captain said, and proceeded to lead us across the lot toward the freeway.

Monk yelped again. I looked at him.

"Candy wrapper," he said.

"You spent the day in thirty tons of trash and you're freaking out about a candy wrapper?"

"I'm unprotected," Monk said. "And that's a big, big candy wrapper."

I turned my back on him and marched on through the weeds.

Monk stepped gingerly through the lot as if he were playing hopscotch on hot coals.

I don't know what he was avoiding, and I didn't really care. It could have been dog droppings or dandelions; to him they are both equally repulsive.

If I sounded irritable, it's because I was. It was bad enough that I'd been yanked off a perfectly good date to go strolling through a urine-stenched

homeless encampment to see some hideous corpse.
Having to deal with Monk's irrational anxieties on
top of all that was asking way too much of me.

But if I'd been really honest with myself on that
cold, windy night, I'd have known it wasn't the
lot, the murder, or Monk that was eating at me;
it was the feeling I'd had when I kissed Joe and
what it meant.

Stottlemeyer took us up the embankment on a
well-worn path beneath the freeway to a cardboard lean-to wedged against the ground and the
base of the overpass. There were two feet, clad in
topsiders held together with duct tape, sticking
out of the entrance of the lean-to. It reminded me
of the Wicked Witch after Dorothy dropped the
house on her in Oz.

"The victim is in there," Stottlemeyer said.

"Yes, I see," Monk said.

"Aren't you going to go inside?"

"Not until my suit gets here."

"Why don't you just wear the damn suit all the
time?" Stottlemeyer said. "Then you'll never have
to worry about breathing or touching anything
ever again."

"It would be awkward," Monk said. "Socially."

"Socially," I said.

"I don't like to draw attention to myself," Monk
said. "One of my great advantages as a detective
is my natural ability to slip smoothly and unnoticed into almost any social situation."

"But just think of all the money you'd save on
wipes," Stottlemeyer said.

Monk took out his key chain and aimed his penlight into the shelter. The tiny beam revealed a man lying inside on his back. He was wearing at least a half dozen shirts and had a scraggly beard. Beyond that he was unrecognizable. His head was bashed in with a brick, presumably the bloody one left beside the body.

I turned away.

Before I met Monk I had managed to go through my life without ever seeing a dead body, without seeing people who'd been shot, stabbed, strangled, beaten, poisoned, dismembered, run over, or clobbered with a brick. Now I was seeing as many as two or three murder victims a week. I wondered when, or if, I'd finally get used to it, and whether I would be a better person if I never did.

"Is he a friend of yours?" Stottlemeyer asked Monk.

"Does he *look* like a friend of mine? Weren't you here for the outbreak-suit discussion?"

"I won't ever forget it," Stottlemeyer said. "Still, I thought you might know him. That's why I called you down here."

"I've bathed more today than he has in the past ten years," Monk said. "What made you think that we could possibly know each other?"

Stottlemeyer motioned to the edge of the embankment. Monk peered over the side and saw a few dozen sealed Wet One packets scattered among the weeds.

"You're the only person I know who carries around that many Wet Ones."

Monk looked at me and we came to the same

realization at the same instant. I felt a chill that had nothing to do with the cold wind.

"You *do* know him," Stottlemeyer said, reading our faces.

"We saw him panhandling on the street near the Excelsior," I said. "He wanted money; Mr. Monk gave him wipes."

"Figures," Stottlemeyer said.

"It's not easy to recognize him," I said. "He doesn't look the same now with the blood all over his face, and . . ."

I couldn't go on. Stottlemeyer nodded. "I understand. It's okay."

"That's not the only reason we didn't recognize him," Monk said.

He turned back to the shelter and crouched at the entrance, letting his flashlight beam sweep over the body and the interior of the lean-to. He sneezed.

Monk sat up, rolled his shoulders, and when he looked at us again, there was a glint of excitement in his watery eyes.

"I know who killed him," he said, and sneezed.

"You do?" Stottlemeyer was astonished. "Who?"

"Lucas Breen."

"*Breen?*" Stottlemeyer sighed wearily. "C'mon, Monk, are you sure about this? You've got him killing old ladies, dogs, and bums. What is he, some kind of a serial killer?"

Monk shook his head and sniffled. "He's just a man who wants to get away with murder. The sad thing is, he has to keep killing to do it."

"Why do you think Breen did this?" Stottlemeyer said.

"Look at you, Captain. You've got your jacket buttoned up to your nose." Monk turned and shined his flashlight on the dead man. "But he's not wearing one."

"Maybe he doesn't have one," Stottlemeyer said.

"He had one when we saw him before," Monk said. "A big, dirty, tattered overcoat."

Only it wasn't dirty and tattered. It was charred and burned. And we missed it. If we'd only known then what we were looking for, and what we were looking *at*, we could have solved the case right there and probably saved this man's life.

I wondered if Monk felt as guilty and stupid as I did at that moment.

"Lucas Breen killed him for his coat and threw out the wipes that were in the pockets." Monk sneezed again. "Which just goes to show Breen's utter disregard for human life."

I wasn't sure what Monk meant. Was it murdering a man for his coat or throwing away disinfectant wipes that revealed the depth of Breen's inhumanity? I didn't dare ask.

Stottlemeyer pointed to the corpse. "You're telling me this guy was wearing Lucas Breen's overcoat?"

Monk nodded and blew his nose. "He must have rooted around in the Dumpster the night of the murder. He was a man with a death wish, and it came true."

"It wasn't going Dumpster diving that killed him," Stottlemeyer said.

Monk took a Ziploc bag from his pocket and

stuffed the Kleenex into it. "If the coat hadn't been the agent of his demise, it would have been a hideous flesh-eating Dumpster disease and a horrible, drooling death."

"Agent of his demise?" Stottlemeyer said.

"Horrible, drooling death?" I said.

"Thank the Lord for Wet Ones," Monk said.

"How the hell did Breen know this guy had his coat?" Stottlemeyer asked.

I knew the answer to that one, and it didn't make me feel clever. Quite the opposite.

"When we were talking to Breen in the lobby of his building, the guy passed by with his shopping cart. Breen saw him."

"Breen must have crapped himself," Stottlemeyer said. "He's sitting there with a homicide detective and the two of you accusing him of murder, and a guy walks by wearing the one piece of evidence that could send him to death row. Breen has probably been searching like a maniac for this guy ever since."

"Yeah," I said. "And we spent the day wading through all the trash in San Francisco for nothing."

Stottlemeyer glanced up at the night sky. "Somebody up there is having a nice laugh on all of us."

"Has the medical examiner been here?" Monk asked.

"She left just before you got here."

"Did she say how long this man has been dead?"

The captain nodded. "About two hours."

"Maybe there's still time," Monk said.

"To do what?" I asked.

"To stop Breen from getting away with three murders," Monk said.

20

Mr. Monk Plays Cat and Mouse

The Bay Bridge, which connects Oakland to San Francisco, is really two bridges—one that goes to Yerba Buena Island and one that leaves it, depending on which side of the bay you're coming from. The two bridges are connected by a tunnel that cuts through the middle of the island.

Adjacent to Yerba Buena Island is Treasure Island, a flat, man-made patch of land that was created to host the 1939 Golden Gate International Exposition and that the United States government seized during World War II for a naval base.

Treasure Island got its name from flecks of gold found in the Sacramento River Delta soil that was dumped into the bay to make the isle. But if you ask me, the *real* Treasure Island is across the bay, north of San Francisco in Marin County.

Belvedere Island is a one-mile-long, half-mile-wide enclave of the superwealthy, who gaze upon

San Francisco, the Bay, and the Golden Gate Bridge from the windows and decks of their multimillion-dollar, bayfront homes. There may not be flecks of gold in the soil, but a handful of dirt on Belvedere is worth more than an acre of land just about anywhere else in California.

So if it were up to me, and for the sake of accuracy in island naming, they'd strip the title "Treasure Island" from that pile of Sacramento dirt dumped in the middle of the bay and slap it on Belvedere instead.

Of course, Belvedere Island is where Lucas Breen lived, because anywhere else just wouldn't have the same cachet. He and his wife inhabited a lavish and ostentatious Tuscan mansion with its own deepwater dock for their sailboat. (Not that I have anything against being rich; I come from a wealthy family, even though I don't have much money of my own. It's the attitude of entitlement and superiority among the rich that I can't stand.)

To get to Breen's house, we had to take the Golden Gate Bridge out of the city, drive across Sausalito, then go over a causeway to the island and wind our way up a thickly wooded hillside. Even with a siren and flashing lights, it took us a good forty minutes to get there. Stottlemeyer did turn off everything as we were crossing the causeway, though. He didn't want to panic the residents.

The gate to Breen's property was wide-open. It was almost as if he expected us, and that couldn't be good.

Breen's mansion was at the end of a circular

driveway built on a hillside that gave him sweeping views of Angel Island, the Tiburon Peninsula, the San Francisco skyline, and the Golden Gate Bridge—when the sky wasn't pitch-black and all fogged in as it was when we arrived.

We pulled up behind Breen's silver Bentley Continental sports car and got out. Stottlemeyer stopped and put his hand on the Bentley's sleek hood.

"It's still warm," he said, and caressed the car as if it were a woman's thigh. "How do you think I'd look in one of these, Monk?"

"Like someone sitting in a car."

"This isn't just a car, Monk. It's a Bentley."

"It looks like a car to me," Monk said. "What else does it do?"

Monk was dead serious.

"Never mind," Stottlemeyer said, and marched up to the front door. He leaned on the doorbell and held his badge up to the tiny security camera mounted over the door, though Breen probably knew we were there from the moment we drove through the gate.

After a minute or two Lucas Breen opened the door. His eyes were red, his nose was runny, and he was wearing a bathrobe over a warm-up suit. He looked miserable. *Good*, I thought, *the more miserable the better.*

"What the hell are you doing here? I was just getting ready for bed," Breen said. "Haven't you heard of a telephone?"

"I'm not in the habit of calling murderers for an appointment," Stottlemeyer said.

"Captain, I've got a terrible cold, my wife is away, and all I want to do is go to sleep," Breen said. "We'll do this another time."

Breen began to close the door, but Stottlemeyer shoved it open and pushed his way inside. "We'll do it now."

"You're going to regret this," Breen said, his stuffy nose and watery eyes making him look—and sound—like a petulant child.

"Fine with me," Stottlemeyer said. "Without regrets I wouldn't have anything to think about and no excuse to drink."

We followed the captain past Breen and into the two-story rotunda, which was topped with a stained-glass dome. Monk covered his nose and gave Breen a wide berth, even though Monk was sniffling, too.

The rotunda overlooked a living room dominated by a set of French doors and large windows that framed a spectacular view of the San Francisco skyline, the city lights twinkling in the fog. To our left, just next to a grand staircase, was a book-lined study, where a fire roared in a massive stone hearth.

"I believe you were told to stop harassing me," Breen said, wiping his nose with a handkerchief.

"I go where the evidence takes me," Stottlemeyer said.

"You'll be going on job interviews pretty soon," Breen said. "What's so important that it's worth throwing away your badge?"

"A homeless man was murdered tonight," Stottlemeyer said.

"That's a shame. What do you expect me to do about it?"

"Confess," Monk said.

"Tell me, Mr. Monk, are you going to accuse me of every murder that occurs in San Francisco?"

"He was wearing your overcoat." Monk sneezed and held his hand out to me for a tissue. I gave him several.

"I told you before, my wife donates my old clothes to Goodwill." Breen strolled into the study and sat down in a leather armchair facing the fire. There was a brandy snifter on the coffee table. It didn't take much detecting skill to figure out that he must have been sitting there when we showed up at his door.

"Gee, it seems like everybody we meet is buying your clothes at Goodwill these days," Stottlemeyer said.

"A fortunate few," he said.

"That homeless guy didn't look very fortunate to me," I said. "Someone caved his face in with a brick."

"The overcoat we're talking about wasn't a Goodwill donation." Monk blew his nose and then tossed the tissue into the fire. "This was the custom-tailored overcoat you wore to the 'Save the Bay' fund-raiser but weren't wearing when you left."

Monk crouched in front of the fire and watched his tissue burn.

"It's also the one you wore when you went to smother Esther Stoval and set fire to her house,"

Stottlemeyer said. "The one you left behind. The one you had to disguise yourself as a fireman to get back. The one you later ditched in a Dumpster outside of the Excelsior hotel, which is where the man you killed found it."

"You're delusional," Breen said to Stottlemeyer, and motioned to Monk, who was still staring into the flames. "You're even crazier than he is."

"You burned it," Monk said.

"Burned what?" Breen said.

"The overcoat." Monk gestured into the fireplace. "I can see one of the buttons."

Stottlemeyer and I crouched beside him and looked into the fire. Sure enough, there was a brass button with Breen's initials on it glowing in the embers.

The captain stood up and looked down at Breen. "Do you often use your clothes for kindling?"

"Of course not." Breen took a sip of his brandy and then held the glass up to the fire, examining the amber liquid in the light. "The button must have come off the sleeve of my jacket when I put the wood in the fireplace."

"I'd like to see that jacket," Stottlemeyer said.

"I'd like to see your search warrant," Breen said.

Stottlemeyer stood there, glowering. He'd been trumped and he knew it. We all knew it. Breen smiled smugly. I imagined he even flossed his teeth smugly.

"It's a shame we don't always get what we want; though, to be honest, I usually do." Breen tipped his snifter toward Stottlemeyer. "You, on the other hand, strike me as a man who rarely does. I can't imagine what that must be like."

"I can't imagine what it must be like on death row," Stottlemeyer said. "Pretty soon you'll be able to tell me."

Monk sneezed again. I handed him another tissue.

"And how would you presume to put me there, Captain?" Breen said. "Let's say, for the sake of argument, that I'm guilty of everything you've accused me of. If that's true, then the one piece of evidence you needed has just been incinerated, along with any hope of ever prosecuting me."

Breen took another sip of his brandy and sniffled, which you'd think would have undercut his menace and smug superiority, but it didn't. That's how secure he was in the knowledge that he'd beaten us.

Stottlemeyer and I both looked at Monk. This was his cue to reveal the brilliant deduction that would destroy the bastard and prove him guilty of murder.

Monk frowned, narrowed his eyes, and sneezed.

Stottlemeyer drove us back to my car. Nobody said a word. Monk didn't even sniffle. There wasn't really anything left to say. Lucas Breen was right. He'd won. He was going to get away with three murders.

Obviously that was bothering us all, but I think what really troubled Stottlemeyer and Monk went beyond the injustice of a guilty man walking free.

It was something deeper and more personal than that.

For years their relationship had been predicated on a simple truth: Monk was a brilliant detective, and Stottlemeyer was a good one. That's not a slight against Stottlemeyer. He became a captain because of his hard work, dedication, and skill at his job. He solved most of the homicides he investigated and had a conviction rate that any cop in any other city would be proud of.

But he wasn't any cop in any other city. He was in San Francisco, home of Adrian Monk. Any detective would have a hard time matching Monk's genius at crime solving. It was worse for Stottlemeyer. He was also Monk's former partner. His career was inextricably linked to Monk. It didn't matter that Monk's obsessive-compulsive disorder had cost him his badge. The captain and Monk would always be partners in their own eyes and the eyes of the SFPD.

As much as Stottlemeyer may have resented Monk's astonishing observational and deductive abilities, he'd nonetheless come to depend on them, unfairly, if you ask me. So had the department as a whole. It was the reason they tolerated all of Monk's considerable eccentricities. I think Monk, on some level, knew this.

Whenever a homicide was too tough to crack, they could always call in Monk. With the exception of one case, the murder of his own wife, he always got his man.

Until now.

What had to make losing to Breen even worse

for Monk was that this wasn't even a case where Stottlemeyer had asked for his help. This was a case that *he'd* dragged Stottlemeyer into. And now Stottlemeyer's badge was on the line because of it.

But more than that, Monk's future as a police consultant was also on the line. If Monk could no longer be counted on to solve every crime, what reason did the police, or Stottlemeyer, have to call on him anymore? What motivation would they have to tolerate his irritating quirks?

It was wrong for Stottlemeyer to expect Monk never to fail, to always make some miraculous deduction at the right moment. But because Monk had done it so many times before, what would have been an unrealistic expectation of anyone else had become the basis of their professional relationship.

That night, Stottlemeyer had gambled on it and lost. And if Stottlemeyer was demoted or booted because of Monk's failure, Monk's career as a consultant to the SFPD was effectively over as well.

And, perhaps, so was their friendship. Because if they didn't have mysteries to solve, what did they have to draw them together? What would they share in common?

Maybe I was overanalyzing it, but as we drove through the darkness and the fog, that's what I heard in the awkward, heavy silence, and that's what I saw in their long faces.

When Monk and I got back to my house, we found Mrs. Throphamner asleep on the couch, snoring loudly, her dentures in a glass of water on the coffee table. *Hawaii Five-O* was on the TV,

Jack Lord in his crisp, blue suit staring down Ross Martin, who looked ridiculous in face paint playing a native Hawaiian crime lord.

Monk squatted beside the glass of water and stared at Mrs. Throphamner's dentures as if they were a specimen in formaldehyde.

I turned off the TV, and Mrs. Throphamner woke up with a snort, startling Monk, who lost his balance and fell into a sitting position on the floor.

Mrs. Throphamner, flustered and disoriented, immediately reached for her dentures and knocked over the glass, spilling everything right in Monk's lap.

Monk squealed and scampered backward, the dentures resting on his soaked crotch.

Mrs. Throphamner reached down for her dentures and inadvertently toppled onto Monk, who squirmed and called for help underneath her, unwilling to touch her himself.

Julie charged, sleepy-eyed, out of her room in her pajamas. "What's going on?"

"Mrs. Throphamner spilled her teeth in Mr. Monk's lap," I said. "Give me a hand."

Julie and I lifted Mrs. Throphamner up. She angrily snatched her teeth from Monk's lap, plopped them into her mouth, and marched out of the house in a huff without so much as a "good night." I didn't even get a chance to pay her.

Monk remained on his back on the floor, staring up at the ceiling. He didn't move. He didn't blink. I was afraid he was catatonic. I leaned down beside him.

"Mr. Monk? Are you okay?"

He didn't say anything. I looked over my shoulder at Julie.

"Get me a bottle of Sierra Springs from the fridge."

She nodded and ran off to get it.

"Please, Mr. Monk. Answer me."

He blinked and whispered hoarsely, "This day has been a nightmare."

"Yes, it has."

"No, I mean really," Monk said. "The city dump. The homeless encampment. The dentures in my lap. All of that didn't really happen, did it?"

Julie returned with the bottle. I opened it and offered it to Monk.

"I'm afraid so, Mr. Monk."

He sat up, took the bottle from me, and guzzled it as if it were whiskey.

Monk tossed the empty bottle over his shoulder. "Keep 'em coming." He looked at Julie. "You'd better go to bed, honey. This is going to get ugly."

21

Mr. Monk and Marmaduke

Monk drank two more bottles of Sierra Springs and carried another four off with him to bed, slamming the door behind him.

In the morning I found him sleeping facedown and fully dressed on top of his bed, the floor littered with empty water bottles. I quietly gathered up the plastic empties and left the room without waking him.

It was my morning to carpool Julie and her friends to school, and I have to admit, I was worried about leaving Monk alone. I wasn't concerned that he was suicidal or anything dire like that—however I *was* afraid of what he might do in my house if left unsupervised. Would I return to find my closets reorganized? My clothes rearranged by size, shape, and color?

I toyed with waking him up and dragging him along on the carpool, but the thought of him stuck in an SUV filled with rowdy adolescent girls made me reconsider. Yesterday was nightmarish enough for him and, frankly, for me, too.

I decided to take my chances and left him alone. I rushed Julie through breakfast, wrote a note to Monk telling him where I was, and hurried off to pick up the other kids and ferry them to school.

Monk was still asleep when I got back forty-five minutes later. I was relieved and worried at the same time. It wasn't like him to sleep in, at least not during the time he'd been staying with us. I was debating whether to call Dr. Kroger when Monk finally got up around nine, looking as if he'd spent the night barhopping. His clothes were wrinkled, his hair was askew, and his face was unshaven.

I'd never seen him looking so rumpled, so human. It was kind of endearing.

"Good morning, Mr. Monk," I said as cheerfully as I could.

Monk acknowledged my greeting with a nod and trudged barefoot into the bathroom. He didn't emerge from his room again until noon, dressed in fresh clothes and looking his tidy best. But instead of coming to the kitchen for breakfast, he simply returned to his room and closed the door to suffer his purified-water hangover in peace.

I wasn't sure what to do, so I busied myself with household chores like paying bills and taking care of the laundry. While I worked, I tried not to think about Lucas Breen and the murders he committed. I also tried not to think about Firefighter Joe and my lingering anxieties about our nascent relationship. So, of course, Lucas Breen and Firefighter Joe were all I could think about.

I couldn't prove that Breen was guilty of murder, but I figured out what was bothering me about Joe. Yeah, I know, it's obvious what it was, and I can see it clearly now, but I couldn't then. That's how it is when you're in the middle of a relationship, even if it's only been two dates. You're too wrapped up in your own insecurities, desires, and expectations to see what's right in front of you.

Maybe it's the same way when you're a detective in the middle of an investigation. You're under so much pressure to solve the case, and you're bombarded with so many facts, that it's almost impossible to see everything clearly. You see static instead of a picture.

I imagine that it was often like that for Stottlemeyer or Disher. I saw how much they invested themselves in their investigations, how hard they had to work at it.

For Monk, it's all inside out. The investigation looks easy and everything else is hard.

We're so distracted by how difficult it is for him to accomplish even the simplest things in life that we don't notice the effort that he puts into solving crimes and how much of himself he puts on the line.

Figuring out the solutions to puzzling mysteries seems to come so fast and so naturally for him, we just shake our heads in wonder and chalk it up as miraculous. We don't stop to consider the mental and emotional resources he has to marshal to pull that "miracle" off.

After all, we're talking about a man who finds it virtually impossible to choose a seat in a movie theater and yet somehow manages to sort through thousands of possible clues in a case to arrive at a solution. That can't be as easy as it looks. There's got to be some heavy lifting involved. And I'm sure even he has times when he can't see what's obvious to everybody else or, in his case, what would ordinarily be obvious to him.

Who can he possibly turn to who can understand his anguish at times like that? Nobody. Because there's no one else like Adrian Monk, at least not that I know of.

Even so, I resolved to give it my best shot. I went to his room and knocked on the door.

"Come in," he said.

I opened the door and found him sitting on the edge of his bed, a book open on his lap. He grinned and tapped a finger on the page.

"This is priceless," he said.

I sat down beside him and looked at what he was reading. It was a collection of single-panel comic strips about Marmaduke, a Great Dane the size of a horse.

In the comic Monk was looking at, Marmaduke was returning to his doghouse with a car tire in his mouth. The caption read: *Marmaduke loves chasing cars.*

"That Marmaduke," Monk said. "He's so big."

"It's a joke that never gets tired," I said.

It was a lie, of course. I couldn't imagine what Monk, or anybody else, found amusing about that comic strip. But at least now I knew the secret to recovering from a night spent binge-drinking purified water.

"He is so mischievous." Monk turned the page and pointed to a comic where Marmaduke takes his owner for a brisk walk, lifting the poor man right off his feet. The caption read: *There's always a windchill factor when I walk Marmaduke!*

"How are you feeling?"

"Dandy," Monk said without conviction. He turned another page.

"You'll get Lucas Breen, Mr. Monk. I know you will."

"What if I don't?" Monk said. "Captain Stottlemeyer could be demoted and Julie's heart will be broken."

"They'll survive," I said.

"I won't," Monk said, and turned another page in the book. Marmaduke jumps into a swimming pool, creating a splash that empties out all the water. *Who invited Marmaduke to our pool party?*

Monk shook his head and smiled. "He's enormous."

"You can't solve every case, Mr. Monk. You're asking too much of yourself."

"If I can find the person who killed my wife, I won't need to solve another murder ever again," Monk said. "So until that day comes, I have to solve them all."

"I don't understand."

"There's an order to everything, Natalie. If I

can't get justice for Esther Stoval, Sparky the fire dog, and that homeless man, how can I ever hope to get it for Trudy?"

That didn't make a damn bit of sense to me. It was also one of the saddest things I'd ever heard.

"How can you put that burden on yourself, Mr. Monk? Those killings have nothing to do with what happened to Trudy."

"Everything in life is linked. That's how you can spot the things that don't fit."

I shook my head. "No, I don't believe that. You really think that if you solve some magic number of cases, you will have done your penance and God will tell you who killed your wife?"

Monk shook his head. "There's nothing magic or spiritual about it. I'm not skilled enough yet to figure out who murdered my wife. If I solve enough cases, maybe someday I will be."

"Mr. Monk," I said softly, "you're the best detective there is."

"That's not good enough," Monk said. "Because whoever killed Trudy is still free, and so is Lucas Breen."

Monk turned another page in the book.

"You can't do this to yourself, Mr. Monk. You're holding yourself to a standard of perfection no person could ever meet."

"That wacky dog gets into one mishap after another." Monk smiled and pointed at the page.

Marmaduke chases a cat up a tree and manages to uproot the tall pine, much to the dismay of several children who are lugging planks of wood, hammers, and nails. *I guess we won't be building our treehouse today.*

"He sure does." I patted Monk on the back and left the room.

Adrian Monk was, without a doubt, the most complex man I'd ever met, and perhaps the most tragic. I wished he could let go of some of that guilt he carried around.

Of course, I was a fine one to talk. How many nights did I stare at the ceiling and wonder if Mitch died because of me? If I had loved him more, he wouldn't have been able to leave us. He wouldn't have been half a world away. He wouldn't have been shot out of the sky. If I loved him more, Mitch wouldn't have needed to fly; he wouldn't have needed anything but me. But I obviously didn't love him enough, because he had to go. And now he was dead.

I knew it was foolish and irrational to blame myself for his death, but even so, I can't deny that the guilt was there and still is.

Were Monk and I really so different?

But he was luckier than I. He knew what he had to do to set his world right again. I didn't have a clue. What penance could I pay to restore order in my world?

I went into the kitchen, looked out the window, and saw Mrs. Throphamner in her backyard, tending her roses, the strong scent of those flowers filling my house. I hoped what happened last night wouldn't scare her away from watching Julie for me. I'd come to depend on Mrs. Throphamner.

The first step toward keeping her happy was probably paying her what I owed her.

I was heading back into the living room in search of my purse, and the cash to pay Mrs. Throphamner, when Monk came charging out of his room, holding open his book, a big smile on his face.

"He's done it," Monk said jubilantly.

"Who's done what?"

"Marmaduke," Monk said, tapping the open page and the strip about the uprooted tree. "He's figured out how to get Lucas Breen!"

Stottlemeyer was in his office looking glum. Monk's Marmaduke book was open on the desk in front of him. Disher stood behind the captain and looked over his shoulder.

"This is the solution to the case," Monk said.

We sat in chairs facing Stottlemeyer's desk and waited for his reaction. Stottlemeyer glanced at the comic, then back at Monk.

"You've got to be kidding," Stottlemeyer said.

That probably wasn't the reaction Monk was expecting. But he shouldn't have been surprised. It was the same reaction I had.

"I agree with the captain on this. I don't think a dog could really uproot a tree like that," Disher said. "Even one Marmaduke's size."

"Sure he could," Monk said.

"That's not my problem with it," Stottlemeyer said.

"But trees that size have very deep roots,"

Disher said. "A car could crash into a tree like that one and it wouldn't move."

"Marmaduke is full of rambunctious energy," Monk said. "Cars aren't."

"Would you both stop it?" Stottlemeyer snapped. "I'm not sure you grasp the gravity of this situation, Monk. This morning I was officially reprimanded by the chief over what happened last night. I have to go in front of an administrative review board next week and explain my actions. They could demote me."

"They won't once you arrest Lucas Breen," Monk said.

"You mean after I confront him with this Marmaduke comic and he confesses?"

"Basically, yes," Monk said, tapping the book. "This ties Breen irrefutably to all three murders."

"Frankly, Monk, I don't see how," Stottlemeyer said.

So Monk explained it, sharing with us the realization he had had while reading the comic and his simple plan for acting on it. I could only smile to myself and marvel, once again, at the mysterious way Monk's mind worked. But I knew he was right. It was our only hope of bringing down Lucas Breen.

Stottlemeyer was quiet for a moment, mulling over what Monk had told him.

"If I go up against Breen again and I lose, they will take my badge," Stottlemeyer said. "I need to know you're right about this."

"I am," Monk said.

Stottlemeyer pursed his lips and nodded. "Okay, then, let's do it."

He rose from his seat and put on his coat.

"What about me?" Disher asked. "What would you like me to do?"

"Stay right here, Randy, and see that those tests that Monk suggested are run on the homeless man and his possessions," Stottlemeyer said.

"I could do that with a phone call," Disher said. "I want to back you up on this, Captain."

"I know you do," Stottlemeyer said. "But if this goes wrong and my career blows up, I don't want you to get hit with the shrapnel. I'm only willing to gamble one badge on Monk and Marmaduke, and it's mine."

Disher nodded. Stottlemeyer squeezed his shoulder and we walked out.

"Marmaduke," Stottlemeyer muttered. "He's one big dog."

"The biggest," Monk said.

22

Mr. Monk and the
Clam Chowder

The ride in the elevator up to Lucas Breen's thirtieth-floor office went a lot faster without Monk. Stottlemeyer had his arms folded across his chest and tapped his foot nervously. I carried Lucas Breen's surprise in my half-open bag and listened to a horrendous instrumental version of Kylie Minogue's "Can't Get You Out of My Head," which, of course, lived up to its name. The bad elevator music was still stuck in my head when we stepped out into the waiting area.

The beautiful Asian receptionist greeted us with her best approximation of a smile. She wore a thin headset that connected her to the phone system. Several flat-screen monitors built into the desk showed security-camera views of the lobby, the garage, and other areas of the building. On one of the screens I spotted Monk sitting at a table outside of the Boudin Bakery in the lobby. He'd covered the seat bottom with napkins before sitting down.

"As our guard informed you downstairs," she said to Stottlemeyer, "Mr. Breen is very busy and would prefer that you return at another time."

She opened her calendar and ran a sharp, red-polished fingernail down the page. "I believe he can accommodate you in March of next year, assuming you're still engaged in your present position on the police force."

Stottlemeyer forced an insincere smile of his own. "Tell Mr. Breen that I appreciate how busy he is and that I need only a moment of his time to apologize."

"You're here to apologize?" she said, arching a perfectly tweezed eyebrow.

"I'm here to prostrate myself at his feet," he said.

"Me, too," I said.

"He likes that," the receptionist said. This time her smile was real and vaguely sadistic.

"I'm sure he does," Stottlemeyer said.

She called Breen and told him why we were there. I don't know what he said, but after a moment she nodded at us.

"You may enter." She tipped her head toward Breen's office. I wondered if she was real or a vaguely lifelike robot, and if when she hummed, it sounded like the music we heard in the elevator.

The doors to Breen's office slid open as we approached. Breen stood in the center of the room, looking nothing like the man we saw the previous night. He was completely recovered from his cold and dressed in one of his custom-made suits.

"You're looking better this morning," Stottlemeyer said.

"You have sixty seconds," Breen said, checking his watch. I could see the monogram on his cuffs.

"That's all I'll need," Stottlemeyer said. "I just wanted to apologize for all the trouble I've caused you over the last few days. You told us from day one that you'd never set foot in Esther Stoval's house."

"I never met the woman," Breen said. "But you wouldn't listen. Instead you accused me of committing every murder in this city."

Stottlemeyer held up his hands in a show of surrender. "You're right; I was wrong. I listened to Monk when I should have listened to you. I don't blame you for being pissed off."

Breen sneezed and wiped his nose with a handkerchief. "Indeed. Speaking of Monk, where is he?"

"He's got a problem with elevators," I said. "So he stayed down in the lobby. But I can call him on my cell phone. I know he'd like to say a few words to you."

I took out my phone, hit speed dial, put it on the speaker setting, and held it out so we could all hear what Monk had to say.

"This is Adrian Monk," he said over the speaker. "Can you hear me?"

"Yes," I said.

"Testing, one, two, three," Monk said.

Stottlemeyer took the phone from me and yelled

into it, "We can hear you, Monk. Get on with it. Mr. Breen doesn't have all day. We've wasted enough of this man's time."

Breen nodded appreciatively at Stottlemeyer, sniffled, and dabbed his nose with his handkerchief. His eyes were beginning to get teary.

"I want to say how sorry I am for intruding on you last night," Monk said. "I hope you will accept this gift as a small token of remorse for the discomfort you've been through."

I reached into my bag and pulled out a big, white, fluffy cat, a Turkish Van with tan markings on her head and tail, and held it out to Breen.

He immediately started sneezing and backed away. "I appreciate the gesture, but I'm allergic to cats."

"So you wouldn't have one in your house," Monk said.

"Of course not." Breen glared at the phone as if it were Monk standing there, then shifted his look to me. "Would you mind getting that cat away from me, please?"

I stowed the cat in my open bag.

"You didn't have a cold last night; you had an allergy," Monk said. "Your overcoat was covered in cat dander from Esther Stoval's house. You trailed dander all over your den when you brought your coat in to burn. That's why I was sneezing, too. I'm also allergic to cats, which is how I know you murdered Esther Stoval, Sparky the firehouse dog, and the homeless man."

It was the cat in the Marmaduke comic that sparked Monk's realization. He remembered sneezing when he first met the homeless man on the street days ago and again at the man's lean-to under the freeway last night. He'd assumed the man slept with cats, but there were no cats anywhere near the man's shelter.

Breen's face reddened with fury. He turned his watery glare at Stottlemeyer. "I thought you came here to apologize."

"I lied. I came to arrest you for murder. Since we're on the subject, you have the right to remain silent—"

Breen cut him off. "I'm allergic to pollen, mildew, and one of my wife's perfumes. A runny nose doesn't prove a damn thing."

"The cat hair does," Monk said. "Esther got that Turkish Van only a few days before her murder. It's a rare breed. I'll bet we're going to find dander from that cat, and others that she owns, in your house and in your car."

"We're searching your house now," Stottlemeyer said. "We'll do a DNA analysis and compare the dander we find to what we've recovered from the homeless man's body and Esther's other cats. It's going to match."

"Yet you said you don't own a cat and that you've never set foot in Esther Stoval's house," Monk said. "That leaves only one explanation. You're a murderer."

It was a strange experience. Monk was summarizing his case and nailing a killer without even being in the same room. It couldn't be half as satisfying for Monk as being able to look his adversary in the eye. It certainly wasn't for me. But it was enough. Breen wasn't going to get away with murder. He was going to prison.

Breen sneered, which was a lovely sight to see. It was a weak, halfhearted sneer. It lacked the sleazy power and smug self-confidence of all the other sneers he'd blessed us with over the past few days.

"You planted the evidence to frame me as part of some twisted, personal vendetta."

"Save it for your trial," Stottlemeyer said. "You're coming with us."

Breen ignored Stottlemeyer and marched out to the reception desk. "Tessa, get my lawyer on the phone immediately."

We followed him out and, just as we reached him, he whirled around, grabbed the cat out of my bag, and flung the screeching animal at Stottlemeyer's face. He staggered back, struggling with the furious, clawing cat.

Breen bolted for his office, aiming his remote at the doors as he passed. Stottlemeyer pulled the cat off of his face, dropped it on the receptionist's lap, and chased after Breen, but the doors slid shut with a solid clank in his face just as he reached them.

"Damn," Stottlemeyer yelled.

"What's going on?" Monk demanded over the phone.

"Breen is getting away," I told him; then I turned and confronted the receptionist, who was casually petting the cat. "Open the doors."

"I can't," she said.

I wanted to strangle her.

"Okay." Stottlemeyer took out his gun and, for a moment, I was afraid he was going to shoot her. "I'll do it."

He aimed at the doors.

"They're bulletproof," she said.

Stottlemeyer swore and holstered his weapon. "Does he have a private elevator in there?"

She didn't answer.

The captain spun her chair so she faced him, leaned down, and got nose-to-nose with her.

Tiny rivulets of blood streamed down his face from the cat's scratches. I don't know how she felt about his scary visage, but the cat was terrified. The cat leaped out of her lap and scrambled up my leg and into my bag.

"I asked you a question," Stottlemeyer said.

"Save your questions for Mr. Breen's lawyer," she said, her voice cracking just a bit.

"How would you like to be charged as an accessory to murder?"

"You can't do that," she said. "I didn't kill anyone."

"You helped a triple murderer escape. I'm sure the jury will be very sympathetic to you."

"Oh, yeah," Monk said from my cell phone. "They'll see right away what a warm, honest person you are."

She blinked once. "Yes, he has a private elevator."

"Where does it go?" Stottlemeyer said.

"To the parking garage," she said.

Stottlemeyer pointed to the security monitors. "Let me see it."

She hit a button, and a view of Breen's Bentley gleaming in its parking space in the underground garage showed up on one of the screens. On another monitor we could see Monk pacing in the lobby, holding the cell phone to his ear.

Stottlemeyer yelled into my cell phone.

"Monk, Breen is making a run for it. He's going to the parking garage. I can't get down there in time. You've got to stop him."

"How am I supposed to do that?" Monk said.

"I don't know," Stottlemeyer said, "but you'd better think of something fast."

Monk rushed out of frame on the monitor. Stottlemeyer handed me back my cell phone, took out his own, and called the police station for backup.

I turned to the receptionist and pointed to the screen that showed the lobby view. I wanted to see what Monk was doing.

"Can you move this camera?" I asked.

"It's fixed in place," she said.

Of course it was. The entire security system had been specifically programmed not to do anything Stottlemeyer or I wanted it to do.

"Can you show me the garage exit and the street outside of it?"

She hit a button and two images appeared on either side of a split-screen display. One camera looked down into the garage from the street. The other camera was outside, showing the exit and the sidewalk in front of the garage.

I glanced at the other screen, the one that

showed the Bentley in its parking space. Breen ran out of the elevator and got into his car.

I looked back at the split screen. Where was Monk? What was he doing?

There was an easy way to find out. I put the cell phone to my ear, but all I got was a dial tone. Monk had hung up.

Stottlemeyer flipped his phone shut and joined me. "Where's Monk?"

"I don't know," I said.

We watched the garage monitor as Breen backed up and sped out of his parking space, burning rubber.

"I've called for backup and put out an APB on Breen's car," Stottlemeyer said. "A Bentley shouldn't be too hard to spot on the streets or on one of the bridges."

"If he doesn't ditch it as soon as he's out of here," I said.

"We'll alert the airports, train stations, and the borders."

That didn't give me much reassurance. Fugitives with fewer resources than Breen succeeded in eluding the authorities for years. Breen probably had an emergency stash of money hidden somewhere. I knew with horrifying certainty that if Breen got out of the building he'd simply evaporate.

He'd never be found.

We watched what unfolded next on the security camera feeds at the receptionist's desk. We saw the Bentley speeding up the ramps toward the exit. And then we saw Monk.

He stood on the sidewalk directly in front of the garage exit, a round loaf of sourdough bread in each hand.

Stottlemeyer squinted at the screen. "Is that *bread* that he's holding?"

"Looks like it to me," I said, shifting my gaze between the monitors. One screen showed Monk blocking the exit and another showed Breen's Bentley racing toward him.

"What the hell is Monk doing?" Stottlemeyer said.

"Getting himself killed," I said. "Breen is going to plow right over him."

Breen was rocketing toward the exit, making no effort at all to slow down as he closed in on Monk. If anything, he was speeding up.

But Monk didn't move. He stood there like Clint Eastwood, stoically facing the car down, holding the loaves of bread. Even Clint would have looked ridiculous and insane.

At the last possible second, Monk threw his loaves at Breen's windshield and dove out of the way. The loaves burst on impact, splattering chunks of bread and thick clam chowder all over the glass, completely obscuring Breen's view.

The Bentley flew out of the exit into the street. Steering blind, Breen fishtailed into a turn and slammed into a row of parked cars. The Bentley crumpled like a crushed soda can, setting off a shrill wail of car alarms up and down the street.

Stottlemeyer looked at me in stunned disbelief. "Did I just see Monk stop a speeding car by throwing two bowls of clam chowder at it?"

"Sourdough bowls," I said, pretty shocked myself.

"That's what I thought," he said, and ran to the elevators. "I can't wait to write that in my report."

I glanced at the monitor and saw Monk stagger to his feet. He took out his phone and dialed. My cell rang just as Stottlemeyer stepped into the elevator.

"You'd better call a paramedic," Monk said.

"Is Breen hurt?" I asked.

"I am," Monk said. "I scraped my palm."

"I think you'll live," I said.

"Do you have any idea how many people walk on that sidewalk each day? Who knows what they have under their shoes. A deadly infection could be raging through my veins as we speak."

While Monk talked, I saw something on the monitor that scared me a lot more than the germs on the sidewalk. Lucas Breen was emerging from his mangled car. He was disheveled, bloody, and covered in broken glass.

And he was holding a gun.

"Mr. Monk, Breen has a gun!" I said. "Run!"

Monk turned around to see Breen staggering toward him, aiming his gun with a shaking hand. People on the street screamed in panic and took cover. Even the receptionist gasped at the sight, and she was thirty floors above the street, safe behind her desk, watching it all on the screen.

But I knew how she felt. It was like watching a horror movie, only these weren't actors.

The only people left standing on the street were Monk and Breen, his face twisted with rage.

"You don't want to do this," Monk said, still holding the phone to his ear.

"I've never wanted anything more in my life," Breen said. "I hate you with every molecule of my being."

I could hear him clearly over the phone, and I could see the whole, terrifying scene playing out from various angles on the security-camera monitors.

"Stall him," I said. "Stottlemeyer is on his way down."

"It would be a big mistake," Monk said.

"Oh, really? Give me one reason I shouldn't blow your head off," Breen said.

"It would be bad for tourism."

Breen grinned, several of his teeth missing. "See you in hell, Monk."

There was a gunshot, only it was Breen who spun around, the gun flying out of his hand.

Monk turned and saw Lieutenant Disher rising from his cover behind a car, his gun pointed at Breen, who was clutching his injured hand.

"Police," Disher said. "Raise your hands and lie facedown on the ground. Now."

The developer sank to his knees, then lay forward, his arms outstretched in front of him.

Disher ran up to Breen, pulled his arms behind his back, and handcuffed him.

"Good shot," Monk said.

"Lucky shot," Disher said. "I was aiming for his chest."

"It doesn't matter what he was aiming for," I said into the phone. "Thank him, Mr. Monk."

"You saved my life," Monk said. "Thank you."

"Just doing my job," Disher said, but he was obviously quite proud of himself. I was proud of him, too.

That's when Stottlemeyer rushed out of the building and over to the men. "Randy, what are you doing here?"

"I figured you might need backup," Disher said. "So I followed you and parked outside."

Stottlemeyer did a quick appraisal of the situation, took a rubber glove out of his pocket, and used it like a rag to pick up Breen's gun.

"In other words," he said, "you violated a direct order."

"I don't recall you phrasing it as an order, sir," Disher said.

"Good," Stottlemeyer said. "Then neither do I."

"Somebody should really call an ambulance," Monk said.

Stottlemeyer looked down at Breen, who was moaning and squirming on the ground. "Yeah, he's in a world of hurt."

"I was thinking about me," Monk said, and held up his hand. I couldn't see his palm on the monitor, but I could see the expression on Stottlemeyer's face.

"That's a scratch, Monk."

"People spit on sidewalks," Monk said. "Dogs urinate on them. This scratch could be fatal."

"You're right," Stottlemeyer said. "Randy, get the paramedics here pronto."

Disher nodded, took out his phone, and made the call.

Stottlemeyer put his arm around Monk. "You did good, Monk. Real good. The clam chowder was an inspiration."

"Not really," Monk said, and showed Stottlemeyer a speck on his jacket. "My jacket is a total loss."

23

Mr. Monk and the Perfect Room

While we were at the police station giving our statements, Monk and Stottlemeyer learned that they were right. Crime-scene investigators found cat dander in Breen's house and in the wreckage of his car that, at least in their preliminary examination, matched the hairs recovered from the homeless man's body and Esther's cats. They sent the samples out for DNA testing, but there was little doubt how it would turn out. Meanwhile, the forensics unit was still processing the prints and fibers they'd recovered from the firefighting equipment.

That was all nice to know, but what really mattered most was that Lucas Breen was being held without bail behind bars in the prison ward of the hospital.

As far as Monk, Stottlemeyer, and I were concerned, the murders of Esther Stoval, Sparky the fire dog, and the homeless man were solved.

We sat in Stottlemeyer's office for our usual post-arrest wrap-up. It was a chance for Monk, Stottlemeyer, and Disher to congratulate one another on a job well-done, since nobody else was going to do it.

"After what happened today," Stottlemeyer said, "we may make sourdough bowls of clam chowder standard equipment in every patrol car. Not only will it cut down on high-speed pursuits, but they're tasty, too."

Monk didn't appreciate the joke, mainly because he wasn't paying any attention. He was too busy trying to rub out the speck of chowder from his jacket with a Wet One, which wasn't easy. Not only was the stain staying put, but Monk had a hard time holding the wipe with his heavily bandaged hand. He had more bandages on his hand for a scratch than Lucas Breen had for his gunshot wound.

"What about your administrative review hearing?" I asked Stottlemeyer.

"Canceled," Stottlemeyer said. "The deputy chief is talking about a commendation ceremony instead."

"For you?" I said.

Stottlemeyer shook his head and glanced at Disher, who was watching Monk wrestle with his stain. "For you."

Disher looked up and his cheeks immediately flushed. "Me? Really?"

"You not only saved Monk's life, but you defused a potentially deadly situation with an armed assailant without anybody getting killed or seriously injured, including the perp."

I liked the fact that Breen was now a mere perp. Oh, how the mighty had fallen.

"What about you, sir?" Disher said. "You deserve some recognition for refusing to back down despite the political pressure from a corrupt police commissioner."

"I'm getting to keep my job, which is enough for me," Stottlemeyer said. "Defying authority and bullheaded stubbornness aren't qualities the department likes to encourage."

"And what does Mr. Monk get?" I asked.

"The department's gratitude and respect," Stottlemeyer said.

"I'd settle for a strong stain remover," Monk said.

All in all it was a good day, a vast improvement over where we were the day before—up to our waists in stinking garbage.

"Is it okay if we let the firefighters know that Sparky's killer has been caught?" I asked.

Stottlemeyer nodded. "Sure, as long as they don't announce it to the media. The chief hates it when somebody beats him to the TV cameras."

So we said our good-byes, and on the way back home Monk and I stopped by the firehouse to announce Breen's arrest.

When we got there, the firefighters were once again cleaning and shining the fire trucks under Captain Mantooth's direction and eagle eye. Monk went straight to the stack of neatly folded towels and picked one up.

"May I?" Monk asked.

"We would be honored, Mr. Monk," Captain Mantooth said.

Monk smiled gleefully and got to work polishing the already gleaming chrome grille.

Joe climbed down off the truck and joined us. He wore an SFFD T-shirt that was one size too small and showed off his tight chest and strong arms. My breath caught in my throat. He was so good-looking.

"Did you solve the murder you ran off to last night?" Joe asked.

I nodded. "I didn't; Mr. Monk did. He also caught Sparky's killer. It was Lucas Breen."

"The developer?" Captain Mantooth said in amazement.

"Yes, that's the guy," I said.

Hearing this, the rest of the firefighters began to abandon their duties and wander over.

"Why would a rich, powerful man like that want to kill a firehouse dog?" Joe asked.

That was a good question, and all the firefighters gathered around me to hear my long, detailed answer, leaving Monk blissfully alone to shine the fire truck to his heart's content.

When I was finished with my story, there was a lot of head shaking and astonished looks. I tugged Joe's sleeve and led him away while his fellow firefighters were occupied discussing what they'd learned.

"This is fantastic news. Let's go out this weekend and celebrate what you've done for Sparky," Joe said. "And for me."

"That's a really sweet suggestion, but—"

He interrupted me. "Let's bring Julie, too. I want to thank her again for bringing Mr. Monk into this. We can make a day out of it. Besides, I'd like to get to know her."

I put my hand on his cheek to stop him. "No, Joe, I don't think so."

"Why not?"

"Because I don't want Julie to start caring for you as much as I have," I said. "It's why we can't see each other anymore."

I took my hand away. He looked as if I'd slapped him with it.

"I don't understand," Joe said. "I thought things were going so well."

"They were," I said. "You're wonderful, and I really enjoy being with you. I can see us becoming very close."

He shook his head as if to clear it. "Then what's the problem?"

"That *is* the problem. Who you are. And all of this." I waved my hand to encompass the firehouse around us. "You're a firefighter."

"So?"

"You risk your life for a living, and that's noble, and great, and heroic," I said. "But it's wrong for me, wrong for Julie. We both lost a man we loved who did the noble, great, heroic thing. You're so much like him. We'd both fall in love with you, and I can't go through it again."

He forced a smile. "What if I promise I won't get hurt?"

"You can't make that promise."

"Nobody can," Joe said. "You could get run over tomorrow by a truck while crossing the street."

"I know, but I don't make a living of leaping in front of speeding trucks every day," I said. "I can't get involved ever again with anyone who has a dangerous job. I can't take the worry and the risk, and I can't do it to my daughter. She needs—we *both* need—a man in our lives who has the safest job on earth."

"I'm not that guy," Joe said.

"I wish you were."

"I wish I were, too." He took me in his arms and gave me a soft, sweet, sad kiss. "If you ever change your mind, you know where to find me."

He smiled, turned his back on me, and walked outside. I watched him go, trying hard not to cry, then saw Captain Mantooth and Monk watching, too. Monk tossed his towel into the basket and came over to me.

"Are you going to be okay?" he asked.

"Eventually," I said.

He saw the tears in my eyes and my trembling lip. "Would you like to borrow my Marmaduke book?"

I smiled and nodded, a tear rolling down my cheek. "That would be great."

When we told Julie that Sparky's killer had been caught, she threw her arms around Monk and startled him with a big hug.

"Thank you, Mr. Monk."

"It's nice to have a satisfied client," Monk said.

"I did something for you," she said. "Can I show you?"

"Sure," Monk said.

Julie motioned for us to follow her, and she hurried ahead of us down the hall to her room. As soon as her back was turned, Monk motioned to me for a wipe. I gave him one.

"Children are so special," he said, wiping his hands thoroughly, "but they're walking cesspools of disease."

I gave him a look. "Did you just call my daughter a walking cesspool?"

"She's also bright and adorable and lovable," Monk said. "From a safe distance."

She stood in front of the door to her room, her hand on the doorknob.

"Okay, prepare yourselves," she said.

Monk glanced at me. "Am I going to need shots for this?"

Before I could reply, she opened her door and waved us inside with a big, proud smile on her face. I peeked in first.

She'd cleaned her room. But saying that doesn't do it justice. It was immaculate, with everything organized.

"You should see this, Mr. Monk," I said.

He hesitantly stuck his head in and then looked at Julie. "What have you done?"

"I've Monked it."

"Monked it?" he said.

"My books are arranged by author, genre, and copyright date, and my CDs are organized in even-numbered stacks by artist." She strolled into her room and opened her closet. Her clothes were arranged by color and type. So were her shoes. "I organized my closet and all of my drawers."

Monk went over and looked at her shelf of stuffed animals with obvious admiration. "You've arranged your animals by species."

"And size," she said. "And whether they are amphibians, reptiles, birds, or mammals."

"That must have been fun," he said, and he meant it. In fact, from the expression on his face, I think he envied her the experience.

"Oh, yes," Julie said. "I had a great time."

I couldn't believe what I was seeing. This was a major change for a kid whose idea of making her bed was picking her pillow up off the floor.

"It must have taken you hours to do this," I said.

"Actually, it's taken me a few days, but I wanted to show Mr. Monk . . ." Julie stopped and shrugged, at a loss for words to explain herself. "I don't know. I just wanted to say thank-you."

I gave her a kiss. "I love you."

"I didn't do this for you, Mom."

"Can't I be proud of you anyway?" I said.

Julie turned to Monk. "What do you think?"

I was curious to know that myself. Monk touched a whisker on one of her stuffed lions and smiled.

"I think I'm sorry that I have to go home tomorrow," he said.

24

Mr. Monk and the Wrong Teeth

I woke up in the morning to find Monk all packed, dressed, and ready to go. He insisted on making breakfast for Julie and me. I figured it would be bowls of Chex all around, but he surprised me by saying he'd be making eggs.

"I'd like mine scrambled, please," Julie said.

"Perhaps you'd like some LSD and some weed with that too." Monk gave her a chastising look, then glanced at me as if to say I'd failed as a parent in some fundamental way.

Julie's brow wrinkled in confusion. "What's LSD? And why would I want to eat weeds?"

"Never mind," I said, giving Monk a chastising look of my own. "So how are you preparing them?"

"There's only one way," Monk said.

He expertly cracked the eggs on the rim of the pan and the yolks spilled out, the egg whites forming perfect circles. I'm not exaggerating—*perfect* circles.

"How did you learn to do that?"

"Lots of practice," Monk said. "It's all in the wrist."

"Could you teach me?" Julie asked.

"I don't think we have enough eggs," Monk said.

"How many does it take?"

"One thousand," Monk said.

Julie and I both looked at him.

"You know the exact number?" I said.

"It was actually nine hundred and ninety-three," Monk said. "But I broke seven more to make it even."

"Of course," I said. "Makes perfect sense."

"Can you buy some more eggs today?" Julie asked me.

"I'm not buying a thousand eggs," I said. "You'll just have to learn two eggs at a time over breakfast each morning."

"That could take years," she whined.

"Now you have a goal in life," I said.

Monk toasted some sourdough bread, which he cut into even halves and served to us on separate plates, along with oranges that were completely peeled and sliced in perfect wedges.

The breakfast was so perfect, in fact, it looked synthetic and strangely unappetizing, as if it were all made of plastic.

Julie had no such reservations. She devoured her breakfast, finishing up just as her ride to school arrived. She gave me a kiss on the cheek and ran out.

Monk cleared the table and I washed the dishes. After that, we were all alone with nothing to do. No murders to solve. No crimes to investigate.

"So what's on the agenda for today?" I asked.

"Moving back into my house and cleaning," Monk said. "Lots of cleaning."

"You haven't been there in days," I said. "What is there to clean?"

"Every inch," Monk said. "The entire building has been tented and pumped full of poison. It's a death trap. We're going to be on our hands and knees scrubbing for days."

"You will; I won't," I said. "I signed on to be your assistant, not your maid. I'll supervise."

"What does that mean?"

"I'll be sitting on the couch reading a magazine and watching you work," I said. "If you miss a spot, I'll let you know."

I picked up my purse and my car keys. He grabbed his luggage and we went out to the car. Mrs. Throphamner was in her garden, already tending to her roses. I remembered I still owed her money.

"Good morning, Mrs. Throphamner," I said. "Your flowers are looking lovely today."

"So are you, dear," she said.

At least she didn't have any hard feelings.

"Oh," Monk said. "I almost forgot."

"Me, too," I said, reaching into my purse. But before I could pay her, Stottlemeyer drove up and got out of his car.

Monk set down his suitcases and we walked over to greet him.

"Monk, Natalie," Stottlemeyer said. "Beautiful day, isn't it?"

"Sure is." It amazed me that he could still appreciate it, considering a typical day meant he had plenty of ugliness and death in store. "Do you need Mr. Monk's help on a case already?"

"Nope," Stottlemeyer said. "I was on my way into the office and thought I'd stop by with the good news. We've got Breen."

"We had Breen yesterday," Monk said.

"We had cat hair yesterday," Stottlemeyer said. "Today we've got a fingerprint. The crime lab found his prints inside a firefighter's glove. He might have been able to explain away the cat hair, but he can't talk himself out of that. You came through for me again, Monk, like you always do."

"You too, Captain," Monk said. "In fact, there's something you can do for me right now."

"Retie my shoes? Adjust my belt to a different loop? Change the license plate on my car so all the numbers are even?"

"Yes, that would be great," Monk said. "And when you get a moment, could you also arrest Mrs. Throphamner?"

I glanced back at Mrs. Throphamner, who was coming out of her backyard with the hose.

"Don't you think you're going a bit overboard, Mr. Monk?" I said. "She fell in your lap by accident."

Stottlemeyer looked past me. "That's Mrs. Throphamner?"

"Yes," Monk said.

"And she was in your lap?"

"Yes," Monk said.

"Maybe it's you I should arrest," Stottlemeyer said.

Monk scowled at Stottlemeyer and went over to Mrs. Throphamer, who was rolling up the hose.

"Excuse me, Mrs. Throphamner?" Monk said. She turned around. "You're under arrest for murder."

"Murder?" I said. Actually, Mrs. Throphamner, Stottlemeyer, and I all said the same thing in unison. We sounded like a chorus.

"Her husband isn't in a fishing cabin near Sacramento," Monk said. "He's buried in her backyard. That's why she planted the most fragrant roses she could find and kept changing them—to hide the smell of his decomposing corpse."

I knew that he was always right about murder, but this time he just had to be wrong. Mrs. Throphamner, a murderer? It was ridiculous.

Mrs. Throphamner sagged and let out a weary sigh. "How did you know?"

"It's *true*?" I said, utterly shocked.

Mrs. Throphamner nodded. "I'm glad you found out. I'm so tired of tending the garden, and the guilt was driving me mad. I loved him so much."

"I know you did," Monk said. "That's why you couldn't entirely let go. That's why you kept his teeth."

"His teeth?" Stottlemeyer said.

"His dentures," Monk said. "She's got them in her mouth right now."

"She *does*?" He narrowed his eyes and stared at her mouth, but she closed her lips and turned her head away. "How could you possibly know that, Monk?"

"When she babysits, Mrs. Throphamner likes to set her dentures on the table beside her while she watches TV," Monk said. "I had the chance to examine them. They're obviously male dentures. The maxillary lateral incisors are prominent and large, while a woman's are narrower. Also, a male's alveolar bone has a heavier arch, and the internal portion of the dentures—"

"Okay, okay," Stottlemeyer interrupted, still watching Mrs. Throphamner's face, waiting for a glimpse of her husband's teeth. "I believe you. What tipped you off?"

"The flowers that Firefighter Joe brought on his date with Natalie," Monk said. "He said they were to cover any lingering smell on him from the dump. That got me thinking about Mrs. Throphamner, and it all fell together after that."

It took me a second, but then it all fell together for me, too. *That was two days ago.* I felt my whole body tighten with anger. My fists clenched. I think my toes did, too.

"Milton was cheating on me after forty years of marriage; can you believe that?" Mrs. Throphamner said. "The only thing he was fishing for in Sacramento was hanky-panky. I had to kill—"

"Wait a minute," I snapped, cutting her off. I turned to Monk. "You've known since *Wednesday* that she's a murderer and you didn't tell me?"

"I was distracted by a lot of other things," Monk said defensively. "I had three unsolved murders on my plate. We were both very busy."

"You let me leave my daughter alone with this monster?"

"I knew how badly you needed a babysitter while we were on the case."

"She's a murderer!" I yelled.

"Well, yes. But other than that she's very dependable," Monk said.

"Dependable?" I took a step toward him, and Monk took five steps back. "She's sucking on her dead husband's teeth!"

"That's exactly my point," Monk said. "She only kills husbands. One husband, actually. She hasn't had a second one yet. And she probably won't. So Julie was safe."

"You aren't," I said, and turned to Stottlemeyer. "Take Mr. Monk with you. Get him away from me before *I* kill him and bury him in *my* garden."

As I stomped off, I heard Monk say something to Stottlemeyer then that any court in the land would agree was a reasonable and excusable provocation for murder.

"Women," Monk said. "They're so irrational."

Read on for an excerpt from the next
book starring Adrian Monk, the brilliant
investigator who always knows when
something's out of place . . .

Mr. Monk Goes to Hawaii

Available from Signet